Crusade

The Perpetual War 1

LEON STEELGRAVE

Published by Ice Pick Books

ISBN: 978-1-8384435-6-6

LEON STEELGRAVE

Books by Leon Steelgrave

Europa City 1: White Vampyre
Europa City 2: Though Your Sins Be Scarlet
Europa City 3: The Violet Hour
Europa City 4: A Life Owed

Europa City One-shot: Cocoa Psycho Killer
Europa City One-shot: Smack Upside The Head

The Perpetual War 1: Crusade

Darkness Visible: The Complete Short Stories

PROLOGUE

At an unseen signal the door slid open, admitting the visitor to the conference room. Despite his host having kept him waiting the better part of an hour, Hannah walked at a leisurely pace, taking in his surroundings. A series of *N'tomo* masks decorated with shells, seeds and brass drew his gaze to the adjacent wall; cultural symbols of the Bambara people, the largest ethnic group in Mali. The opposite wall told a different story. Was the collection of rusting chains, shackles and ancient planks a permanent feature, or was it intended as a none-too-subtle reminder of the previous relationship between their two nations? Hannah parked the speculation and turned his attention to the figure at the opposite end of the conference table.

According to records, Toumani Coulibaly, CEO of the Bamako Tech Corp, was in his late fifties, but looked a good decade younger. The tailoring of his suit accentuated an athletic build, its purple hue contrasting with Coulibaly's ebony skin. But it was the material and not the man that caught his visitor's attention. Hannah noticed a faint iridescence and, depending on the way the light caught it, a fuzziness along its edges: nano-weave, capable of stopping small-arms fire or turning the thrust of a knife. Even in the seat of BTC power his host was taking no chances. Not so unusual when you considered that industrial espionage among the African Tech Corps centred around the physical elimination of their rivals opposed to the more traditional cyber-attacks and theft of intellectual property.

'Apologies for your wait, Mr Hannah. Please take a seat.'

Hannah reached into his pocket as he sat, activating the signal jammer to prevent any visual or audio recordings of the meeting. If ordnance didn't appear on an invoice or shipping manifest, it didn't exist.

Coulibaly motioned to a pitcher of water and a bowl of fruit on the table. 'A drink? Something to eat?'

'I'm good, thank you.' Hannah reached into his inside suit pocket and pulled out his com-unit. 'Shall we get straight to business?'

'As you wish.' Coulibaly tapped a button set into the edge of the table and a mahogany panel hinged back to reveal a screen. He presented his right eye to unlock the screen and swiped his way through several documents.

'Here we are: two hundred and fifty AI units – third-generation combat pilot interface. Ship to Tessler in Europa City for installation into SB Defiant XV attack helicopters. Two hundred and fifty AI units – seventh-generation fire control, suitable for terrestrial or orbital deployment. Finally, five thousand nano-med units – tissue regeneration. Yes?'

'And the other nanotech we spoke of?'

Coulibaly's expression stiffened. 'Didn't the Religious States of America sign up to the North–West Frontier Accord forbidding the use of such technology for military purposes?'

'We did more than that – we pretty much wrote the Accord. As such, I'd direct your attention to Article Two, Section Four, Clause Three, which allows the use of limited materials for research purposes, primarily the development of countermeasures.'

'Five thousand units?'

Hannah said nothing, letting the silence stretch. The Agency held extensive files on the Bamako Tech Corp; they had no claim to the moral high ground.

A tic twitched below Coulibaly's right eye as he weighed up potential blowback against the huge profits BTC would reap if, as all the signs indicated, the Americans were about to launch a fresh crusade. Greed won out.

'Very well. Five thousand units as per your specification.'

'And you can commit to the delivery dates?'

'For the most part, yes. The specialist nanotech might have to slip to the second quarter of 2089. I trust this is acceptable?'

'We can certainly work around that.' Hannah stood and proffered his hand. 'A pleasure doing business with you, Mr Coulibaly.'

CHAPTER 1

Cooper felt the unfriendly eyes staring at him from darkened windows. He had come to liberate this country, and yet its inhabitants hated and feared him. Sweat trickled down his spine, the armour plates in his vest chafing against his chest and shoulders. Just one more discomfort in this godforsaken land. He must have missed the section on heat, flies and hostility in the recruiting pamphlet.

Signs of war were visible wherever he looked: shattered glass, wooden shutters that dangled drunkenly from a single hinge, tumbled adobe walls pockmarked by small-arms fire. Who in their right mind would want to fight, let alone die, for this village in the middle of butt-fuck nowhere? But according to intel, insurgents were using this as a base to strike at Templar armour, so the squad had drawn the short straw of MOUT duty.

Cooper froze as Sergeant Jackson held his palm out before cupping it to his ear. He saw nothing himself but trusted Sarge's instincts; learned from three tours in the Saudi campaign, they had made him into an experienced veteran. Cooper risked a glance at Walker and Mackinlay, the tension in their faces doubtless mirrors of his own. He heard a tinkling noise and a door swung open two houses down. The chatter of his assault rifle drowned out his scream as he blasted the door.

'Stop firing!'

Silence descended as Cooper's rifle stuttered to a stop. He heard the tinkling sound again, followed by a bleat. A slotted iris fixed him with a reproachful stare. Even the goats hated them.

'Damn it, Cooper! Wait until you have eyes on the target. That could have been a child!'

Cooper eased his finger off the trigger. He stared at his boots, worried he had compromised their mission.

The squad moved off in single file, the sarge in the lead, Cooper bringing up the rear. The goat emptied her bowels as he passed, a sure sign she wasn't big on liberty and democracy. The street gave way to a square, and the squad sighted their first civilians huddled next to a fly-swarmed market stall: three women, a girl of around four years of age and a shawl-wrapped infant. Jackson raised his rifle in the air and motioned the interpreter, Goodman, forward. Mackinlay, Walker and Cooper kept their weapons trained as they approached. The girl gripped her mother's skirt as the sergeant and Goodman stopped a dozen feet away.

'Tell them we mean them no harm. We're only interested in Caliphate soldiers. We know these men take their food, force their husbands and sons to fight. But we can protect them. They don't have to be afraid.'

Goodman relayed the sarge's words. Even with their faces covered, their distrust of the soldiers was obvious. Fear showed in their eyes and the rigid lines of their bodies. They had seen the red cross pattée on the sarge's tunic and had linked it to the Caliphate's propaganda. Templars: the most fanatical and dangerous of the American soldiers. Monsters who would make them watch as they slit the girl's throat, dashed the baby's brains out, took turns at raping and mutilating them, condemning their heathen souls to hellfire.

'They don't have to say anything. Just point us on our way.'

Cooper tried to follow the exchange. It seemed longer and more involved than the sarge's original words. The woman rocked the baby back and forth, looking nervously at her companions. From her stance and attitude, Cooper thought her the youngest, probably still in her teens. Just like Mackinlay and himself. She stepped forward, provoking the mother of the little girl to unleash a string of invective. The other woman interceded. Whatever hierarchy existed between them, she seemed to have the most juice. She turned to Goodman and initiated a rapid back and forth. The sarge, Cooper noted, kept his eyes on the youngest. With a newborn to protect, all she wanted was for these American infidels to be gone. With the other women's focus on him, Goodman moved directly into her line of sight. She turned her head and nodded at the door of the house behind. The only one with closed shutters.

'Wrap it up, Goodman. Cooper – link cams and hold here with the civvies. The rest of you – with me.'

The head woman stepped forward to block the squad as they attempted to follow Jackson. Walker raised his rifle but Goodman was quicker, uttering some placatory phrase in Arabic. The head woman moved aside in response, her body language making it clear she was far from happy as her eyes burned into the backs of the retreating soldiers.

Cooper pulled down his HUD and initialised the uplink on his helmet cam. He took a few steps away from the women and split the HUD display, simultaneously monitoring his comrades and the civilians. He keyed on the motion detection overlay and watched the arrow formation of four dots close on the building. The dots blinked out one by one as the squad entered the house – signal jammer! Cooper took a step towards the house and stopped. The sarge's instruction had been clear: he was to watch the women. He checked on his charges. The young mother cradled her baby on her shoulder as she picked through dates on one of the stalls, the older women hovering protectively nearby. Dismissing them, he cut back to monitoring the squad's progress through the house.

A bare entrance hall opened onto the main living area. Sunlight shone through the shutters, casting a series of bars across the threadbare rugs. Cooper took in the mismatched, mended and patched furniture, doubtless reclaimed from the bombed remains of the surrounding towns and villages. He cycled between the various feeds, trying to pinpoint the source of his growing discomfort. He saw no art, ornaments or other signs of the personal. Nothing to suggest they were in a home. It felt staged.

Jackson shouted, 'Clear!' and the squad moved on, examining the floor for tripwires and other booby traps. Walker passed through the remnants of a beaded curtain and into the central hallway. He covered Mackinlay as he breached the first room; empty except for a rolled prayer mat.

'Clear!'

Walker moved to take point as they reached the kitchen. Cooper saw him tense in response to a patch of desert camo. He relaxed as it resolved itself into a tunic hanging on the back of a chair. Mackinlay checked the remainder of the room as Walker crossed to the stove. He touched the cast iron pot on top of the range with the back of his hand. The casual speed with which he withdrew his hand indicated the pot to be cool. Could be their target had already bolted, the informant moving the Templars on without consciously betraying the Caliphate soldiers. Cooper checked the other half of his HUD. The women had moved closer to the stalls, their backs turned to him.

Mackinlay's voice sounded in his earpiece: 'Clear!'

Jackson and Goodman pushed open the next door, which opened onto a bathroom with a chipped enamel bathtub and a rusting shower head. A pair of enormous cockroaches scuttled down the hole of a squat toilet. Anger replaced Cooper's earlier foreboding as the sarge's distorted image stared back at him through the crazed glass of the mirror. Their would-be informant had played them. Nothing but dust and vermin here.

A final door awaited the squad at the end of the hallway. They moved less cautiously now, convinced that the op was a bust. Maybe it was the noise that alerted Mackinlay. Not that it mattered in the final analysis or changed the outcome. The door swung open to reveal a man dressed in combat fatigues. Goodman shouted a warning, but fear or instinct made the man reach for the rifle slung over his shoulder. Mackinlay emptied half a magazine into him, Walker also spraying the room as he went down. By the time the firing stopped Cooper was already at the door of the house.

The target was down, but Mackinlay's cam focused on the woman and two children who lay sprawled across the bed, eyes fixed accusingly on their murderers.

Walker turned at the sound of Cooper's approach, the feed from his cam pivoting to show fresh horror approaching. Cooper froze. The girl from the market had swapped her baby for a satchel charge. He watched it leave her hand and arc towards the squad. A flash. A bang. Wreaths of thick smoke.

Jackson checked his watch. 'MOUT simulation terminated at fourteen twenty-two hours. Congratulations, Cooper; you just got everyone killed.'

The sarge's words jolted Cooper back to reality. The young woman had removed her niqab to reveal reddish-brown hair and sharp, fox-like features. Like the other 'hostiles', she was a member of the OPFOR based at Fort Irwin. Cooper followed her and Jackson back to the market square at the centre of Razish, the largest of the training villages.

Jackson took out his datapad and interrogated the MILES sensors that covered the squad's bodies. He read out casualty probability look-up table results for each member of the squad.

'Cooper – killed outright. Goodman – also killed

outright. Guess you were the lucky ones. Mackinlay – blinded in right eye, right arm removed at the elbow, right lung punctured by shrapnel. Survivability: eighteen per cent. Walker – both legs removed at the knee, left arm removed at the shoulder. Survivability: seven per cent. Even assuming you manage to overcome your shock and treat your injuries, you're surrounded by hostiles with no immediate backup or evac. In other words, game over.'

The entrance of the colonel interrupted the debrief. He strode across the square, a tall straight-backed oak of a man. Close-cropped blond hair and beard almost white against his sun-darkened skin, uniform somehow immaculate despite the ever-present dust. Grand Master Thaddeus Vanderbilt might be the leader of the Order, but Colonel Martin Tyler was the de facto public face. His blue eyes had stared out at the American public from a hundred vid-casts; whether standing over the bodies of Caliphate soldiers or handing out aid to civilian refugees, he remained the man in charge. Tyler's political ambitions were well known; he had a lot riding on the success of this latest crusade. Failure was not an option.

Cooper snapped to attention, his stomach knotting. This was bad; the OCTs usually handled the debrief. Shit was definitely about to go down and he had little doubt he would be at the centre of it.

'Novitiate Cooper, step forward.'

Cooper felt nauseous and lightheaded as he took up position in front of Colonel Tyler. Was this the moment he had been dreading?

Tyler touched his index finger to the red cross pattée on the left breast of his tunic. 'The Templar Cross isn't some simple insignia. It's a badge of honour worn by an elite few. To earn that badge a man must undergo the harshest selection process in the whole of Creation – the so-called Templar Trinity. To the physical and mental hardening demanded by traditional special forces we add the third element of spiritual purity. A man who makes it through selection to take his vows is not only a highly trained and disciplined solder; he is the physical embodiment of God's will on earth. He has earned the privilege of the elite, but with privilege comes grave responsibility. The Order becomes his family, each man his sworn brother, and unlike Cain he is most certainly his brother's keeper. Instinct might tell a common solider to run to the aid of his comrades, but discipline would hold a Templar firm to his duty. Novitiate Cooper, your orders were to guard the civilians. You disobeyed those orders, left your post and exposed your brothers to danger. This neglect of duty must have consequences. Report to the chaplain-commander for punishment. Ten lashes followed by forty-eight hours of fasting and confinement. Pain to remind you of the consequence of your failure. Solitude to reflect on your failure and seek guidance from God.'

'Sir, yes, sir!' Cooper barked out the reply, his face white with shock. He took a deep breath, raised his head and marched off to his fate. Only twenty-eight per cent of applicants passed the selection process. He was hanging on by his fingertips; one more mistake and he would be out, forced to slink home in shame or take a regular army post. The former was unthinkable, while the latter meant accepting a vastly inferior pay scale. More than that, it meant foregoing the extensive benefits package that extended to the families of serving soldiers.

Cooper loved his family more than his country or his God. The desire to help them, to make their lives better, had already taken him further than he thought possible. He focused on them now as he sought to dig even deeper, to summon the strength to succeed. The pain, the conflicted feelings and doubts, were unimportant. He would earn the right to wear the fabled red cross pattée for the benefit of his family. Get his father nanotherapy for his arthritis, his sister a place on the preferred jobs list and his brothers the opportunity for a college education. Family was everything.

CHAPTER 2

Cooper turned his head away and raised his arm in front of his eyes to block out the sudden glare of sunlight as the door swung open. He squinted, trying to make out the features of the silhouetted figure.

'Time's up, Coop. You're a free man.'

Cooper nodded, his mouth too parched to speak. When Mackinlay stepped forward to help, he waved him away. He slid his right leg forward and upward until his foot was flat against the floor and then bent forward to brace his hands. A sudden push brought him out of his kneeling position. His head spun but he kept his footing as he stumbled towards the door and freedom. Like the other applicants, he had given little thought to the purpose of this three-metre cube of windowless concrete with its single steel door. Walker had given them their first practical demonstration: consigned to the box for deliberately ducking a blow during a milling exercise. Cooper had watched him crawl out on his hands and knees. He might not be the toughest applicant, but he had more grit than Walker.

Mackinlay caught his elbow as he stepped outside. 'Easy.' He passed Copper a canteen. 'Not too much. Not too quick.'

Cooper unscrewed the cap and raised the canteen to his mouth. He let the water trickle against his parched lips, moistening them before taking his first cautious mouthful. If anything had ever tasted sweeter, he couldn't remember. He took another mouthful, easing the rawness in his throat, and handed the canteen back.

In the distance, the shadowy outlines slowly resolved themselves into the familiar buildings of Fort Irwin as his eyes adjusted to the light after forty-eight hours of darkness. A klick along the blacktop, the mass of the main barracks blocked out most of the horizon, with the officer quarters visible to the right and the buttresses of the main chapel to the left. Cooper squinted apprehensively at the road.

Mackinlay pointed to the buggy parked opposite, painted, like all the training vehicles, in desert camouflage.

'Don't worry, I brought a ride.'

This time Cooper offered no protest as Mackinlay helped him into the two-seater vehicle and fastened his seatbelt. He leaned back, trying not to flinch as the seat back came into contact with his wounds. Mackinlay pretended not to notice as he cranked up the air-con. The cool, crisp air carried a faint hint of cedarwood.

'Med centre,' Mackinlay instructed the vehicle. 'Drive at casualty speed.'

The electric motor hummed to life and the buggy slid smoothly along the road, ramping up to 40 kph. Mackinlay patted the dash affectionately before slouching back in his seat.

'Did I miss much while I was in the box?' Cooper asked.

Mackinlay's expression darkened. 'Ortiz is dead. Came off the aerial assault course yesterday and broke his neck. They'd deliberately wetted it down – expect the unexpected.'

'Shit.'

'Guess God wasn't with him, huh? Still, he signed the waiver. Same as the rest of us. How you doing?'

'All right, I suppose.'

Mackinlay eyed him speculatively. 'Your mistake was projecting your own values onto the enemy. The Islamists aren't like us. They don't have the same family values or respect for the sanctity of human life.'

'So they keep telling us.'

'That's 'cause it's true.'

Cooper lapsed into silence as the buggy made a left turn, the road taking them past the chapel with its extended west wall flanking the main body on either side. With its buttresses and vaulted roof it looked archaic, a relic from a bygone age. But, like the Order itself, the chapel was little over thirty years old, its intricate carvings and pillars achieved through 3D printing. It had been a gift to the newly founded Order from President Lyndhurst, the founding father of the Religious States. A sign of the goodwill and wealth bestowed upon it.

The buggy came to a gentle halt and Cooper hit the release on his belt. He clambered from the buggy and took a deep breath to steel himself. He summoned a smile for Mackinlay as he walked around the front of the vehicle.

'I can take it from here, Mac. Thanks for the ride.'

'Want to keep the buggy?'

'No. Best stretch my legs. Send it back to the motor pool.'

Cooper paused at the door of the med centre, watching Mackinlay's retreating figure. He would report back Cooper's physical and mental state to the other applicants. Their trainers expected it, even encouraged it, as a means of support and, more pertinently, of weeding out the ideologically unsound.

Even those few seconds exposed to the sun had caused Cooper to break out into a sweat, and he felt it cool almost instantly on his skin as he entered the med centre. Cams tracked him along a sterile white corridor to where the reception AI identified him with a biometric scan. After four months at Fort Irwin Cooper still felt like a rube. With American industry decimated after the Great Flood, the cost of tech imported from the manufactories of Europa City and Africa had grown exponentially, and yet the Templars had access to it all. Another demonstration of how much the Order's wealth had grown since its inception.

'Consulting Room 3C – third door on the right,' the AI instructed.

Cooper followed its directions and rapped smartly on the door with his knuckles before entering. The doctor, a lean, fit-looking man of middle years with salt-and-pepper hair, looked up from the terminal on his desk. A name plaque identified him as Dr Gerhardt.

'Novitiate Cooper. Please take off your shirt and lie face-down on the couch.'

Cooper gritted his teeth as he peeled the shirt from his back, pulling the scabs from his lash marks. Pain, as their instructors constantly reminded them, could be controlled. He turned his head to face the doctor and watched as he thumbed an ampoule into the chamber of an air needle-gun.

Gerhardt stepped up to the couch and bent to examine Cooper. A polymer-encased finger probed the edges of the cuts left by the chaplain-commander's whip.

'Mild infection – nothing we can't knock out. Ready?'

Without waiting for the affirmative, Gerhardt pressed the needle-gun to the base of Cooper's spine and triggered it. A narrowly focused blast of compressed air punched through the flesh and delivered the ampoule's payload.

It started as an itch that grew steadily in intensity until it felt like insects crawling beneath the skin, creating an almost unbearable heat. Cooper knew the insect analogy wasn't far from the truth: millions of microscopic nanobots were rebuilding his muscle and skin in a matter of minutes. The Church frowned on such interference with God's design, but the Templars' Charter granted them a dispensation. As Copper understood it, medical nanotechnology was meant to be limited to the treatment of injuries. And yet, two months into the selection process, the surviving applicants had each received a course of nano-treatment designed to increase bone density and muscle mass. He had put on twenty pounds of muscle in less than two days.

The heat faded, and this time Gerhardt's probing finger produced no sensation of pain. Satisfied, he swapped out the needle-gun ampoule and injected a course of antibiotics.

'There we go. Fit for duty.'

Cooper swung his legs off the couch and stood. His throat still felt raw and he had a headache. The doctor, apparently picking up on his distress, pointed to a couple of packs sitting on the table adjacent to the door.

'Drink both rehydration pouches and keep your fluids up for the rest of the day.'

'I'm free to go?'

'Until the next time.'

Cooper didn't doubt there would be a next time. Injuries, from cuts to broken bones, were common, and, as Ortiz had demonstrated, fatalities not unknown, particularly once the applicants moved to training with live ammunition. First, however, he would have to survive tomorrow's endurance march.

The 4am bell sounded, the thirty-minute warning before morning prayer. Cooper stretched the stiffness out of his muscles, feeling a slight pull across his shoulder blades as the newly regenerated skin settled. He showered quickly and dressed in the dun-coloured fatigues of the novitiate before making his way outside for roll call.

Sergeant Jackson walked the line, calling out their names alphabetically from memory while inspecting them. All present and correct, he formed the men into pairs and marched them side-by-side to the chapel. Once inside, the pairs peeled off left and right, filling the arcade of twelve arches formed by the supporting pillars. No pews being present, the men knelt on the stone floor.

Chaplain-Commander Du Pont stood in the east, his body shielded by a simple lectern and framed between two pillars. Stylised vines decorated both pillars, but where the ones on the right rose in strict vertical rows, those on the left climbed its trunk in a helix pattern to reach the profusion of plants at the top. During the hours of darkness an outside light illuminated the recently decorated rose window, bringing to life the battle scenes of the Templars' first, doomed yet heroic, attempt to recapture Jerusalem from the Caliphate. Two further crusades had followed with no greater success.

Du Pont's measured tones, amplified by pick-up mikes, sounded throughout the chapel.

'Lord, we beseech thee to impart your grace to these your humble servants, so that they may emerge tempered by the fires of their training as instruments of your will. Let them know neither doubt nor fear in the face of the enemy as they go about their holy duty. Give strength to their arms that they might smite all who oppose the will of the one true God, who has no other name. Grant them the wisdom to faithfully serve these Religious States of America and the fortitude to resist temptation, so that when they at last lay down their arms they may ascend to the heavens above and take their rightful place at your side. Forever and ever, amen!'

The morning blessing, in Cooper's opinion, was always thankfully short; a spiritual stiffener to set the men up for the day. High Twelve, or noonday, prayers were considerably more involved, focusing on their duty to God, to America, and finally, the many sins of their enemies and the justification for their destruction. The Islamic Caliphate might be the accepted enemy, but it didn't take much reading between the lines to recognise the prevailing view: that the Templars' mission should stop at nothing short of the total extermination of the Islamic faith. Cooper thought that extreme, but knew better than to contest it with the chaplain-commander.

The first rays of dawn coloured the horizon a vibrant red as the applicants filed from the chapel. A stillness in the air warned of the heat to come, which did not bode well for the trials of the day. Cooper caught up with Mackinlay and Walker as they made their way to the mess hall. They welcomed him with a smile but, like himself, he could see they were already looking inward. The endurance march would be hell on earth.

Breakfast consisted of a protein shake and water laced with electrolytes. Cooper found he had little appetite, but drank the malt-flavoured sludge regardless. You learned quickly in the military to always take food when offered it. Besides, he would soon be burning plenty of calories.

Cooper adjusted the straps on the tactical vest, pulling it tight to his torso. The ballistic plates were old-style ceramic, chosen for no better reason than to add to the weight. The shoulder plates moved awkwardly as he settled the rucksack on his back: forty pounds of weight comprising an integrated three-litre water reservoir, medical kit, rappelling rope, grenades, detonation cord, blasting caps and extra magazines. At least the helmet was light, its shell made from thermoplastics. Lastly, he slung the M42 assault rifle over his shoulder.

The sharp blast of a whistle cut through Cooper's thoughts and he moved off at the double, making his way from the barracks to the parade ground and its waiting line of JLTVs. Jackson moved quickly along the line, giving each of the men a number between one and eight. At his signal, they loaded up into the JLTV matching their numbers. Cooper found himself sharing with Walker, Garcia and Pedersen. The auto-drive kicked in as soon as they had fastened their belts, jolting them back in their seats. Cooper caught a final glimpse of the box as the glass polarised to opacity. He hoped it wasn't an omen. The crackle of electricity and the clang of metal told him the fence had been de-energised and the gate opened, which meant they were heading out into the desert.

They travelled for over an hour, bouncing and sliding their way off-road before coming to an abrupt halt. Silence fell, interrupted only by the ping of cooling metal. Cooper raised a questioning eyebrow to which Walker shrugged in reply. They checked their weapons and popped open the doors.

Striated walls of rock rose on either side of the JLTV, the defile opening out in a funnel shape away from the vehicle. Cooper synched his earpiece to the com-unit strapped to his right wrist. He checked the motion sensor: friendly contacts only. A map reading identified their position as fifteen klicks north-east of Fort Irwin. A ping alerted him to an incoming message, which detailed a route back to base. Cooper noted that the bearing would take him over the exposed high ground at the mouth of the defile before striking out over open desert.

Static crackled across an open comms channel. 'You have two hours to return to base following the designated route. You will set off at ten-minute intervals, starting with Novitiate Cooper.'

Cooper checked the position of the tube from his water reservoir to ensure he could access it on the march, then pressed the polarising setting on his goggles. Walker gave him an encouraging thumbs-up as he set a two-hour countdown on his com-unit.

Plumes of dust rose up around him as he set off at a brisk marching pace, following the curve of the defile. The walls on either side sloped gradually downwards as they neared the entrance, before meeting the rising ground of the hill to the south-west. Cooper felt the sweat gathering beneath the straps of his backpack and a tightness in the recently repaired skin on his back. Two days in the box had left him depleted, making an already difficult challenge an even greater feat of endurance. While he could have asked for a medical deferment, Cooper knew it would have meant being marked down. After his mistake during the MOUT exercise he couldn't risk any more demerits. He checked his progress and slackened his pace a little. One hour fifty-nine minutes and fifty-nine seconds would still be a pass. Let others worry about coming top of the class.

Cooper breasted the top of the hill and paused to take a fresh bearing. The ground dropped sharply towards an open plain, its expanse littered with boulders and scrubby vegetation. Ten klicks by his calculation with little or no shade. He adjusted his backpack, sipped some water and started down the slope. He had taken less than twenty paces when the friable sandstone crumbled beneath his boots and his right foot slid away from him. Unable to halt himself, he increased his momentum instead, sliding down the side of the hill in a cloud of dust and scree, arms windmilling for balance as he fought to avoid a crippling fall. Looking to slow his descent, he spotted the grey and lifeless wood of a stunted tree and turned his body towards it. It filled his vision a second before the jarring impact that spun him about the trunk, spending most of his momentum.

Breathing heavily, he brought himself to a halt and checked his respiration, heartbeat and pulse on his com-unit. OCT would be monitoring the same telemetry as part of his evaluation. Cooper gave himself a minute for them to return to something approaching normal before setting off again. Might as well make use of the adrenalin while it was still coursing through him.

With the main obstacle overcome, Cooper settled into a steady march. The sun beat mercilessly from a cloudless cerulean sky and there was a metallic tang to the air that seemed to taint his water. He drank as sparingly as he dared, aware of the imminent danger of heatstroke. As his feet ate up the klicks, he realised the march was not only a feat of physical endurance but also one of mental fortitude. The discomfort of the merciless heat, aching muscles and exhaustion could all be suppressed, but there was an oppressiveness to the open and unrelieved landscape that made him constantly question the progress shown on his com-unit compared with that seen by his own eyes. Hadn't he passed that same clump of gorse ten minutes before? Perhaps the heat had fried his com-unit? He pushed the doubts aside and forced his legs to keep moving.

An hour and a half into the march, his com-unit showed three klicks remaining. What should have been a comfortable margin, had the route not thrown up a fresh surprise. Ahead, a dustbowl stretched across the horizon. Cooper checked the map and confirmed the specified route passed through the centre of the bowl. He did some rough calculations and worked out that skirting round would add a minimum of five klicks. It was time he didn't have, particularly when his water was already running low.

Cooper pressed on, his feet sinking up to the ankles in the soft sand. Each step required additional effort, driving him closer to exhaustion. He gritted his teeth, ignoring the ache in his thighs and the sting of sweat in the abraded skin beneath the straps of his pack. Every step he took was a step closer to the finish, a step closer to success. He reminded himself that failure had consequences for not just himself but for his family. This was the last of the great physical tests; he had never been stronger or fitter in his life. As he had done in the box, he slowed his breathing, entering a meditative state. Anxiety and pain faded and he redoubled his effort. His pace quickened and he realised the sand was giving way to firmer ground again. Half a klick to go and five minutes left on the countdown. It was going to be tight.

The gate, with its twin rows of razor wire, filled Cooper's vision as he forced one foot in front of the other. His breathing was ragged, his muscles on fire, but it no longer mattered. With only metres to go, he increased his pace. Servo motors hummed to life and the gate slid back on its rails to admit him. He was home. Was it enough?

Sergeant Jackson consulted his datapad. 'One hour, fifty-seven minutes and twenty-three seconds.'

Cooper couldn't quite suppress his smile. They could bang on about humility all they wanted, but he saw no sin in taking pride in having passed.

'Stop grinning and hit the showers. Advanced knife fighting in one hour.'

Cooper stumbled in the direction of the barracks. It was going to be a long day.

CHAPTER 3

Hopkins rolled onto her side, the warmth of her orgasm already starting to fade. Tyler lay on his back with his right arm behind his head, staring up at the lazy rotation of the ceiling fan. Wherever his thoughts were, they were no longer in the room or with her. Her fingers brushed across his bicep, moved to his ribs and came to rest on the firm muscle of his right pectoral. She hesitated for a moment before reaching out with her index finger and tracing the outline of the puckered bullet scar.

'Don't.'

'Don't what?'

'Say what you're thinking of saying. You of all people know I have to go back. We've both got too much invested in this to stop now.'

Hopkins withdrew her hand and turned away. She sat up and snatched her cigarettes and lighter from the bedside table. Her steps were brisk and angry as she crossed to the bedroom window and drew back the curtain to look out at the neatly mowed lawn. Tyler's eyes would be on the long auburn hair that fell to the small of her back, the swell of her hips and ass, those long, well-muscled legs he liked to lie between. Weak with the sins of the flesh, just like all the others. She lit a cigarette, drew in a lungful of smoke and then exhaled it in the direction of the fan.

'At least open the window if you're going to smoke in here.'

'Given where you're headed, a little passive smoking is the least of your worries.' Sighing, Hopkins opened the window anyway. The autumn air raised goosebumps on her skin.

'I came back from the Saudi campaign. I'll come back from this one.'

'This one's different, Marty. Williams is coming to the end of his second term and he's determined to leave a legacy behind him. He doesn't care how many American corpses he builds that legacy on. You need to play it smart – you're no good to either of us dead. It's not like Grand Master Vanderbilt is going to be out there risking his ass to get the Jews their homeland back.'

'We've talked about this, Susanna. Vanderbilt has already proven himself, both at the Fall and during the First and Second Crusades. I need battle honours of my own to have any hope of succeeding him. Trust me, I've no interest in being another fallen hero. I've worked too hard for that. We've worked too hard for that. Come back to bed. Don't spoil what's left of our time together with this ... foolishness.'

Hopkins stubbed her cigarette out on the windowsill and flicked the butt into the garden. She turned to face Tyler, who patted the bed beside him. Agreeing to the truce, she slipped back under the sheets, warming herself from the heat of his body. It was a moment she would have liked to extend, but Tyler had other business on his mind.

'What was the feeling like in the House today? Will the bill approving the crusade pass the Senate?'

Hopkins' lips puckered in distaste. 'It's going to be close. The Southern Democrats might control the House but even the hawks have become wary of the cost of the war. Public disapproval grows with each body bag sent home, and that's before you take into account the failure to prevent terror attacks on our own soil. I've lobbied all I can, but with a week left before the vote we need to dig up fresh dirt on the holdouts.'

Tyler chuckled dismissively. 'That's why I prefer war to politics. It's far cleaner just to shoot your enemies.'

Hopkins turned away as Tyler leaned in for a kiss. She'd had enough of his condescension. When they first met, he was just another grunt with a propensity for violence heightened by Templar indoctrination. She had deprogrammed the worst of his zealotry, starting with the offer of herself as the forbidden fruit. Once he had broken that taboo the rest came easy. She had stoked his ambitions, moulded him, coached him to use his media appearances to his advantage and aid his climb through the ranks. Success had made him arrogant, and while this was not necessarily a bad thing for his political ambitions, he needed reminding she wasn't subservient to him. But now wasn't the moment.

'News, Fourth Crusade Bill.'

A holo-screen fizzed into existence at the foot of the bed in response to Hopkins' command, automatically loading Fox News. As spokesperson for the SDNC she'd written many of the headlines and didn't need an echo chamber. Better to take a temperature reading from the opposition.

The FSTV banner flashed up on the screen and faded out to reveal a tall, gangly man in his late thirties with thinning black hair, eyes hidden behind mirrored aviator shades. His limbs moved animatedly as he gestured to camera and launched into his monologue, speaking in a distinctive Southern drawl.

'People call me a terrorist sympathiser, a liberal limp dick, even a betrayer of the American dream. Well, let me tell you that no one believes in the American dream more than I do, which is why it breaks my goddamn heart to see it traduced by those swine masquerading as our government in Richmond. Chester Williams is a buffoon, backed by a corrupt Senate whose only interest is in prolonging this war in order to profit from it. The current campaign in the Middle East is approaching its fourth decade and has claimed the lives of more than three million American soldiers. Three million of our sons and daughters – if that isn't the destruction of the American dream right there, I don't know what is! How much more of a wake-up call do the lovers of this grand republic of ours need for them to say enough is enough? Despite what some would have you believe, I'm not in denial about the Caliphate. We all know and recognise it's an oppressive regime, one that violates human rights and dignities on a daily basis. But the truth of the matter is that many of the Arab nations have chosen to embrace their twisted doctrine, and it's not America's job to act as policeman to the world. You can't give people democracy at gunpoint.'

Tyler cut across the broadcast. 'Are you seriously going to listen to this lunatic, Susanna?'

'Last time I checked we still had a little something called freedom of speech in this country.'

'Depends on your definition of free speech. Jefferson Lynch is a hack, a has-been, courting controversy to prop up his flatlining career. We ought to lock him up for spouting that kind of sedition.'

'We lock him up, we're going to have to lock up a lot of others besides. Like it or not, he represents the views of a whole lot of Americans. Those are the hearts and minds you're going to need to win over in order to pursue this crusade. Lose sight of that and you'll have lost before you've even begun.'

Tyler's scowl informed her that he was going to sulk for the rest of the night. The more influence you gave a man, the more he would act like a child when you told him something he didn't want to hear. She often wondered how America had risen to become a superpower in the first place. More by luck than grace of God, she reckoned.

'End feed.' Hopkins lay on her side, presenting her back to Tyler. She felt his body tense and then relax almost immediately as he mastered his anger. Was that civilised instinct or the pragmatic realisation that violence, in this instance, would gain him nothing? That was the trouble with keeping a dangerous dog: you never knew when it might turn.

CHAPTER 4

Lynch unfolded his six-foot-three-inch frame from the seat and groaned. There was never enough legroom in coach, but he couldn't deny that his circumstances were much reduced, as much as he'd like to. Seven years on from his book covering the '81 presidential campaign, he'd failed to produce another hit. Back then, it really did look as though the Republicans would sweep to power on a tide of anti-war sentiment. Instead, after a bitter and disputed count, Chester Williams had been inaugurated as the fifth president of the RSA and had cycled up the war machine to maximum revs. As public opinion moved behind the president, the talk show appearances, book signings and lectures dried up, as did slots on the prime-time news channels. Lynch was last year's man, reduced to playing an angry caricature of himself, engendering chaos and anarchy wherever he went. Only now, amid all the booze and the pills, he had lost track of the dividing line between fantasy and reality.

He retrieved his leather satchel from the overhead locker and put on his aviator shades. Time to get into character for his public. He swept an armful of Wild Turkey miniatures off his tray and into his bag, earning a glare from the flight attendant. Lynch leered at her, safe in the knowledge she was unlikely to pepper-spray him while in the cabin. He set off at a jolting walk, his legs apparently containing too many knees. The passengers, having already endured five hours of Lynch's strident attempts to engage with all and sundry since leaving Mexico City, shuffled out of his way while avoiding eye contact. Lynch smiled to himself and saluted the male cabin attendant stationed at the top of the steps at the rear of the aircraft.

An Indian summer sun shone in the sky above the tarmac of Lexington airport. Lynch took a moment to enjoy the heat on his skin before loping down the steps. A bus sat idling beyond the wingtip of the plane, waiting to transport passengers to the international arrivals terminal. Lynch clutched his satchel to his chest as he uttered a series of terse pardons in order to thread his way to the rear of the bus. Run the gamut of airport security, take another bus to the car park, collect his car and head out on the interstate, and he would be home and dry.

The bus jolted to a halt with the hiss of compressed air. Lynch let the other passengers swarm out of the bus and make their way through the glass doors of the terminal. No point rushing; he had to wait for the unloading of his checked-in luggage. He ambled his way onto the escalator and tucked into the side to let others pass. As he approached the top the irrational fear that he would somehow fly off took hold, and he cleared the end of the escalator with a long, jerky stride.

Lynch's head whipped side to side before coming to rest as his gaze fixed on an arrow labelled 'arrivals'. He stepped onto the travelator, sweating in spite of the air-con, and let it carry him the length of the corridor. Midway along, he realised he was still clutching his satchel to his chest, and slung it over his shoulder. Airports always spooked him.

A right turn at the end of the travelator led to the baggage reclaim hall. Lynch studied the monitor and identified the belt for his flight. It stood depressingly still as he took up position behind the yellow line. The monitor read 'expected in five minutes'. He needed a cigarette and a drink. As he shifted his weight from foot to foot the clinking from his satchel reminded him that he could at least do something about the latter.

Lynch unscrewed the cap from a miniature and swallowed its contents in a single gulp. He paused for a moment before extracting a second bottle. The woman standing next to him pursed her lips in disapproval. Lynch looked her up and down: fortyish, bottle-blonde hair, still with a good figure. He remembered how she had studiously ignored his advances during the flight, but he could work with that. Show her that her manners and graces were nothing more than repression, unleash her desires. He'd need another drink or two first, and so would she, before they got over the line.

Lynch's fingers slipped off the miniature as the flashing light and rumbling movement of the baggage belt brought him back to the now. He scanned the belt, his eyes flitting across an array of dull cases until they finally alighted on the Hawaiian spray-painted Samsonite. Didn't matter how wasted he got on the flight; he was sure to collect the right bag.

He heaved the bag off the belt, snapped out its pull handle and trundled towards the exit. The automatic doors swished aside and he passed through the turnstile. Ahead, the corridor forked and Lynch steered his bag to the right – nothing to declare. He nodded to the customs officer behind the desk: he was just an ordinary Joe returning from down Mexico way. Why the hell had he done that? Was he crazy, trying to attract attention? Eyes front. Keep on walking. No reason for the hammer to drop.

Lynch froze. He liked dogs; he had grown up with them. And there was no denying that the German shepherd padding towards him with its handler trailing behind was a beautiful example of the breed. Close to three feet at the shoulder with a thick black-and-tan coat and dark, intelligent eyes, it looked pleased to see him. Very pleased.

He turned round. As expected, a pair of customs officers were closing in on him. Lynch let go of the handle of his case and stepped to one side. The garish paint job suddenly seemed a lot less clever.

The shepherd sat down opposite his case and started to bark.

The dog handler cracked a knowing smile. 'Mr Lynch, if you wouldn't mind accompanying us?'

Lynch sat staring at the pitted surface of the table. Links of chain rattled through the eyebolt on the table as he reached up to scratch an eyebrow. He lowered his hands and stared at the cuffs. They had taken his watch and other personal effects when they detained him. Since then, he had sat alone in the interview room. Alone but presumably observed. A pair of wall-mounted cams tracked his movements, red recording lights blinking malevolently. Classic softening-up technique. But if they expected him to squeal, they had another think coming.

An indeterminate period of time later, the door swung open and a figure stood silhouetted in the harsh light beyond. Dramatic pause established, he entered the room and closed the door behind him. Lynch looked at the dark suit, white shirt, black tie and earpiece: government spook, the stereotypical Man in Black. Interesting. Could there be an outside chance he wasn't about to spend the next twenty years in prison?

Lynch watched as his visitor took a remote from his inside suit pocket and disabled the cams before pulling out a chair and sitting opposite. Up close, from the lines around his eyes and grey at his temples, Lynch put his interrogator's age at around forty. The man smiled, revealing the perfectly straight and evenly spaced white teeth of expensive orthodontics. Lynch's fists clenched in response to a sudden urge to smash those teeth.

'Jefferson Lynch, age thirty-seven, Lexington native, journalist, writer and drug mule.'

'You got me there, bubba. The question is, who are you?'

The man flipped open his wallet to reveal a card identifying him as Operations Officer Hannah. 'Right about now I'd say I was your best, and realistically only, friend in the world.'

'That's a pretty bold claim for someone I just met.'

Hannah shrugged dismissively. 'Not from where I'm sitting. There are no cameras or audience for you to play to, Lynch, so why don't you cut the crap? Your career is in near terminal decline and you're facing a felony conviction for drug smuggling with intent to supply. Because, legendary dope fiend or not, there isn't a defence attorney in the country who can convince a jury that four kilos of cocaine are for personal use.'

'So why are you here? If it's such an open and shut case, why not let justice take its course? Unless there's something you want. For example, my supplier?'

'Your supplier, his enforcers and much of his distribution chain were arrested shortly after your flight left Mexico City this morning. The conclusion to a two-year operation.'

Lynch spoke aloud before he could stop himself: 'Then what the hell do you need me for?'

Hannah treated him to another flash of perfect white teeth. 'We need you to go to war. Or, more precisely, to cover the war as a correspondent attached to the First Templar Division's Combat Aviation Brigade, under the command of Colonel Martin Tyler. His mission, as part of the Templar special forces unit, is to liberate Israel from the Islamic Caliphate and restore the holy city of Jerusalem.'

'Look, I know I don't get much coverage on the mainstream news networks these days, but in case you hadn't noticed, I've spent most of the last decade protesting the war. Wouldn't one of your Fox News sock puppets be a better fit for writing puff pieces on our latest round of military adventurism?'

'They'd only be preaching to the converted. As you're aware, this is an election year, one that marks the end of President Williams' second term. In order to secure a continuity candidate who will continue to prosecute the war we need to fully control the narrative. That means taking all the nut-jobs and refuseniks that live below the comment line of your posts with us.'

'I'm sure it does. But even supposing I can sell this crazed Damascene conversion of yours, what makes you think I'll betray every journalistic principle I've ever held? You're right, I don't have much left at this point, but I still have my reputation.'

'What you have are crippling alimony payments, an eleven-year-old daughter you're not allowed to visit, spiralling debts and a serious substance abuse problem. None of which will be helped by doing federal time. No hope of rapprochement with your daughter, no prospect of anything beyond the most menial employment, no more guns to play with. In short, everything and anything that makes your life meaningful will be gone. Are your principles and reputation really worth that? Alternatively, we can make the charges disappear, give you a chance to serve your country. Once you're actually out there with our boys you might come to find yourself thinking differently about the war. If not, well, having the president's gratitude and the opportunity to cover national politics again ought to be compensation enough.'

Lynch sucked at his teeth, hollowing his cheeks. 'The last time the Caliphate got hold of a war correspondent they tortured him live on air before beheading him.'

'Shouldn't be a problem, Mr Lynch.' Hannah smiled. 'As long as you don't let them take you alive.'

Lynch ran his hand across his shaved skull as he stared at his reflection in the mirror. The incision behind his right ear where they had implanted the interface still looked raw, but the skin around the fasteners on his temples had healed much faster. Compared to some of the more extreme body modification he'd seen, they looked relatively normal. He picked up the wrap-around HUD, which hummed to life as it neared his eyes, and clicked it into place.

'Camera one, active. Camera two, active.'

A pair of small drones rose from the table behind him, the feed projected directly onto his retinas. In the mirror they looked like bats.

Lynch cut the feed and bowed his head. He could do this. Play their twisted game for as long as it took to figure out a way of turning the tables. Then it would be payback time. Old school investigative journalism – penetrate to the heart of this rotten war and expose it for the sham it was. This time it would be different; no editors to slap him down, no vested interests burying the story. This time, the dead would have a voice. Eighteen years since the Second Crusade started, and their faces still haunted his dreams. Time to pay his dues.

CHAPTER 5

Cooper focused on his breathing, willing himself to be calm. This was the final test of the programme, strictly pass or fail with no middle ground. He pressed his palm to the sensor and the door to the VR suite slid open. A technician looked up from the star-shaped configuration of five couches and motioned him forward. The door closed behind Cooper with a disturbing finality.

The technician, now standing with his back to Cooper, motioned vaguely to his right as he checked the readings on a set of holo-displays.

'Strip down to your shorts. You'll find a suit in one of the cubicles.'

Cooper walked over to the nearest cubicle, which was little more than a U of extruded plastic that came up to his chest. He stripped off his clothes, stacking them on top of his boots on the floor, and unhooked the VR neuro-link suit from the back wall. The black neoprene resembled a wetsuit but was noticeably heavier. Cooper suppressed a shudder as he zipped up the suit and felt the multitude of tiny needles penetrate his skin to establish contact with his nerves. Wired for sight, sound, smell, touch and taste.

The technician handed Cooper a helmet as he stepped

out of the cubicle, and he strapped it on before swinging his legs onto the couch.

'Ready?'

Cooper nodded, lowered the helmet's faceplate and lay back on the couch, which moulded itself to the contours of his body. The technician connected the suit's umbilical to the couch's console and checked the readouts again. Pre-checks complete, he inserted a black metallic disc into the console.

'We're good to go here. You might experience some nausea, a sense of falling, on connection. It's perfectly normal.'

'Got you.'

The technician hit the simulation button. Cooper felt his stomach, closely followed by his mind, go into freefall. He opened his eyes to find himself bound to a chair with a thick rope. He felt the coarse fibres biting into his naked flesh and the heat of compacted sand on the soles of his feet. The metallic taste of blood filled his mouth and he probed experimentally with his tongue, discovering several missing teeth. Green and yellow bruises covered his torso and his limbs, the sight of which triggered a series of dull aches and pains. Standard operating procedure prior to interrogation. Unable to remember how he had got there, his eyes flitted around the room looking for clues. Stone walls covered in flaking whitewash, a single light in a stained bulkhead and a steel door pitted with rust offered no clues. A sudden flash of memory recalled an explosion and his JLTV rolling down an embankment. Flashes of gunfire, screams, and then darkness. Cooper wondered if he were the only survivor.

Thirst and hunger, along with the stench of his own waste, added to Cooper's increasing discomfort. Pain and exhaustion permitted only the briefest moments of sleep before his body jerked back to consciousness. With no windows and the light constantly lit, he had no means of accurately measuring time, but estimated a good twelve hours to have passed before the door opened.

The man framed in the doorway kept his thick black hair neatly trimmed and wore a spotless olive drab uniform and knee-high leather boots. His nose, cheekbones and forehead were weathered by exposure to the elements, the remainder of his features concealed behind a beard. He walked with a rolling gait that bordered on a swagger.

'Back in the land of the living? Good. I have some questions for you.'

'Templar Novitiate Billy Ray Cooper. Service number 26647155.'

Cooper's interrogator sighed. 'We can go down that route, yes. But I would prefer avoid such ... uncivilised methods.'

Cooper said nothing and the interrogator shrugged. At an unseen signal the door opened again and a second man, short and more compact, entered, pushing a trolley in front of him. He wheeled it into position next to Cooper, allowing him to see the battery, jump leads and thick rubber gauntlets.

'Thank you, Qasim.'

'Will there be anything else, Commander?'

'Send in the drone.'

Qasim nodded and marched from the room. A few seconds later the whir of rotors announced the arrival of a camera drone, which took up position above Cooper. Ignoring the instruments of torture for now, the commander picked up a metal water bottle from the lower shelf of the trolley and unscrewed the cap. Cooper's tongue licked at his cracked lips.

'You are thirsty, yes? Answer my questions and I'll see you are brought food and water.'

When Cooper remained silent, the commander upended the bottle above the Templar's head, letting its contents run down his face and neck to soak his chest and back. Cooper's tongue licked greedily at the drops, which only made his thirst worse.

'Still nothing to say? Perhaps if I start with what I know,

you will continue? You are a member of an advance scouting party for a covert Templar force operating deep within Caliphate territory. What is the strength of your unit? Where are they based? What is the mission objective?'

'Templar Novitiate Billy Ray Cooper. Service number 26647155.'

The commander shook his head sorrowfully as he pulled on the rubber gauntlets. He attached the leads to the battery and touched them to Cooper's chest. Cooper gritted his teeth as electricity jolted through him, paralysing his muscles. His torturer repeated the procedure a further two times, increasing the duration of the shock with each repetition. Cooper retreated into his mind as he had been trained, suppressing the pain.

The punch caught him by surprise, a different kind of pain to the electric shock. It snapped his head to the side, where a second punch snapped it back again. His torturer repeated his questions, following up with fresh punches when he met with silence. He worked methodically, without anger, gauging how much punishment his subject could take before blacking out.

Cooper felt himself weakening. A few simple words – numbers, positions, target – and the pain would stop. But he knew those words would finish him. He had to bury the information deep. Instead of the treacherous words he began to recite the catechism; doctrine drilled into each applicant by rote.

'What is the chief end of man? Man's chief end is to glorify God, and to enjoy him forever.

'What is God? God is a spirit, infinite, eternal, and unchangeable, in his being, wisdom, power, holiness, justice, goodness and truth.

'Are there more Gods than one? There is but one only, the living and true God, who has no other names.'

The next blow landed with sufficient force to knock Cooper to the ground. His torturer took a step back, breathing hard. He permitted himself a faint smile as he hauled Cooper and the chair he was bound to back into the upright position.

'Very good. You won that round. But you won't anger me again.' He took another bottle of water from the trolley and permitted Cooper to drink. 'We might be enemies, but I respect you nonetheless. You Templars are good soldiers and brave warriors. Worthy opponents. I take no pleasure in this, but you have information I need. For both our sakes, tell me what I need to know and I promise you a clean death.'

Cooper spat out a mouthful of blood. 'Fuck you.'

The torture continued for another two days, alternating between beatings and electrocution. They gave him just enough water to stay alive and conscious, with random breaks of sufficient duration to allow the faint glimmer of hope that the torture might finally be over before it started once more. Cooper fell silent, the 107 questions and answers of the catechism playing on a repeat loop in his head. He had learned them because the programme required it, but in truth he struggled with his faith, particularly when faced with the certainty of the other applicants. Accordingly, the fear of being found out persisted. But he understood duty and loyalty, and clung to them both.

There was something in the commander's demeanour that triggered a warning when he next entered the room, the ever-present camera drone buzzing above him. Cooper squinted through a swollen eye, the white of which was filled with blood. The squat silhouette behind the commander resolved itself into Qasim, and there was no mistaking the purpose of the heavy scimitar he held in his hand. This was it. The words of Psalm 23 came to mind but died on his lips. In the end they were only words and he doubted that saying them would have any effect on whether or not he received his eternal reward.

'Intel has a limited shelf life, as you know. Yours has reached its expiry date. As have you.' The commander addressed the hovering drone directly. 'Templar Novitiate

Cooper, you have been found guilty of war crimes against the Islamic Caliphate, and in the name of Caliph Abu Ahmad al-Nasr al-Qurayshi I sentence you to death by beheading. Qasim, you will carry out the sentence.'

Qasim took up position behind Cooper. It seemed the Caliphate had no interest in any last words he might utter. He felt the movement of air as the scimitar swept back and then forward, the keen steel biting deep into his neck.

Cooper sat bolt upright on the VR couch. He raised the helmet's visor and felt his neck cautiously. He was thirsty and hungry but otherwise unharmed by his VR ordeal.

The technician finished typing on the holo-screen and smiled. 'Congratulations, Novitiate Cooper; you've made the grade.'

Cooper nodded, still not entirely anchored to the present. The reality of the technician's words slowly dawned on him. He had done it: passed the most intensive and brutal military training programme in existence, earned the right to wear the red cross pattée. All that remained now was the taking of his vows, after which he would be set for life. Not only would he receive a generous pension after twenty years of service, the consulting options for ex-Templars paid top dollar: bodyguard, police firearms training, Homeland Security; the list went on. The hardest part was surely behind him now.

CHAPTER 6

Grand Master Thaddeus Vanderbilt looked out through the armoured glass of the Panopticon's Central Office, situated at the top of the Watchtower. From here, the President enjoyed a 360-degree view of the Outer-Circle, with its Cabinet, Situation and Lyndhurst rooms: the ability to observe without being observed. It echoed the all-seeing eye of God, reminding the people that the president served as father to the nation. The current holder of that office, Chester Williams, a heavyset middle-aged man of average height with grey hair to match his eyes, sat opposite Vanderbilt, separated from him by an expansive leather-topped desk. He wore a well-tailored suit of navy blue with a crisp white shirt and knitted silk tie. Gold shone on his left ring finger and wrist, the latter in the form of a heavy watch bracelet.

Vanderbilt glanced at his own watch and suppressed a yawn. Ten minutes into the briefing and Williams had yet to say anything of substance. The president was dancing around some unspoken issue, an issue he knew Vanderbilt wouldn't like. The age-old struggle between church and state, a testing of the limits of temporal power. More than two decades on from its inception, there were still those in government who felt uneasy about the existence of a religious military order, those who grew more concerned by the day by the Templars' influence and power. Vanderbilt, having reached the conclusion that a theocracy would better serve the people, knew they were right to worry.

The two secret service agents stationed either side of the president tensed as the door opened. Vanderbilt took stock of the newcomer as he crossed to the desk and sat in the unoccupied chair next to him; the rank insignia on his uniform identified him as a *seren*, a captain in the Israel Defense Forces, a member of the army in exile. Both his bearing and physique indicated him to be operationally active.

'Grand Master Vanderbilt, this is Captain Katz of the IDF Special Forces Unit 212. I've ordered him to be attached to Templar forces in an advisory capacity for the duration of the campaign. He will be the eyes and ears of the Israeli government, reporting directly to Prime Minister Ben-David.'

Vanderbilt had heard of Unit 212, Maglan, a reconnaissance unit that specialised in operating behind enemy lines using advanced technologies and weapons. It meant the man before him was an augment and, more pertinently, a spy.

The president motioned Katz to the swivel chair next to Vanderbilt. The two soldiers nodded curtly to one another.

'Prime Minister Ben-David is pleased to hear the Senate has voted in favour of further military action against the Islamic Caliphate. He looks forward to the continued cooperation between our two nations.'

'You may assure Mr Ben-David that the American people stand shoulder to shoulder with the sons and daughters of Israel, as we have done ever since those dark days of '63. Together, we will overthrow the Caliphate and restore your homeland, as God intended.'

'Thank you, Mr President. Believe me when I say there's no greater gift you could give to the Jewish diaspora.

Pleasantries aside, my understanding is that I'm here to discuss my assignment?'

Williams nodded. 'You'll be serving with the Second Battalion, Two Hundred and Twenty-Seventh Aviation Regiment of the First Templar Division's Combat Aviation Brigade under the command of Colonel Martin Tyler. Israeli forces will accompany you during the final assault on Jerusalem.'

'I've heard of this Colonel Tyler. He's a good soldier. A brave man.'

Vanderbilt narrowed his eyes. 'I'm glad our choice meets with your approval.'

Katz turned to Vanderbilt. 'I apologise, Grand Master, if I've somehow given offence?'

'I'm sure the Grand Master simply misspoke. We're grateful for the support of the Israeli military during our operations. Isn't that correct, Thaddeus?'

Vanderbilt offered up an insincere smile of apology. 'Of course, Mr President.'

'If that's all, Mr President?' Katz asked, ignoring the tension.

'Yes. Report directly to Colonel Tyler at Fort Irwin on Monday for your orientation.'

Williams waited until the door had closed behind Katz. 'What the hell was that?'

'About not wanting an Israeli spy embedded with my men.'

'You don't know that for certain.'

'Chester, don't kid a kidder. The Israelis watch their friends twice as closely as their enemies.'

'Be that as it may, the Israeli government in exile has been a very generous donor to the party over the years. It's only natural for them to expect a return on that investment, particularly when it relates to the restoration of their homeland.'

'That's another thing – you're asking me to put my men through the meatgrinder only to let the Israelis step in at the last moment and take all the glory.'

'If I didn't know better, I'd say I was hearing the sin of vanity. Surely there's no greater honour for a Templar than to lay down his life in the service of God, particularly in the pursuit of His glory? At least, I assume that's why Congress spends all that money on training and equipping your warrior monks.'

'A Christian glory, yes. Not a Jewish one.'

'I'm sure they can be one and the same. As to feeding this meatgrinder of yours, don't forget we have almost a million volunteers from the Greater Russian Collective and Eastern Europe.'

'And when they lose control and start slaughtering civilians?'

Williams shrugged. 'They'll be Muslim civilians.'

Vanderbilt stood without waiting for Williams' dismissal. The trouble with second-term presidents was their belief that they had nothing to lose, their obsession with building a monument to their time in office. He would have to ensure Williams' successor proved more amenable to the Church's agenda.

Vanderbilt sat at his desk, staring into space. A twinge in his right shoulder reminded him he still carried the fragments of a Caliphate bullet. He massaged the deltoid, easing the tension in the muscle. The wound always played up when his conscience was troubling him. Like some peculiar moral weathervane.

He pressed the intercom, patching him through to his adjutant. 'Lachlan, cancel the remainder of the day's meetings. See to it that I'm not disturbed.'

But disturbed he was, both by Williams' spoken and unspoken criticism. Had he indulged the sin of pride? And if he had, was there not some justification? When Grand Master Merrick had finally succumbed to wounds received during the final days of the Third Crusade, Vanderbilt had taken control of a very different Order. He had transformed the Templars from a purely military-religious concern into an organisation of wealth and political influence in the space of five short years. It had taken courage and skill, had created enemies along the way, but who could deny the result? True, he had not done it alone; his family's wealth and political contacts proved invaluable, as did the confidence of his old college roommate, Williams, then serving his first term as president. Yet it remained an undeniable fact that the Templars' meteoric rise would not have occurred under the mastery of his rivals. Surely knowledge of your own worth wasn't a sin? Was it not written that a proper love of God came from a proper love of yourself? If his acts brought honour and fame to himself, that was a subsidiary to the glory he sought to do unto God. Everything he had done, did now, and would do in the future aspired to the final realisation of one nation under one flag under one God. An America weakened by environmental and economic disaster would rise again as a power to make the world tremble. He, Thaddeus Vanderbilt, had vowed as such and would make it so. Not for his own fame and aggrandisement, but for the salvation of the American people.

Vanderbilt sighed, opened the top drawer of his desk and took out the scourge. Blood had stained the once-tan leather tails dark. Of all the deceptions a man might practise, self-deception was surely the worst. To achieve purity of purpose he must drive the pride from his body. He unbuttoned his tunic and shirt and hung them over the back of the chair before kneeling at the edge of the Persian rug in front of his desk. His fingers traced the intricate geometric patterns. Where was it from? Aleppo? Idlib? Most certainly somewhere in Syria; the spoils of an earlier campaign to punish the heathens. He rolled the rug up and knelt on the boards below. The first strokes of his self-mortification were tentative as he worked up his conviction and rhythm. Speed and force increased, opening wounds in the already scarred flesh, bringing with them the rush of pain. But it was in the spaces between the pain that Vanderbilt found his clarity and focus.

Vision, Vanderbilt saw, was key, and the lack of it the reason why so many of his contemporaries failed to understand the purpose of the crusades. Uniting a nation divided by class, colour, education and wealth required a common goal. Jerusalem, to the majority of Americans, was a faraway city in a faraway country that appeared on their screens in largely negative terms. As a symbol, however, it represented a far greater ideal. The place where their lord and saviour, Jesus Christ, had died upon the cross for their sins. Home to the Church of the Holy Sepulchre, containing two of the holiest sites in Christianity: Calvary and the tomb of Christ. Sites of pilgrimage down through the centuries, access to them had served as a spur to the original crusades a millennium ago. Admittedly, today, even among the faithful, such symbolism had become subservient to the political and military reasons for reclaiming the city from the Caliphate. The Jews remained a powerful political voice in Richmond, one that could sway voters and determine the presidency, and even in exile Israeli cyber and weapons tech was second to none, with the RSA covertly funding much of their R&D.

Williams' apparent naivety troubled him. He was an old enough hand to understand that one should always temper political necessity with caution. The Jews in general and the Israelis in particular were a duplicitous people, and it should never be forgotten that they had allowed Christ to be sacrificed upon the cross. They stood to gain much from the liberation of their homeland at little cost to themselves. Vanderbilt found himself minded to keep a detachment of Templars in Jerusalem following its liberation for security purposes. Any objections the Knesset might make would be easily overridden by the presence of hostile forces on Israel's borders with Jordan and Syria. Then there would be the need for permanent military bases as they continued to push back the Caliphate forces towards their final extinction.

Securing a fourth crusade brought Vanderbilt's attention to the presidential succession. Republican or Southern Democrat made no difference as long as the candidate was suitably pro-war. Williams' choice of Charles Gerrard as the continuity candidate through which to continue his legacy was sound enough. But should the voters swing from blue to red there was little doubt that John Haversham would take the presidency. A former RSAF pilot and third-term senator for Texas, Haversham's campaign promises included increased military spending and the reintroduction of the draft. While Vanderbilt was always happy for Congress to throw money at him, he had to concede Haversham's policies played poorly with young and liberal voters, enough to cost him the presidency. But the man could still serve a purpose as a stalking horse. He made a note to divert funds to backing Haversham's campaign. The more the voters saw of him, the more they would come to favour Gerrard.

With the presidency secured to a suitable candidate, there was the matter of his own succession. Not that he intended going anywhere, but even in an order founded on the virtue of piety there were ambitious underlings to consider. The wiser and therefore more dangerous challengers were keeping their powder dry, which brought him to enfant terrible and current media darling Colonel Martin Tyler. A good soldier, and brave and loyal in his way, only lacking the conviction of a true believer. He said the right words to fool a willing public, but those capable of looking deeper saw the truth. The war represented nothing more than a means to an end for Tyler, and that end was his political ambition. Give the man his due, he possessed a native cunning that he had put to admirable service in the accumulation of wealth and power. But at heart he remained a common thug and singularly unsuited to the rank of Grand Master. He had a duty to entrust the future of the

Order to safer hands. One of the old families, not some vulgar nouveau riche upstart.

Vanderbilt stood up, shook the blood from the scourge and returned it to the drawer. He sprayed his back with an antiseptic coagulant and resumed his seat. The air stung his wounds, triggering a mild endorphin rush. It faded quickly, allowing him to return to the moment. He called up the metrics on his workstation. His troublesome colonel was riding high on a current wave of public approval, which made direct action such as sidelining him inadvisable. But his ambition made him reckless, both with the lives of his men and his own. Keep him in the vanguard of the action, a position he naturally gravitated towards, and there was every chance of a Caliphate bullet eliminating the problem. After which he would enjoy spending the political capital of Colonel Martin Tyler's martyrdom. In the meantime, there were other matters to attend to.

Vanderbilt activated the intercom again. 'Lachlan, I want you to put out a dinner invitation to Senator Gerrard. I suppose you'd better invite that dreadful campaign manager of his. What's her name?'

'Hopkins, sir.'

'Yes, her. Dreadful woman. But sometimes you have to sup with the Devil.'

CHAPTER 7

Katz looked out across the makeshift barricade. The plaza that had teemed with life and joy during his childhood stood empty, its surface cratered and strewn with debris. The stalls and families were gone, replaced by the tanks and soldiers of the enemy. He turned and looked up at the ancient and scarred stone of the Western Wall and the Temple Mount it partially enclosed, taking comfort in their long endurance. Enemies had driven the Israelites from their homeland many times during the long and bloody centuries; Caliph Khaled bin Hasan al-Masri al-Qurayshi was simply the latest in a long line of aggressors who had tried and failed to crush the Jewish faith. From the destruction of the First Temple by King Nebuchadnezzar and the long years of the Babylonian exile that followed, through to the destruction of the Second Temple by Roman legions under the command of Titus, they had endured. And, God willing, they would endure again after this latest fall.

Katz looked along the length of the barricade, taking in the grim features of IDF soldiers interspersed with the equally grim Templars. The Caliphate's siege of Jerusalem was almost a year old when he had received his call-up papers. Now, a year later, it was over. A year of American airlifts spiriting away the remaining civilian population. A year of food and supply drops while the Caliphate slowly tightened the noose between exploratory attacks. The IDF and Templar numbers dwindled while the Caliphate army swelled. They scented blood and went in for the kill.

The Templar officer in charge, Commander Maxwell Lewis, passed down the line, pausing to share a few words of encouragement or a joke with each of the defenders. Lewis was a bear of a man with a great salt-and-pepper beard. He acted as if nothing could touch him, and for the most part it worked, he having so far emerged from the conflict without a scratch. Katz admired his courage and faith, but most of all his indomitable zest for life. He stopped beside the IDF captain and Katz saw the fatal truth of their situation pass wordlessly between them.

'Scanners show Caliphate armour and troops massing for an assault on the plaza. I've ordered an evac for you, your men and the wounded.'

'Commander, surely you don't expect us to abandon our post? We will fight to the end in defence of our country.'

'That's a noble gesture, but also a futile one. For now, Israel is lost. Better to retreat and live to fight another day. One where you can make your enemies pay.'

'With respect, Commander, the same could be said of you and your men.'

'Indeed. But this a question of logistics. There's not enough room on the transport and someone has to cover the evac.'

'Commander.' Katz pointed across the barricade to where two figures had emerged from the smoke, a white flag fluttering between them. They stopped and the slightly shorter, more heavily built man stepped forward.

'I am Major Abu Ahmad al-Nasr of the Eighth Army of the Islamic Caliphate,' he gestured to the other officer positioned to his right, 'and this is my aide, Captain al-Hashimi. Commander Maxwell, you and your men face overwhelming odds, but you need not die here. There's little honour in slaughtering men trapped like rats in a cage, particularly those who have fought bravely. I propose a compromise. Hand over the Israelis and your weapons and I will allow you to walk away.'

'And what of the Israelites? Will they be treated fairly as prisoners of war?'

'They have committed crimes against Islam and must face punishment.'

'Then it's no deal.'

'This saddens me, Commander. But if it is the will of Allah then so be it.'

Al-Nasr bowed and turned away. He and al-Hashimi retreated slowly across the plaza, as if enjoying a Sunday constitutional stroll. Katz raised his rifle but Captain Moshe pushed the barrel towards the ground.

'The eyes of the world are watching. They must not find us wanting. Go help prepare the wounded for evac.'

Katz had just finished tightening the strap on the stretcher when a gunship appeared overhead. It hovered long enough to launch a series of rockets at the approaching Caliphate armour before banking to take up position over the barricade. He turned away and squeezed his eyes shut as the larger transporter helicopter touched down, scattering dust and grit. The soldier behind tapped him on the shoulder and together they lifted the stretcher and ran for the copter. A pair of medics relieved them of their burden and carried the wounded Templar into the hold. Katz and his companion made two more trips and then stopped to help the walking wounded board.

Over by the barricade, Maxwell was arguing with a young lieutenant whose right arm was in a sling.

'Dammit, Vanderbilt, you're no good to me with one arm. Get on that transport. That's an order, soldier!'

Vanderbilt looked mutinous for a moment and then snapped off a salute. 'Been a pleasure serving with you, sir.'

Maxwell simply nodded, accepting his just due before

turning to face the approaching column of Caliphate tanks.

Katz helped Vanderbilt aboard. He looked at the now pitiable huddle of Templar soldiers manning the barrier and then at Captain Moshe's outstretched hand. The helicopter rotors were already revving up for departure. All he had to do was turn and walk away. Later he would tell himself it was common sense and not a lack of courage that made him take Moshe's hand. The commander had said it himself: to stay would mean a futile death.

As the gunship laid down covering fire, Katz stood framed in the open door of the transporter as it lifted away. The first of the tanks had already breached the barricade, its defenders, now reduced to just seven men, falling back to form a circle around the recognisable figure of Commander Maxwell, who knelt in prayer. Two more tanks joined the first. There was a pause, possibly while the tank crews awaited orders, and then the machine guns opened up. They continued to fire long after the Templars had fallen.

'B''al'ma d'hu 'atid l'ithaddata.'

By the time Katz finished reciting the first line of the Kaddish he had been joined by every Israeli aboard the transport.

'Ul'aḥaya metaya,

'ul'assaqa yathon l'ḥayye 'al'ma,

'ul'mivne qarta dirush'lem,

'uleshakhlala hekhlehh b'gavvah.'

It didn't matter if it took a single generation or a hundred. They would rebuild Jerusalem.

Katz started awake. It had been several months since he had last had the dream. Always there was that long, agonising moment as he willed himself to join the Templars in their last stand. And yet, as a member of Mossad's Kidon unit, had he not struck down enemies aplenty? His was the justice of the knife, the garotte, or the gun. Delivered with swift, clinical precision.

Katz looked at the faint scars still visible on his chest, at the shoulders, elbows and wrists; legacies of an implanted hardwired nervous system that increased his reaction time by fifty per cent. Groundbreaking in the late Sixties, but since supplanted by body-enhancing nanotech coded to the recipient's DNA to avoid rejection. What troubled him most about the acts he had committed in the service of his country was not guilt, but the lack of it; the knowledge that he would repeat each act without question if ordered to do so.

He reached across the bed in response to a beep from his com-unit. The message contained a single image: Abu Ahmad al-Nasr al-Qurayshi. The fifth and, according to prophecy, final caliph of the Islamic Caliphate. His was a face well known to the Israeli, but he seared it into his memory anyway, matching it with information stored in mnemonic implants to call up a full biography and psychological profile. Know your enemy like you know yourself. Think like him to anticipate his moves and defeat him.

CHAPTER 8

Commander al-Hashimi regarded the line of troops arrayed along the Western Wall. They stood straight and proud, dressed in immaculate uniforms with their weapons oiled and cleaned. The soldiers of the Jerusalem Guard before him were the pride of Islam and the envy of special forces the world over. The trouble with the West was that many still thought of the Caliphate as little more than a rabble of fanatical goat herders armed with AK-47s. These men were third-generation soldiers. He had fought alongside many of their fathers on that glorious day when they liberated this city from the Jewish infidels. The plaza had looked very different that day. Now the brightly striped market stalls and shoppers were back; the bustle of conversation and the scent of spices carried on the wind. While some bullet scars remained, the majority of the plaza had been rebuilt with intricate geometric designs set into the plascrete. Contrary to what many in the West believed, they were neither monsters nor cultural savages. Indeed, there was a mathematical purity to their art and architecture.

Al-Hashimi raised his eyes to the Temple Mount, on top of which shone the golden Dome of the Rock. That sight alone justified all that he had done in the service of the

Caliphate. With Mecca and Medina once again in the hands of the Saudi apostates, relinquishing control of Jerusalem was unthinkable.

The sound of approaching feet made him turn irritably, a rebuke on his lips for the interloper who dared disturb his inspection. Instead, he found himself bowing to Abu Ahmad al-Nasr al-Qurayshi.

'Forgive me, my caliph, I was not told of your arrival in the city. If I'd known I would have prepared a suitable welcome.'

The caliph smiled. 'And I would not have known the real state of the city's defences.' Al-Qurayshi held out his hand. 'Come, old friend, walk with me. We have much to discuss.'

Al-Hashimi turned to his second-in-command and ordered him to take over the inspection. An honour guard of six men formed up front and back of the old comrades as they made their way across the plaza.

'Do you remember that first day when we stood here together?'

'That glorious day is indelibly marked in my memory.'

Al-Qurayshi paused and his guard paused with him. 'I remember no glory, only failure. My predecessor, the illustrious Khaled bin Hasan al-Masri, long may he dwell in Paradise with the prophets, was most specific in his orders: no martyrdom for the Americans. He saw the wisdom of driving a wedge between the Christians and the Jews. Instead, we let those who hate our way of life, our very existence, escape.'

'I am sorry to have failed you.'

'You did not command that day. The stain of dishonour is mine and mine alone. I have spent the long years since battling our enemies to atone.'

The caliph moved off again. Al-Hashimi felt uneasy. He had known his friend for close to thirty years, from the time they were simple soldiers, and had never seen him this troubled. Normally he was not a man to dwell on the past. Twice the Americans had tried to take back Jerusalem and twice the Caliphate had sent them home to lick their wounds and think again. They had fought together bravely during those campaigns, but it was Abu Ahmad al-Nasr who had displayed a talent for strategy that saw him promoted to the rank of brigadier general. Al-Hashimi did not begrudge his friend that honour, any more than when, in the fullness of time during the short years of peace that followed, the council of elders elevated him to caliph. But the American infidels were nothing if not cunning. This time, when their armies returned, they struck at Saudi Arabia, working together with rebels and dissidents to wrest control of the country and its resources, depriving the Caliphate war machine of fuel and materials while driving them back to the borders of Syria and Jordan. For the first time in almost two decades the Caliphate tasted defeat. Since then, another uneasy peace had followed.

Al-Hashimi's reflections came to an end as they both reached the mobile command centre parked on the opposite side of the plaza. Two guards followed them inside while the others took up their posts at the door. A pair of technicians sat in front of a bank of monitors displaying real-time satellite feeds. The caliph pointed to the first screen, which showed a squadron of fighter-bombers parked on an airfield. At his command, the image zoomed in on one of the jets to reveal the RSAF markings.

'Akrotiri Air Base in Cyprus. The first of the Hellcats arrived two days ago.' The image zoomed out again and panned to the left to the blue-green water of Episkopi Bay, where a flotilla of ships sat at anchor. 'We have identified an aircraft carrier, an amphibious transport dock, two amphibious assault ships, a destroyer and three cruisers. We also suspect the presence of at least one attack submarine.' He pointed to the next screen. 'Tessler Corporation R&D base, Europa City. Currently home to twenty VTOL "hopper" attack craft. No doubt they will claim to be testing them prior to delivery to the RSA, but they are fully armed and we have identified American drone operators in the city.' A third screen showed tanks, mobile artillery, AMPVs, JLTVs, transporters, dozers, fuel carriers and infantry. 'Georgia, in the Greater Russian Collective. Our spies estimate they have mustered close to half a million Russian Orthodox volunteers to assist in retaking Jerusalem. They will push towards Israel through Lebanon, Jordan and Syria. We have also intercepted communications with the Egyptian government granting a temporary air corridor. Our enemies are massing on all sides in preparation for a fresh crusade, and this city is surely the ultimate prize. We cannot allow Al-Aqsa Mosque to fall into the hands of the infidel. The Sixth Army mobilises to reinforce your troops and I myself will oversee the defence of the city. We fight together again, old friend. Possibly for the final time.'

'Should we begin evacuation of the civilian population?'

'No, their presence will discourage drone and long-range missile attacks – at least initially. They know their duty. As, I trust, do you. In the meantime, we will take such action as we can against our enemies.'

'As you command, my caliph, so will it be done.'

Al-Hashimi left the command centre a troubled man. He had the greatest respect for his old friend, but the caliph's decision to employ the civilian population sat ill with him. While it was clear that they were facing overwhelming odds, he felt they should meet them honourably as devoted soldiers of Islam, not cower behind women and children. But he could no more be disloyal than he could pluck out his heart. Al-Qurayshi would not have arrived at such a decision lightly. A greater strategy surely existed; one he would have to trust his friend to reveal in the fullness of time.

A sharp trill alerted him to an incoming call on his com-unit. His wife's image flashed up on the screen and al-Hashimi glanced around the plaza to make sure he was alone before answering.

'Amina.'

'Husband, you are well?'

Al-Hashimi thought he detected a level of stress in Amina's voice. Dark circles were visible around her eyes, even on the low-res video.

'I am. And you and Imani?' The latter referred to his youngest daughter, who he had not seen in person for almost two years and whose fifth birthday was approaching.

'I am fine, but our daughter is of an age now where she … senses things. The rationing, power cuts, the lack of husbands, fathers, uncles and brothers. It's difficult for a child to understand the sacrifices we make.'

'As a loyal and devoted wife and mother I'm sure you've impressed the necessity and wisdom of the caliph's decrees on our daughter, despite her tender years.'

Al-Hashimi's voice was steady but sharp. A tone Amina interpreted as meaning someone else might be listening in on the call.

'Of course, husband. She misses her father and brothers but she knows you defend our way of life from the infidel. Allah willing, we shall soon be victorious.'

'Allah willing, indeed. Perhaps you should get out of Karbala for a few days? Visit your aunt in Baghdad. I'm sure Jamila would appreciate a visit from her favourite niece and little Imani. Family must stand by one another.'

He picked up the hesitation before her reply as his wife tried to work out if there was some coded message in the words. Sometimes a trip to visit relatives was just that. But Jamila was no fool and could be relied on to instil some sense into her niece.

'Yes,' al-Hashimi reinforced his message, 'a trip would do you both good.'

'As you say, husband. I'll make the necessary arrangements.'

'Good. Give Imani my love and I'll call you tomorrow before her bedtime.'

Al-Hashimi ended the call. Some days, he found

submitting to the will of God more difficult than others. But the conflicting duties of husband, father and soldier had surely not changed in a thousand years. He missed the certainty of his youth when he saw the world and its problems in black and white absolutes. Not that he doubted the righteousness of the jihad or the authority of the caliph. But, and here he knew he trod close to blasphemy, al-Qurayshi was still a man, and men could be mistaken in their beliefs and resulting actions. While he had no desire for elevation to such high status, he would prosecute the war differently if he were caliph. That, of course, might simply result in him making different mistakes. After all, he was a frail creature of flesh and blood.

CHAPTER 9

Kai plipped the key fob, unlocking the SUV. He steered the trolley to the back of the vehicle and opened the rear door. As he reached for the first of the tins of paint his wife let out a sigh and stepped back with her hands on her hips. Kai looked at the swollen mound of her stomach and felt the now familiar mix of joy and concern. In four short weeks their son would be born. The first, he hoped, of several children.

'Do you need a hand to load up?'

'I got this, honey. Just you relax. I still think you should have stayed at home.'

'And let you choose all the paint and paper for the nursery? I don't think so. You'd have everything white or magnolia. A baby needs colour, some stimulation.'

'I know that,' Kai protested, provoking a knowing smile from his wife.

He set to work with renewed vigour, loading the rest of the paint, paper, paste, rollers and brushes into the SUV, stacking them neatly and tightly to prevent the load shifting. It was a little after midday and the sun beat from a clear blue sky, reminding him to be thankful. He took out a handkerchief and mopped his brow before running a finger along the inside of his clerical collar.

'That's us good to go, Jess.'

'There's no hurry, is there?'

'Well, I was hoping to make a start on the nursery this afternoon.'

'It'll surely keep another hour or two? It's a beautiful day – be a shame not to enjoy a little of it.'

'I guess you're right at that.'

Kai locked the SUV and took Jessica's arm, leading her across the parking lot. The rear of the mall backed onto a square, the centre dominated by an ornamental fountain. Water sparkled in the sunlight as they threaded their way through the Saturday afternoon crowds. As they neared the fountain a blond-haired youth collided with Kai. They spun apart and the boy stood with his mouth open, hands thrust deep into the pockets of his jacket. Jessica took a tighter hold of his arm as he stared the boy down.

'Something you want to say, son?'

The words seemed to break whatever spell the boy was under.

'Apologies, preacher. Ma'am.' With that he was gone, making for the far corner of the fountain.

Kai shook his head dismissively. 'I hope we raise our son with better manners than that kid.'

'I don't think he meant any harm. You know what teenagers are like – probably obsessing over some girl. Stop being a grouch and let's sit by the fountain.'

Kai got them settled on the low stone wall that surrounded the base of the fountain. Jess was right; it really was too nice a day not to enjoy. The nursery would still be there come Monday, or even Tuesday.

'Ooh, he's kicking.'

Jessica took his hand and placed it on her belly. In that moment Kai forgot the boy and his lack of manners. Truly there was nothing more powerful than two people coming together in love and producing the miracle of life together.

'I think Junior would like an ice cream.'

'He told you that, did he?'

'Hey, a mother knows these things.'

Kai smiled and pecked her on the cheek. The ice cream cart was on the other side of the square, a briskly moving queue indicating that Jess wasn't the only one with a craving for something cool.

He took his turn in line, ordering Jess a scoop of vanilla and one of pistachio, while he went for chocolate and rum 'n' raisin. He had just tapped his com-unit to pay for it when he became aware of the commotion by the fountain.

The blond-haired boy stood on top of the basin wall, right arm raised above his head, fist clenched, thumb held down. Kai saw all the signs he had ignored in that split second: the jacket zipped to the neck in spite of the heat, the look on the boy's face when he saw his clerical collar; not surprise or shock as he'd first thought, but what he now recognised as disgust. In his peripheral vision he saw a figure running towards the boy, the haircut identifying him as off-duty military. Jess, terrified, trying to waddle along the edge of the fountain. Too late. Far too late.

'This war is wrong! We must stop this unjust persecution of Islam!'

The explosion knocked Kai off his feet, overturned the ice cream cart. As he scrambled to his hands and knees the ice cream, already melting on the hot tarmac, was cold and sticky between his fingers. He saw the nails sticking out of his forearm but felt no pain. The ringing in his ears was somehow impossibly loud and silent at the same time. He stared at the melting ice cream, which had taken on a raspberry swirl of blood. He told himself not to look up, to keep believing in the possibility of miracles.

Kai looked up. He saw the bloodied figures, some of whom were missing limbs, crawling or staggering across the square, their mouths open in silent screams. He saw the other things, the lumps of raw meat and shattered bone, no longer identifiable as human beings.

'Jessica!'

The *beep-beep* drew Kai back to consciousness. Not the shrill urgency of an alarm, but a more languid rhythm. Smell was the first sense to return, closely followed by touch: fresh linen and the warm cocoon of a bed. Must be Monday, his day of rest. Instinct made him reach out for Jessica, but he only felt a tug on the back of his hand. The absences assailed him: the familiar pine scent of the bedroom, bacon and eggs cooking on the stove. Grit had glued his eyes together, but he forced first the left and then the right to open, saw the sterile white of the hospital room. The beeping noise sped up as his heartbeat increased. The bandaged forearms and the cannula in the back of his hand couldn't be real; they belonged in the same dream as the bomb. That's all this was, a terrible nightmare from which he would shortly awake as Jessica brought him his breakfast.

The door opened to reveal the concerned features of a nurse. 'Please try to remain calm, Mr Schreiber. You're perfectly safe here.'

Kai tried to back away as the nurse approached, but found nowhere to go. Cool fingers wrapped around his wrist as she took his pulse while consulting the readout on the monitor next to his bed.

Visions of bloody carnage filled his mind, but still he denied the truth.

'Jessica … the baby.'

The nurse's fingers left his wrist and took his hand in a comforting grasp. 'I'm so very sorry. They're gone. There was nothing anyone could have done.'

The beeping increased in pitch and speed, but failed to rival the howl of rage that accompanied it.

Kai regarded the face in the mirror. It looked like his, with the intense blue eyes, thick black hair and slightly sunken cheeks. When he raised his eyebrows or twitched his mouth the image responded. Why did he feel so detached, so remote from himself? Because the better part of him was surely dead.

Superficial. That's what the doctor had said of his injuries. Irrigation, a coagulant to seal the wounds, a nano-shot to knit the flesh back together, morphine to wrap him in a warm hug. Sure enough, here he stood three days later, buttoning up his shirt and attaching his clerical collar. Healed in flesh, but what of the spirit? No physician could fix the wounding of his soul. Only faith might achieve such healing, and the preacher currently found his in short supply.

The previous day had seen various visitations from the members of his congregation, bringing their gifts of fruit, candy and, in one instance, the Bible itself. Kai had dutifully thumbed to the passages that he had often directed the bereaved towards, but he found no relief in the words of Matthew: 'Blessed are those who mourn: for they shall be comforted.' Where was his comfort, or even his God, in this darkest of hours? The only answer to his prayers was the constant ringing in his ears, which the doctor had assured him would fade with time.

There are none so blind as those who won't see: a fact amply demonstrated by his doctor's insistence that he was a lucky man. The yardstick he used to measure this luck was nine dead, including Kai's wife and unborn son, and twenty-six wounded, eighteen of whom had life-changing injuries – the loss of sight, hearing and/or limbs. But wasn't Kai's life irrevocably altered? He saw it in his parishioners' eyes as they sat at the side of his bed. They told themselves they had come to comfort their preacher in his hour of need, but they had come instead to confirm that the horror belonged to someone else. Kai forgave them this trespass as he offered up the bland pleasantries they so desperately sought. Broken as he was, he still had a duty to his flock.

The spiritual having failed him, Kai turned to the temporal, but the vid-casts offered no solution either. The bomber, Bradley Foster, was a regular teenage Texan from a good Christian family. There were signs, of course, that all was not well: his grades had dropped and he had become increasingly withdrawn in the months leading up to the attack, but nothing indicative of the radicalisation he had demonstrated. Hadn't Kai looked him directly in the eye before the attack and seen nothing? Was that the test the Lord had set him, and which he had failed? Or was his loss preordained to put him on some greater path? If so, he rejected it in the face of this cruel and barbarous treatment.

Kai pulled on his jacket and ran a comb through his hair. The face in the mirror still seemed separate from his person, but he guessed the two would merge in time as he came to terms with his loss. In the meantime, he had a wife and son to bury. The mortician had coyly skirted around the need for a closed casket, as if there were any doubt after he'd had to supply a DNA sample to ensure the remains that went in the coffin actually belonged to Jessica and their unborn son.

He called an automated cab and instructed it to take him home. Hunched in the back, his fingers flitted across the screen of his com-unit as he surfed through the news feeds related to the bombing. Most repeated the same lack of information he had previously trawled through, prompting Kai to move on to the president's response:

'While our thoughts and prayers are with the victims of this cowardly attack and their families, we, the American people, will not be cowed or broken by this assault on our great nation. The time has come to take definitive and crushing action against the Islamic Caliphate, not just militarily but financially, depriving it of the resources it directs against our country. As of two o'clock this afternoon, the Senate has approved military action in Israel. Templar forces will spearhead the campaign, working in close partnership with the Israel Defense Forces and the government in exile. Where previous administrations have tried and failed, we will succeed in the liberation of Israel and the restoration of Jerusalem to those of the Christian and Jewish faiths.'

Kai terminated the feed. The government might shy away from the term but the media was already calling the campaign the Fourth Crusade. Here was the opportunity to strike back at those who had taken all that he loved in life away from him. This, surely, was what God intended.

The recruiting sergeant swiped his finger across the datapad, his eyes flicking from the screen to Kai and then back again as he attempted to reconcile what he was reading with the calm blue eyes regarding him from across the desk.

'Austin.' The sergeant's voice caught and he cleared his throat before continuing. 'That was a terrible tragedy that day. My condolences for your loss. I can't imagine what it must be like to lose a wife and unborn child. Must turn a man inside out and upside down.'

'Can't deny it's been a trial, or that I was powerful angry for a time, as any man would be. But my faith and the support of my congregation got me through. Made me realise I had a duty beyond my suffering.'

'That's why you've applied for the Templar chaplaincy programme?'

Kai smiled benignly. He knew it looked benign because he had spent time in front of the mirror perfecting it while practising his lines over and over. Love. Not hate.

'I don't pretend to know the will of the Lord, but I do believe He set me on this path for a reason. I see it now as my Christian duty to provide spiritual guidance to our brave soldiers, to ease their consciences and hold them fast to the difficult path that lies before them. After all, God is on our side.'

The sergeant typed 'Check Stability/Psychiatric' on the datapad and highlighted it. He swiped to the next screen and handed the pad over.

'If you'd sign here and here, we'll get your application processed.'

'When do you think you'll have a decision?'

'Should be through in a couple of days.' The sergeant took the pad, checked the signatures and then scrolled back. 'Your PULHES gradings from your medical are all within range, so there shouldn't be any major issues.'

Kai stood and shook the sergeant's hand, keeping his expression as neutral as possible. God had a plan for him, and he would carry it out with the full righteous anger of the Lord behind him. Eye for eye, tooth for tooth, hand for hand, foot for foot.

CHAPTER 10

Rivera twisted the joystick, and seven thousand miles away the C8 Ultra Galaxy banked ponderously to the right, the arid and rocky landscape flitting below. She had been flying below radar for over a hundred klicks now. The mission was classified, pre-programmed into the flight computer by the spook standing behind her. For the little it was worth, he had given his name as Hannah, another faceless cog in the world of CIA black ops. Judging from their initial heading and previous recon, the Galaxy was somewhere over what had formerly been Jordan.

The first tumbledown houses of a bombed-out town came into view on the display screens, and she turned the transporter to follow the freeway. It steered like a bus compared with the F-27 Hellcat she normally operated. More importantly, it didn't have cannons, let alone rockets or missiles. She dropped the transporter another forty feet, bringing the burnt-out cars, lorries and busses into sharp focus. Some sat where their drivers had abandoned them; some had been pushed to the side of the road to allow other vehicles to pass. A few klicks down the freeway she spotted the burnt-out hulls of tanks and Humvees, the remnants of a recent battle.

Hannah leaned in closer. 'Switch screen three to the cargo hold and give me comms.'

Rivera toggled between external and internal cams: two JLTVs sat in their anchors of webbing surrounded by various pallets of arms and munitions. A trio of soldiers, dressed in desert camouflage with all rank and regiment insignia removed, sat checking their weapons.

'Fresh intel – we've got incoming,' Hannah spat. 'The LZ will be hot. Can you handle it?'

The nearest soldier turned and looked directly into the cam. 'Are you kidding? This is what me and the boys live for.'

A series of red flares lighting up a cleared section of highway came into focus on the screen.

'Take her in, Rivera.'

Anticipating a short runway, Rivera brought the plane in fast, the Galaxy bouncing twice before slewing down the road at an angle as the brakes squealed in protest. She completed the manoeuvre by turning the plane around ready for take-off before lowering the aft cargo bay door system and ramp.

The indignant voice of the squad commander crackled across comms: 'What the hell kind of landing do you call that?'

'As my dear old dad used to say, any landing you walk away from is a good one,' Rivera replied.

Hannah interrupted. 'Egginton, cut the chatter and get a shift on. Wheels up in ten.'

The squad moved into action, hitting the quick release on the straps of the nearest pallet and pushing it down the ramp. The Galaxy was kneeling, the cargo bay floor sitting about three feet from the ground, but the pallet still gathered enough momentum to clear the ramp. Egginton squinted against the glare of headlights from a parked truck and motioned the pair of waiting rebels forward. He mimed loading it onto the truck and the men nodded.

'Look out!'

Egginton jumped to the side as another pallet slid off the ramp and came to a halt where he had been standing. 'That's enough damn horseplay, Fairbairn!'

'Thought you lived for this kind of shit?'

Egginton gave him the finger and headed back up the ramp. He and Fairbairn released another two pallets, pausing to allow the JLTVs to roll off first.

Hannah checked the time as he watched the approach of incoming hostiles on the screen: three Humvees with rear-mounted machine guns. 'Gonna be close.'

'Just what exactly are Santa and his little helpers dropping off?' Rivera asked.

'Body armour, M4A3 carbines, RPGs.'

'So this is a black op with RS of A stamped across its ass?'

'Most of this shit is manufactured in Europa City, which is a lot closer.'

'That's your plausible deniability? Shit.'

'Just get the transporter ready for take-off. That's one asset we can't afford to leave behind.'

Rivera shrugged and powered up the engines. She ran through the rest of the pre-flight checks by rote, her attention focused on the drama on her screens. Egginton's men had fired up the JLTVs and put on their body armour. One of them threw Egginton a vest and helmet. He buckled himself in with an ease born of familiarity.

The rebel leader appeared and hailed Egginton. The conversation appeared to grow heated, the Jordanian gesticulating at the truck while Egginton shook his head. Finally, Egginton signalled with a chopping hand motion that he should go. Rivera didn't need audio to recognise the explosive curse that followed, but the Jordanian turned, pulled open the passenger door and climbed into the cab.

The first arc of tracer fire came as the truck sped away. Two more bursts scythed in front of the lead JLTV, sending Egginton and his men diving for cover. As they crawled towards the rear of the vehicle a grenade or rocket exploded nearby.

'Get our bird out of there, Rivera.'

Rivera hit the ramp controls and released the brakes, letting the Galaxy lumber forward. She willed it to go faster as the headlights of approaching vehicles lit up the road. Hannah looked questioningly at her as the distance between the plane and the lead Humvee shrank.

'No going back now!'

The driver belatedly realised his mistake and attempted to turn. As it skidded to the side of the road the nose of the Galaxy sent it into a roll. A second Humvee, not wanting to share the fate of his comrade, slammed on the brakes and disgorged a trio of soldiers who took up position at the side of the road. They opened fire as the plane took to the sky, hitting the outer starboard engine. Rivera cursed as it started to flame and hurriedly cut the fuel supply.

'Keep her steady,' Hannah advised. 'We'll be out of range soon. Don't want to make ourselves a target for surface-to-air missiles.'

'Gee, I'm glad you're here to advise. I'd never have thought of that.'

Hannah glowered. 'Guess you can take it from here, Rivera.'

Rivera kept her eyes on her screens as Hannah turned on his heel and exited the UAS pod. She concentrated on nursing the transporter back to Cyprus on three engines and made a mental note to avoid any more of these fucked-up missions. Hannah had refused to say what they were training and equipping the rebels for, but it didn't take a genius to figure out they were prepping for another war against the Caliphate. The joke of it was that twenty years from now they'd probably end up fighting those same rebels. The spooks never seemed to learn.

She contacted flight control at Akrotiri Air Base and told them to prep for an emergency landing. With the exception of the starboard number one engine the systems checks were all normal, but that was no guarantee. She lowered the undercarriage and throttled back, and the runway filled her screens. The fire trucks formed up either side of the runway as the transporter touched down. Rivera braked hard, bringing the damaged aircraft to a standstill before cutting the engines. She killed the satellite link and the screens went dead. The groundcrew could take it from here.

Rivera deleted the flight logs as instructed and powered down her console. She looked around the UAS pod as she stretched the kinks out of her muscles: a basic cockpit inside an air-conditioned steel box. Eight years' flight experience and her feet had never left the ground. She supposed she should be flattered that the RSAF considered that the investment her training represented in terms of time and money made her too valuable to risk in the air. But part of her still wondered what it was like to actually be inside the aircraft you were flying.

Rivera leaned in close, partly because of the hubbub in the bar, but mainly through artifice. She knew the kid could smell the faint odour of fresh sweat cutting through her deodorant; the tickle of an errant strand of hair against his cheek. His Adam's apple bobbed up and down as he swallowed. She hid her smile as her lips brushed his ear.

'What say you get us another beer, Coop?'

'Yeah. Of course.' He stood up, faced the bar, then spun around. 'Stay right there, okay?'

'Don't worry, I'm not going anywhere.'

This time she couldn't hold back the good-natured laugh as Cooper all but ran to the bar, pausing only to look over at his friends sitting nearby: the tall, dark-skinned one and his blond companion. What were their names? Mackinlay and Walker. This year's intake was the same as the last, and the one before that. Good ol' country boys, the sort who didn't know shit from Shinola. But had the girl who came out of Cedar Fort, Utah, eight years ago really been so very different? Join the RSAF and see the world, the recruiting poster had said. Trouble was, she usually saw it right before she dropped a bomb on it. But that was the gig she had signed up for. As her old flight instructor would have said, *Suck it up, buttercup.*

After the recent black op with Hannah, the current training came as something of a relief. No denying the latest generation of F-27 Hellcats were mean machines. Trouble was, MILES hit you with beams of light, not bullets. You could run training sessions indefinitely, but none of them prepared you for the moment when the head of the man next to you exploded like a melon. She knew these kids were in for a rude awakening, just as she knew it would be pointless trying to convince them that they hadn't seen anything yet.

Cooper battled his way back to the table. Rivera could tell by the way he was walking that he already had a burgeoning erection. She accepted the bottle of beer and raised it slowly to her lips, making deliberate eye contact. Cooper took a hurried gulp of his own beer and set it aside. She could almost see the wheels turning inside his skull as he groped around for some suitable small talk. If she wasn't careful, she'd be getting a reputation as a cradle snatcher. Then again, what did she care? They didn't know enough to make demands of her and took direction where necessary. If the odd one got clingy and started mistaking a rush of hormones for true love, well, she knew how to deal with that.

Cooper pressed his lips to her ear and hollered, 'Do you like country music?'

Rivera looked over to where a bluegrass band was struggling its way through the American Standards. 'Not when it's played this badly.'

'Oh.'

Cooper looked like a puppy that had just been bopped on the nose with a rolled-up newspaper. *Boring conversation, anyway,* Rivera thought. She leaned forward and kissed him. Enjoyed the way his eyes went wide when she slipped her tongue into his mouth. Maybe not the smartest move in public. Command discouraged the Templars from wearing their uniforms on furlough, but the buzzcuts tended to be a giveaway.

'Maybe we ought to take this outside?'

'I'm not sure that's such a good idea.' Cooper looked over to where his friends sat watching. 'We're not supposed to … fraternise.'

'You're still in training, right? Haven't taken your vows?' Cooper nodded. 'Then look on this as a last chance to sin. Or maybe you don't like girls?'

'I like girls.'

'Then what you waiting for?'

Rivera stood and walked confidently from the bar, ignoring a dozen or so staring pairs of eyes. She caught Cooper following meekly behind, out of the corner of her eye.

She had parked her car in an area of shadow between two streetlights. Its lights flashed in response to her press on the fob. Cooper hopped nervously from foot to foot as she opened the passenger door and racked back and reclined the seat.

Rivera slid onto the seat and scooted her way back.

'Well, come on then, soldier. Time to get it on.'

Cooper glanced nervously up and down the street, his attention going back to the door of the bar. *How much encouragement does this mutt need?* Rivera pulled her T-shirt over her head and unclasped her bra. Cooper all but leaped into the car, his hands reaching for her breasts.

'Whoa! Easy there.' She reached across him and pulled the door closed. 'We got plenty of time.'

She felt his erection pressing against her belly and put her feet up on the dash, pushing herself back until it was rubbing against her groin. She started to grind and Cooper groaned in response. He buried his face in her breasts and she let out a yelp as he bit her nipple. His thrusting became more urgent, already approaching a crescendo. Rivera knew how this ended and it was fine. She dug her fingers into Cooper's ass and writhed against him, dry-humping him until he came with a scream.

'Oh, God. I'm sorry. I don't normally, y'know?'

Rivera reached up and stroked his cheek. 'Don't worry about it. I'm sure there's plenty more where that came from. Meantime …'

She unbuckled her jeans, slid them and her panties down to her ankles. Cooper looked confused, so she pushed his head between her legs and held it there. She let out a gasp as he got the idea.

CHAPTER 11

Cooper soaked up his surroundings: so familiar and yet somehow now alien. The scarred surface of the dining table, the cheap, extruded plastic chairs, the rusting range, blackened pots and pans, flaking paint and peeling paper all spoke of a hardscrabble life lived at the edge of subsistence. His father hadn't worked in over twenty years, not since they'd closed the pharmaceutical plant, while his mother had slavishly looked after home, husband and children.

Wayne Cooper's heavily seamed face testified to the fact that he found his enforced inaction a burden. Yet he remained a proud and pious man, as evidenced by his arthritically swollen clasped hands and bowed head as he recited grace. On this occasion there truly was much to be thankful for. The table groaned under a roast turkey, potatoes, corn cobs, biscuits, peas and gravy. A spread normally only seen on Thanksgiving, and only then if his mother had managed to squirrel away enough of her meagre housekeeping. That the money Cooper sent home had paid for this largesse in no way detracted from it. He truly felt like the prodigal son on the receiving end of the fatted calf.

Cooper's sister winked at him as the prayer droned on.

Shania had turned sixteen in his absence, her body filling out accordingly. Cooper hoped she was smart enough to keep herself out of trouble, given the attention she must be attracting from the local boys. He looked over at the twins, Dale and Wade: they had grown at least four inches, hitting a growth spurt as they entered their teens. Their legs swung impatiently as they waited for the meal to begin. Lastly, he looked to his mother. Her once-blonde hair was now mostly grey but sometimes, when the light was right, he could still see the beauty his father had married. The same beauty that now shone out of Shania. His mother caught his eye and frowned disapprovingly before bowing her head by way of example.

His father, having duly thanked God, stood and started to carve the turkey. Any lingering doubts Cooper possessed about his newly elevated status evaporated when his father placed the meat on his plate before serving himself. Feeling he had still not paid sufficient honour to their newfound provider, his father handed him a beer. Meantime, the meat platter had reached his mother as it worked its way down the table.

Cooper popped the cap and clinked bottles with his father. The gesture seemed to please the old man, who took a long swallow of beer before bending to his meal.

For a time there was only the clatter of cutlery on plates, interrupted by occasional requests for this or that dish. Towards the end of his second helping Cooper felt fit to burst, but knew he could not leave anything on his plate. As the pace of the meal slackened conversation started up, beginning with inane pleasantries.

'You look very handsome in your uniform. Don't he, Ma?'

'He does that. You should get yourself out and about before you leave. Let those Jonesboro girls see what they're missing. Might even find yourself a sweetheart before you leave.'

Cooper flushed red as images of Rivera flashed through

his head. He'd known it was wrong at the time, but he couldn't quite bring himself to regret it. Mackinlay and Walker could disapprove all they wanted, but technically he'd broken no rules.

'Hush now, can't you see you're embarrassing him?'

Dale and Wade, as they so often did, spoke together: 'Can we see your gun after dinner? Please? We promise to be good.'

'Sorry guys, but we ain't allowed to take our weapons off base. But I'll tell you all about our training later. We've got some really cool simulations.'

'Your letter was a bit vague about how long you'd be staying.'

'Yeah, sorry about that. I wasn't sure I'd passed the programme when I wrote you. I mean, I thought I had, but you never know. Anyway, I've to report back to Fort Irwin six days from now to take my vows. Expect we'll ship out pretty soon after that. Nothing confirmed yet, but rumour has it we're headed for Cyprus in preparation for a fresh crusade. You know, what with the bombing and all.'

His father put down his knife and fork and cast awkwardly around as he searched for the right words to say.

'I'm proud of you. Always have been and always will be, whatever happens. You know that, right? You got to do your duty, no doubt about that. But there's no need to take any unnecessary risks. You got to come home to us.'

There was a clatter as his mother dropped her fork. 'What kind of talk is that to bring to the dinner table?'

'Smart talk is what it is. Billy Ray has already done us proud and there ain't no call for him to do more than that. Tell me you understand?'

Cooper hesitated, but his father's intense gaze wouldn't accept silence for an answer. 'Of course.'

The remainder of the meal passed in an awkward silence, one that not even pancakes and syrup could lift. It came as something of a relief when Cooper finally stood to excuse himself from the table.

Shania looked uncertainly at the proffered bottle of beer. Beads of condensation frosted the glass, indicating that the golden contents were ice-cold.

'Don't worry, little sis. What Pa don't know won't hurt him.'

Cooper sat beside her on the front step of the porch and stared out into the night. It was warm with a slight breeze blowing in from the south. The kind of evening he used to enjoy just shooting the shit with his friends. He needed to catch up with Donny and Mike before he left, even though he knew what their reaction would be. Neither of them approved of his decision to enlist or believed in the righteousness of the war. In spite of the best efforts of his instructors, he wasn't convinced either. He found it easier to put his faith in the guarantee of three meals a day and a regular pay check. No one in Jonesboro could offer him that. As to war, how bad could it be?

'Pa was in a strange mood tonight.'

Cooper took a swig of beer and nodded thoughtfully as old, forgotten memories surfaced.

'Do you remember Uncle Cyrus, Pa's younger brother?'

'Can't say as I do.'

'Right enough, I think he died round about the time you were born. He volunteered for the Second Crusade and got hisself killed during the final evac. From what I remember overhearing as a kid, Pa didn't approve of his decision to join up. Thought the rich folks were just doing what they'd always done – using the poor as cannon fodder.'

'Is that what you think?'

'Don't rightly know, if I'm being honest. What I do know is none of those folks in Congress with their expensive suits and fancy manners is going to do a damn thing to help the likes of us. This is my out, Shania. It helps all of us, you know that. So I gotta take it. Whatever the risks.'

His sister leaned in close and rested her head on his shoulder. There was a floral scent to her hair and a faint tremble in her body.

'Pa's right. Don't you go taking no chances over there.'

The 'y' and the 'c' were out on the neon sign above the door of Tipsy McStagger's, and Cooper noticed the emerald green door and window frames were badly in need of a fresh coat of paint. Had it always been like this? Probably. When you grew up with everything in a state of dissolution it came to be the norm. His time at Fort Irwin and furlough visits to Barstow had changed that, made him acutely aware of his hometown's poverty and general air of despair. He pushed open the door, ringing an old-fashioned bell.

Dark wood panels lined the walls of the bar, decorated with rusting tinplate advertisements for long vanished brands. A series of shelves ran along the walls close to the ceiling, displaying beer bottles and cans from around the world. Cooper guessed they were meant to impart an international air, but bitter experience informed him the only beers on draft were a piss-weak domestic ale and a local stout that tasted of cigarette ash. So much for good cheer.

At a little after two o'clock in the afternoon, McStagger's was doing brisk trade in response to Welfare Wednesday. Cooper scanned the crowd, identifying a pair of familiar figures at the bar. One tall and lean with a tousled mass of dirty blond hair and a week's beard growth, the other shorter and more heavily built, his brown hair already thinning with male pattern baldness. Sporting the uniform of the Jonesboro youth, Donny and Mike wore plaid shirts, faded denim and variety store sneakers, which Cooper's new comrades had persuaded him to upgrade from. He ran his hands self-consciously down the front of his slacks as he approached. Ignoring his mother's advice, he had decided to dress casually; the uniform tended to polarise people.

Donny turned on his stool and stared myopically at

Cooper. He scratched at his beard while trying to clear the fog of alcohol from his brain. The severe haircut and new duds had thrown him, but recognition dawned and his upper lip curled in a sneer.

'Well, lookee here, Mike. Soldier-boy has decided to pay us a visit.'

'Good to see you too, Donny. Mike.' Cooper pointed to their near empty glasses. 'Can I get you boys a refill?'

'You sure can, Billy Ray. And shots of straight rye all round, seeing as you can afford it.'

'Guess I can at that.'

Cooper called over the barman, a young kid in his twenties who had been assiduously polishing a glass, and ordered a round of beer and whiskey. He waited until they had been served and the barman had turned his attention to another customer before he asked, 'What happened to old man Priestly? He was practically a fixture of this place.'

Mike picked up his shot and downed it before answering. 'Didn't your folks or Shania tell you? Cancer got him.'

Donny snorted. 'What got him was the three-fifty-seven he stuck in his mouth when he couldn't pay his medical bills.'

'Same thing, Donny.'

'Guess it all depends on your point of view.'

'Why do you always have to be such an asshole when you drink?'

'Because guys like you, Mike, need assholes to tell them the truth. Ain't that right, Billy Ray?'

Mike muttered, 'Fuck you,' and stared into his beer.

Cooper knocked back his rye and pulled up a stool next to Donny. He tried to steer the conversation back to less troubled waters, hoping to find the easy camaraderie that had previously existed between them.

'You seen much of Selena lately?'

Mike shook his head in warning, but by then it was too late.

'Not since she started going with Mason Davenport.' Donny drained his beer and banged the glass down on the bar. 'Joe, another beer. Put it on Billy Ray's tab.'

The barman looked at Cooper who nodded in return.

'What the hell does she see in a dweeb like Mason?'

'A job at the meat processing plant, for one thing, which is more than the rest of us have got.'

'Thought there was a waiting list?'

'There is. But when your uncle's the foreman and union rep it's easy to jump the line. Ain't what you know, but who you know. Same as ever.'

'Sorry to hear that, man.'

Donny shrugged. 'Don't matter much. I was only kidding myself thinking a girl like Selena would give me the time of day. I'm a loser, from a long line of losers.'

'That's the beer talking.'

'Fuck you, man! I don't need your sympathy. Still can't believe you sold out and joined up. Not like you believe any of that holy bullshit. Is money really that important to you?'

'No, but having some sort of life is. Look around you, Donny. This town is on its knees, dying a little more by the day. Don't see no point hanging round here waiting on my welfare payment while my life slowly slips away. Not when I can be earning enough money to look after my kin.'

'Now don't you be forgetting the opportunity to spread liberty and democracy to the heathens.'

'Okay, so maybe I don't believe in everything, but you watch the news – the Caliphate is doing terrible things to its own people and inciting atrocities over here. Look at that suicide bombing in Austin.'

'Last time I checked Brad Foster was American. Born and bred. Just like Mom's apple pie.'

'Yeah, but someone must have radicalised him.'

'Probably the CIA. It's an election year, after all.'

'Seriously? You believe that shit?'

'Don't have to believe it. Just have to look at the facts. You can check 'em for yourself – every time there's an election or a drive for a new crusade, terrorist attacks on our home soil go up. You want to fool yourself into believing that's a coincidence, that's your business. But maybe before you go and put a bullet in some Muslim kid you ought to ask yourself what's the real reason you're out there killing. Sure as shit I can guarantee it ain't truth, justice and the American way.'

'So we should just let the Caliphate continue to occupy Israel?'

'Why not? When was the last time the Jews did anything for us? Let them fight their own wars, is what I'm saying.'

'Jesus, Donny.'

'Jesus ain't got anything to do with this, Billy Ray. Any more than God. This is all about keeping the military-industrial complex going.'

'Now you're just being paranoid.'

'That don't mean there ain't nobody out to get me. Wake up and smell the coffee. Country's been on a war economy for most of this century. This crusade is just the latest means of cutting down on the surplus population. Every kid like you that goes out there and comes home in a body bag is one less sucker they have to pay a lifetime of welfare for. Not me. I ain't dying just to keep the arms manufacturers in business. Can't believe you're dumb enough to. But that's your lookout.'

Cooper scrapped back his chair and stood. 'Now you listen up, Donny, and listen up good, 'cause I ain't gonna take that sort of shit from you no more.'

Donny moved his stool and lurched to his feet, swaying uncertainly. 'Reckon you got the sand to take me, do you? Well, c'mon!'

Mike moved between the two men, palms held aloft. 'Whoa there, boys. Settle down. We're all friends here, having a drink.'

Donny looked from Cooper to Mike and then back again. He shook his head. 'Don't reckon I got any friends here. Leastwise not ones I recognise of old.' He picked up his glass and drained it. 'Thanks for the drinks. I'll be sure to come to your memorial when they ship you home.'

'Donny,' Mike protested, as he walked away.

Cooper just shrugged and sat down again, trying to ignore the voice in the back of his head that agreed with Donny. He looked first at Mike and then around the bar, saw the same hopeless and beaten-down expressions. Donny be damned. He had no choice.

'Joe, get us another round.'

CHAPTER 12

Kai paused, enjoying the moment of power as he held the congregation in his grasp. He looked out over the Templar ranks kneeling with heads bowed on the cold stone floor of the chapel, awaiting his final word.

'Amen.'

Over a hundred throats echoed the word back at Kai and he raised his hands to dismiss them. They rose in union and filed from the chapel in two orderly rows, boots striking the floor to a steady beat. A few of the faces were known to him from basic training, but most were strangers. There was no mistaking, however, the figure that now closed on the pulpit. A six-footer with close-cropped blond hair and a full beard, the blue eyes of whom had stared out at him from a hundred vid-casts.

'A rousing sermon, Padre. Just what the men need before they take their vows.'

'Thank you, Colonel Tyler. Is there something I can do for you?'

'As a matter of fact, there is a little something you can maybe clarify for me.'

'The Holy Trinity? Transubstantiation?'

Tyler permitted himself a tight smile. 'No, nothing of a theological nature; I know the catechism as well as any other man. A request has been brought to my attention – your request, in fact – that you want to be assigned to combat duties.'

'That's correct, Colonel. My instructors will confirm my physical fitness and marksmanship are all within tolerance.'

'Yes. I've reviewed your basic training records.'

'And?'

'As you say, perfectly acceptable for any … rank and file member of the Order. But military chaplains are traditionally non-combatants.'

'Yet you and your men are self-confessed soldiers of Christ. Surely a chaplain can be one, too?'

'A man can be anything on a piece of paper, Padre. My concern is what he is in reality. I'm going to be blunt here – I've read your file, all of it – and I understand your desire to strike back at those who have wronged you. But when it actually comes to taking another human life, you might well find your conviction fails you. If it does, you could end up putting the lives of your brothers at risk.'

'I understand your concerns, Colonel. But let me assure you that I won't be found wanting.'

Tyler stared into the middle distance and Kai got the impression the colonel was considering far more than just his fitness to serve. His deliberations complete, Tyler's focus returned to the chaplain.

'Very well. Report to Sergeant Jackson tomorrow at oh-six-hundred. We'll see what you're made of.'

The matter apparently concluded, Tyler turned on his heel and left without another word. *Out of the frying pan and into the fire,* thought Kai.

Jackson was waiting outside the hangar complex when Kai got back from his morning run. The sergeant's features remained impassive, giving nothing away. The silence stretched too long for comfort, forcing Kai to fill it.

'What's the plan?'

'We see if you can shoot.'

Kai fell into step with the sergeant as they headed back towards the main complex, passing the barracks and mess hall to arrive at the base armoury. The quartermaster, clearly anticipating his arrival, stood behind a trestle table. He pointed to a pistol, rifle and shotgun in turn.

'Standard sidearm, Sig Sauer M19, 9mm caseless. Standard rifle, M8 carbine, 5.56mm caseless. And last, but definitely not least, M1040 combat shotgun, chambered for SCMITR shotshells.'

'Scimitar, like the sword?'

'No: S-C-M-I-T-R.' The quartermaster held up a shotgun cartridge. 'Twenty-gauge – contains eight metal darts. It's a variation on the flechette, but the flat, wide shape produces a larger, more disabling wound. Good for penetrating body armour. Has an eight-round capacity.'

Kai's eyes lit up as he reached for the SCMITR only for Jackson to push his hand away.

'One thing at a time, Padre. Let's try you on the range with the sidearm to begin with.'

'You know I passed my firearms training, right?'

'Yeah, but between you, me and the gatepost, let's just say there are different grades of pass.'

Kai bit back his anger at what he took to be a slur on his training and accepted the proffered pistol and magazine. He followed Jackson to the shooting range and donned safety glasses and ear defenders in preparation. As Jackson wound the target out to seven metres, Kai checked the safety, inserted the clip and pulled back the slide to chamber a round.

At the nod from Jackson, Kai raised the pistol and fired ten shots, emptying half the magazine. He placed the pistol down and Jackson recalled the target. The grouping was tight, just below and left of centre.

'Okay, let's see how you do at fifteen metres.'

This time the grouping was slightly wider and slightly lower, but still close to centre. Jackson nodded his approval. He handed Kai the M8 and set the target to the maximum twenty-five metres.

Kai went through the process again with ten single shots and three three-round bursts. The semi-automatic fire was predictably looser but still within the target. Finally, they handed him the combat shotgun and brought the target back to ten metres. Kai pumped off three rounds, shredding the target, then fired another three, revelling in the devastation. He lowered the SCMITR and stood grinning.

'Reckon we have a winner.' Jackson took the gun from him and laid it down. 'Probably your funeral, Padre, but I'll inform Colonel Tyler you're cleared for combat.'

'Was there ever really any doubt?'

'Say what?'

'This was never about my capabilities, but weighing up how it would play with the public. Tyler's no fool. He'd already made his decision when he told me to report to you.'

Kai took Jackson's silence as confirmation. It made no difference to him. He had what he wanted: the opportunity to make the heathens pay in person.

'I'll be hearing confession this evening, if there's anything you need to get off your chest. If not, I'll see you around, Sarge.'

Kai heard Jackson's amused 'motherfucker' as he walked away.

Maybe it was simply a question of demographics, but Kai noticed that those seeking his counsel were predominantly African American, Hispanic and Latino. Templar Private Arturo Garcia was a prime example as he sat with his brow furrowed and his fingers knotted together around the crucifix he wore.

'What you have to remember, Arturo, is that there's no sin in killing these heathens. His Holiness Pope Alexander

IX has promised all sins will be expunged for partaking in this holy war against the Caliphate, so you need not fear for your immortal soul.'

'I understand that, Padre. It's more I'm having doubts about taking my vows. Asking if this is the right path for me.'

'When God places a heavy burden on our shoulders it's natural to ask yourself, why me? To seek someone else to carry the load. But a man of faith, of conviction, soon pushes these doubts aside and accepts his duty. Tomorrow, God willing, you will swear your oath to overthrow the Caliphate, to trample its evil underfoot. Rest assured, that is the path of righteousness.'

Garcia didn't look convinced, but as with so many born into and raised in the Catholic faith, he found it almost impossible to question the authority of the Church and its servants. Kai fought the urge to shake him, angered by what he viewed as refusal to face up to the facts. The Caliphate represented a clear and present danger to everything America stood for. Admittedly, he himself had been blind to that fact prior to the bombing, wilfully burying his head in the sand. But his eyes were open now. He had seen the evil first-hand and knew no good Christian soul could stand idly by and leave it unchallenged.

Kai sighed inwardly; better to save his righteous rage for those who deserved it. Arturo Garcia was young, untried in the fires of war and, as likely, untouched by personal tragedy in life. He needed a reminder of who and what he was fighting for.

'Are your parents still with us? Do you have siblings?'

'Yes, Padre.' The young soldier's face lit up. 'My mother and father live in San Marcos with my three brothers and two sisters.'

'You signed up to protect them.' Kai made it a statement of fact.

'My father, he wanted to, but he has a bad leg. As the eldest son it was my duty to enlist instead. I just want him to be proud of me.'

'You had some furlough before receiving your orders to deploy?'

'A week's leave. Felt good to see my family again. I … I'm ashamed to admit it, but I almost didn't want to leave. Everyone was so happy to see me. But they were only pleased because I am going to fight the Caliphate.' He screwed up his face. 'I don't think I'm explaining myself well.'

'The words you say to me are not as important as what you feel in your heart. God knows the truth and requires no explanation. You must put your doubts aside and trust in His judgement. Can you do that, Arturo? Trust the Lord.'

'Yes, because you tell me this is the right thing to do.' Garcia stood and proffered his hand, which Kai clasped in both of his own. 'Thank you, Padre. This is a weight off my mind.'

Kai kept a benign smile on his face as Garcia walked away. *Some are lambs of God, others are only sheep, but they all like to be led.*

With Garcia's departure, Kai's ministry was complete for the day. Tomorrow would see him take his vows along with the regular enlisted Templars. A watershed moment: the opportunity to avenge his wife and unborn son was almost in his grasp. More than ever, he must give the impression of normalcy while trusting God to guide his hand.

Having retired to the barracks, Kai opened the locker at the foot of his bed and took out the uniform tunic and name tape he had received from Sergeant Jackson. He laid them flat on the bed and retrieved his sewing kit. He stitched quickly and neatly, attaching the name tape above the right breast pocket. Schreiber: it was a name the heathens would have cause to long remember.

Cooper fastened the collar of his dress uniform. It felt a little tight, but he guessed that was the point. He checked the crease on his trousers and the shine on his shoes: all as per regulation. The face that stared back at him from the mirror had a brutal cast to it due to his hair being shaved close to the scalp. Was there a hardness to his eyes that hadn't been there before, or did he imagine it? He pushed his doubts aside, pulled on his white gloves and settled the peaked cap on his head.

Cooper filed into the chapel alongside his fellows and knelt in his appointed place. Two hundred applicants had signed up for the programme six months previously; now only fifty-four remained. He flicked his eyes left and right, not daring to turn his head, and managed to pick out the familiar profile of Mackinlay staring straight ahead. A faint murmur rose as Chaplain-Commander Du Pont took up position in front of the low altar, on which an open Bible rested. The scarlet silk marker pointed to Deuteronomy 20:4: 'For the Lord your God is He who goes with you to fight for you against your enemies, to give you the victory.'

The man nearest the altar reached out and placed his right palm on the Bible, while the remaining initiates placed their right hands on the right shoulders of the men nearest to them.

'You will repeat your several names where I say mine and repeat after me,' Du Pont instructed.

'I, Billy Ray Cooper, in the name of Almighty God, hereby declare, on oath, that I will be a true solider of Christ in the battle against the heathen; that I will support and defend the Constitution and laws of the Religious States of America against all enemies, foreign and domestic, with my life's blood; that I will be the protector of my brother's life and honour; that I will take no wife and father no children while in God's holy service; and that I take this obligation freely without any mental reservation or purpose of evasion; so help me God.'

'You may cease repeating and rise.'

Cooper let his hand drop. He felt dizzy as he climbed to his feet. Sergeant Jackson and Colonel Tyler joined

Chaplain-Commander Du Pont at the altar. Jackson held a cushion on which fifty-four red cross pattée badges rested.

'Templar-Private Adler, you will come forward to the altar,' Tyler instructed.

Cooper watched Adler march to the front of the chapel and stand to attention. Tyler instructed him to stand at ease and Jackson handed the colonel the first of the badges.

'Templar-Private Adler, I present you with the badge of a Templar. Wear that badge with honour and pride, and I trust you will never disgrace it.'

Adler accepted the badge and shook hands with Tyler, who then dismissed him. Four presentations later, Cooper received his summons to the altar.

CHAPTER 13

Interview Transcript #1: Jefferson Lynch in conversation with Colonel Martin Tyler, prior to the Palmachim Beach landing.

Jefferson Lynch: Firstly, Colonel Tyler, I'd like to thank you for taking the time to speak with me. I know things are moving fast and you're a busy man.

Colonel Tyler: You and your viewers are welcome, Mr Lynch. It's important we give the American public an accurate overview of the war. Cut down on some of the misinformation out there.

JL: But you'd agree this is more than a simple military campaign? Given your unit shares its name with a historic order of Christian knights who sought to liberate Jerusalem a thousand years ago, there are many who view this as a religious and ideological war. Some would even go so far as to say it amounts to a direct persecution of those who follow Islam.

CT: That's exactly the kind of misinformation I was talking about earlier. Yes, ours is a country founded on staunch Christian principles, and my men are true soldiers of Christ. But we are not, by any metric, engaged in an ideological war with the broader Islamic faith – our fight is with the Islamic Caliphate alone. Lest people forget, we are here to liberate Jerusalem at the direct request of the Israeli government in exile. Historically, Jerusalem has long been an important city of pilgrimage to Christians, Jews and Muslims alike. As the foremost Christian power in the world, it falls to the Religious States to use its economic and military powers to end the Caliphate's illegal occupation of Jerusalem and secure the city for the peaceful faiths of the world.

JL: Interesting you should mention illegal occupation. Wasn't the Israeli government accused of exactly the same in the former West Bank territories of the Palestinians? It was—

CT [interrupting]: I don't believe that's relevant to the discussion at hand.

JL: No? The international community certainly thought differently when Israel annexed the West Bank, leading to thousands of displaced Palestinians fleeing to Egypt. It isolated Israel, leaving her without allies when the Caliphate threatened her borders.

CT: Since you're so interested in giving your viewers a history lesson, I would remind you that America stood by our Israeli allies during the dark days of the Fall in '63. Templar soldiers gave up their lives then, as they are about to do now.

JL: You could argue that makes it more than a religious duty – that it makes it personal.

CT [sound of mike being torn free]: If you're only here to do a hatchet job, I don't have time for this bullshit.

JL: Just trying to present all sides of the argument, Colonel.

CT: Doesn't sound like that from where I'm sitting. Seems to me you're presenting opinion as fact, like some second-rate tabloid hack.

JL: You said it yourself, Colonel: Jerusalem has a long and complicated history. One that makes it all but impossible for Christian, Jew or Muslim to be purely objective in their reasoning.

CT [scornful]: You're keen to paint us as bigots and unreasoning zealots. Contrary to what many seem to believe, this isn't a sectarian war. The Islamic Caliphate is the aggressor; we are simply adhering to our sworn and sacred duty as defenders of the faith. While I take no pleasure in war, in killing, I will not flinch in my duty, and nor will the men under my command. We have our orders and we will obey them.

JL: And those orders originate from Grand Master Thaddeus Vanderbilt?

CT: Where they relate to Templar operations in Israel, yes. Grand Master Vanderbilt coordinates strategy with the president and our allies from the Greater Russian Collective.

JL: I'm kind of surprised the Grand Master isn't here to oversee the campaign in person. After all, he was on the last transporter out of Jerusalem in '63. Him, five other Templar wounded and twelve members of the IDF.

CT: Is there a point to this, Lynch?

JL: Only that I'm surprised he's delegated what is, after all, the Templars' fundamental mission to a subordinate – regardless of how qualified and decorated.

CT [long pause]: Fuck you, Lynch. And don't think for one minute you're putting that bullshit on air.

Transcript Ends.

Lynch rolled the data-disc over his fingers like a coin, staring all the while into space. A smile played on his lips as he recalled the vein throbbing in Colonel Tyler's temple, fading almost as quickly as it was born. He knew antagonising Tyler was stupid, so why had he deliberately gone out of his way to rile him? Whatever perverse pleasure he might derive from the interview, it remained worthless. Another dissident piece blocked by the censors. And still he went on recording them. Told himself he would find the means of getting them out into the world once he was home. Make the truth of this shabby little war known across the globe. Wasn't he Jefferson Lynch, hard-bitten political pundit? Whiskey in one hand, a cigarette in the other, nose full of powder as he blazed his truth across the satellite feeds.

A goddamn fraud was what he was. He had spent so long playing a caricature of himself that he no longer knew where the fiction ended and fact began. What he did know for certain was that he couldn't do twenty years in federal prison. They had him on the hook, and, wriggle as he might, he wasn't getting off. He could record all the interviews he liked, but who was he fooling? Assuming they kept their word and didn't put a bullet in the back of his head once this was over, he would slink home with his tail between his legs and let them parade him across the news networks. In return, they would let him back into the presidential press corps. But whereas before he had been the rabid dog everyone was afraid of, now he'd be a lapdog, ever ready to roll over and have its tummy rubbed. And before you knew it, they'd be gearing up for another damn war. Same as always.

Lynch pulled the Glock from its holster, racked back the slide and pressed it to his temple. His pulse thundered in his ears as he squeezed the trigger. Less than six pounds of pressure and it would all be over. *Boom!* Jefferson Lynch has left the building! No prison. No angry comments below the line accusing him of selling out. A cordite full stop to a life lived on the edge. Didn't he owe this to his public?

'You're a fucking pussy, Jefferson Lynch!' Lynch slammed the pistol on the table and pulled out his hip flask.

He unscrewed the cap, threw back his head and upended the flask.

Like the hack he'd become, he was continuing the story long past its natural conclusion. He could delude himself he still had something to say, but the law of diminishing returns would win out.

Cooper checked the time on his com-unit: four hours until zero hour. Tension was high onboard the RSS King David as it rode at anchor in Episkopi Bay off the southern coast of Cyprus. He looked enviously at Walker in the bunk across from him: fast asleep without a care in the world. Mackinlay had asked him to accompany him to the ship's chapel to pray, but Cooper had made his excuses. He might believe in God, but he found it hard to accept God believed in him, leastwise not when it came to the mission at hand. He looked again at his com-unit. Like every military com-unit in the area, it was in lockdown mode; no communication in or out. But that wouldn't prevent him from doing what he needed to do. He swiped open the message app and started to type:

Dear Ma, Pa, Shania, Dale & Wade,

If you all are reading this letter then the worst has happened and I've fallen in the service of my country. I hope you won't be angry with me or feel disappointed. I know my decision to join up was difficult and confusing for you all. But I did it out of love. I did it so we all could have a better life. It hurts in my heart to think I won't be there to share that life with you, but if I've one final wish it's that you not be bitter about my sacrifice. I knew what I was doing and I did it willingly. I did it for you.

Pa,

You're the best example a young man could hope for in life. No matter what life threw at you, and it threw plenty, you faced up to it with courage and dignity. You never blamed others for your misfortunes or took your anger out on anybody unjustly. Times were mighty tight, and we never had much of anything as a family, but we always had your love and guidance. You taught me how to be a good man, and I don't think there's any greater gift than that in the world. Be proud of that.

Ma,

You're one of the most beautiful, kind souls I know. Your heart's so big it surprises me it don't burst. Always, you knew the right words to say – whenever the other kids picked on me for my clothes or I didn't get the grades I wanted in school, you made it all better. I hope you can find some comfort in knowing that your little boy did the best he could.

Shania,

When we were little, I wasn't always the best big brother, and I want you to know I'm sorry for all those times I pulled your pigtails, and for telling Sonny Nelson you had cooties in sixth grade. You've grown into a smart and pretty young woman that any brother would be proud of. I know you'll help Ma and Pa and the twins get through this difficult time so that you all can pull together as a family. Live the best life that you can, little sis. I'll be looking down on you all.

Dale, Wade,

No denying that you come together as a pair, and all the better for it. Like most little brothers you can be as annoying as a skeeter at times, but I wouldn't have it any other way. But things are going to be tough on you now as you're gonna have to do some growing up afore your time. Be good for Ma and Pa, and keep an eye on that big sister of yours. She can be real tricksy when she's a mind to.

Love, your dutiful son and brother,

Billy Ray.

Cooper saved the letter and threw his com-unit down on the bunk, his eyes squeezed tight to hold back the tears. He swiped the back of his hand across his face and swung his legs from the bunk. Since he couldn't sleep, he might as well go and get some coffee. He pulled on his boots without bothering to lace them and crept past Walker, though he doubted much of anything would wake him. Now there was a man of implacable faith.

Cooper spun the wheel on the hatch to open it and stepped out into the corridor. Featureless grey-painted steel ran in both directions and he took a moment to orientate himself. The galley was two decks up, the nearest stairwell twenty metres to the left. Bowing his head slightly in deference to the low ceiling, he set off. Midway up the stairs he collided with someone descending in the opposite direction.

'Shit, sorry—' Cooper's words trailed off as he met Rivera's frank gaze. He'd heard the remote piloting crew were operating from the aircraft carrier and should have known she would be onboard. Even in the unflattering lines of combat fatigues, she looked good.

'Hey there, Eve. I was just going to get a coffee. Fancy joining me?'

Rivera stepped back from him. 'I don't think that's such a good idea. Do you?'

Cooper searched her eyes for some hint of warmth and found none. 'Guess not. Mind how you go.'

Rivera pushed past and headed down the stairs. He watched her blonde ponytail bob up and down in rhythm with her steps, trying to ignore the swell of her hips. Why the hell had he followed her from the bar to her car that night? His life had enough complications without adding this to the mix.

Cooper checked his earpieces as the SB Defiant XV attack helicopter lifted off from the deck of the aircraft carrier. They doubled as hearing protection and coms, normal conversation rendered impossible by the roar of the rotors. As the deck fell away, the nine copters formed a diamond formation with his, under the command of Colonel Tyler.

Cooper eyed the instrument panel nervously; were the flashing LEDs good or bad? Funny how he thought nothing of letting an AI drive his car, but balked at one piloting him.

Then again, his car wasn't several hundred feet in the air and flying into a combat zone.

The sarge, picking up on his concern, cracked a smile. 'Don't worry, you're in capable hands. More so than any human pilot.'

Cooper wondered what Rivera would make of that. Probably very little. She didn't appear to have strong feelings on any subject, including him. Shrugging it off, he looked across to where Mackinlay was manning the other M60 and received a thumbs-up. Cooper nodded back. Locked and loaded; ready to rock.

Cooper's eyes flitted around the cabin, taking in the rest of the Defiant's crew. Colonel Tyler was reading the instrumentation on the flight console. Sergeant Jackson sat braced against the side of the copter, his assault rifle slung across his chest, jaw moving ponderously as he chewed gum. Katz, their Israeli advisor, sat opposite, running a whetstone along the edge of a wicked-looking combat knife. He'd called it an *Ari* something or other; some Hebrew shit. Both men being experienced veterans, Cooper guessed this was their pre-combat ritual. In time he would find one of his own, but for now his nerves jangled like stretched wire.

The Defiants accelerated to attack speed, leaving the first wave of landing craft with their crews of Templar shock troops behind. They would soon be disgorging their contents onto the sands of Palmachim Beach, but first the air cavalry had to prepare the way for them.

Prior to the Caliphate occupation the beach had been a resort, famed for its dunes, limestone ridge and sea turtles. Now the geometric shapes of anti-tank traps, bunkers and gun emplacements broke up the dunes and ridge, a convoluted trench system zig-zagging between them. Following the failure of the Second Crusade, the Caliphate had had years to prepare for the inevitable return of the Americans.

At Tyler's command, the first three copters peeled off and commenced their attack run. They swooped low, jinking in and out of the flak, firing Hellfire missiles at the first line of defences on the beach. As the ensuing fireballs rose into the sky, Cooper and Mackinlay strafed the infantry cowering in the trenches. The second wave rode in behind them to commence their attack on the next line of defences. This time the air-to-ground missiles impacted against the reinforced concrete of the bunkers with mixed results.

The third wave met increased flak as the Caliphate gunners found their range. Cooper swore as the lead Defiant took a hit and plummeted to the beach in a fireball. It was one thing to acknowledge that they would lose men in the attack, but the reality of seeing his comrades die felt very different. Anger and fear vied for supremacy as the ammunition belt rattled through the M60.

The second copter went into its attack, closing in on the bunker for maximum effect before releasing its entire complement of missiles. The bunker split apart, orange tongues of flame and dark billows of smoke rising into the sky. Nearby, a heavy machine gun traversed, following the banking Defiant, spitting out tracer. The fire-bright rounds struck the fuselage of the copter, and as it rose up Cooper saw the left-side gunner hanging lifeless from his lanyard. He pushed the image from his mind and concentrated on laying down cover fire. The AI angled the copter's nose down, releasing the last of their missiles into the beach defences. With the resistance now quelled, it went into hover mode, moving the copter from side to side as it raked the trenches with the minigun. The two wingmen followed suit, all but obliterating the beachline as the first wave of landing craft approached the shore.

'Take her down,' Tyler ordered the AI. 'We're making history here, boys, and my boots are going to be the first to touch Israeli soil.'

Jackson shifted uncomfortably. 'Our orders were to provide air support for the ground assault.'

'And that's what these flying calculators are gonna do while we spearhead the attack.' Tyler turned in his seat. 'I assume you don't have a problem with that, Captain Katz?'

The Israeli officer readied his Tavor assault rifle by way of reply.

'That's what I thought.' Tyler toggled open a channel. 'All troops prepare for ground assault. Weapons hot, boys. We're going in!' He addressed the AI again: 'Once we're down, return to the carrier, refuel, re-arm and resume your attack.'

The helicopter's runners were still two feet from the ground when Tyler jumped. Goggles down and scarf up, he used the whipped sand for cover as he sprinted to the nearest trench. He slid down its broken side, aimed left, then right, but only corpses opposed him. Cooper adjusted his own scarf and goggles and followed, the rest of the squad following close. They moved cautiously to the right, checking the Caliphate bodies for signs of life and finding none. Ahead, the remainder of the air cavalry troops breached the trench, moving along its length as they advanced towards one of the remaining bunkers.

A Caliphate soldier, head bloodied, emerged from a shattered dugout, hands raised in surrender. Chaplain Schreiber raised his SCMITR combat shotgun and fired, decapitating the wounded soldier.

'What the fuck, you maniac!' Cooper shouted. 'He was surrendering!'

Tyler fixed him with a basilisk stare. 'Remember your training, son. We move fast and hard. No prisoners.'

As they moved on Schreiber blasted two more wounded. 'Death to the heathens!'

Jackson shook his head and muttered, 'Could tell from the minute I set eyes on him that motherfucker was crazy.'

Cooper pressed on through the trench system, heart hammering in his chest as he followed Tyler's lead. The squad came to halt in the lee of a bunker. Missile strikes had scratched and cracked the concrete, which otherwise looked intact.

Jackson held out his hand. 'Satchel charge.'

Mackinlay passed the explosives to the sergeant and pressed himself flat to the side of the trench as Jackson crept across the face of the bunker. He stopped on reaching one of the gun apertures, primed the charge and pushed it inside.

'Fire in the hole!'

The thick concrete walls concentrated the explosion, expelling smoke and flames from the apertures like the hot breath of Hell itself. Jackson waited for it to clear before poking his assault rifle through the gun slit and emptying the magazine. The following squad was already moving up the trench to neutralise the next bunker.

The game of leapfrog progressed up the beach until they came in sight of the freeway, where Tyler called a halt. Behind them, the first landing wave had beached, with the Templar shock troops advancing unopposed. Tyler raised his field glasses and looked out to sea, taking in the approaching second wave before looking further out to where a pair of amphibious assault ships were already disgorging the third wave.

Tyler faced inland and scanned the horizon. The road stretched away, bounded either side by dusty scrubland. He handed the glasses to Jackson.

'Kind of expected more of a welcoming committee. What do you think?'

Jackson scanned the scrub, looking for telltale tracks, footprints or the betraying glint of the sun reflecting from optics. Finding none, he handed the glasses back. 'Too damn empty, sir. We should wait for the shock troops to catch up.'

'No, we secure the area. Can't risk Abdul flanking us.'

The squad moved out, fanning across the road with Cooper taking point. They advanced slowly, searching the scrub for booby traps and mines. At a hundred metres out, Jackson called a halt and crouched down. He pressed his left palm against the ground.

'Feel that?'

Cooper pressed his own hand to the ground.

'Vibration. Close. But how—'

The Templars fell back along the road as the tremors increased, scanning the horizon for the source. A low rumble joined the vibration as the earth fell away either side of the road to reveal a series of ramps. Engines growled to life as the first of the old Type 99A main battle tanks gunned its way onto the road.

'It's a goddamn trap,' Tyler spat, 'and we walked right into it!'

CHAPTER 14

The T99As opened fire as the Templars retreated, shells arcing high overhead to explode among the concentrated ranks of shock troops on the beach. The screams of the injured and dying carried over the shelling. Cooper looked at Tyler out of the corner of his eye, seeking some sign that his commander had an exfiltration plan. He had gone through his training believing Tyler to be infallible, but out here in the thick of combat, where judgement mattered most, he appeared all too human. Having gotten them into this mess, Cooper could only hope Tyler would get them out of it.

A burst of heavy-calibre machine gun fire punched through the body of the man beside him, erupting through his chest in a spray of crimson. Cooper stood frozen, staring at Horowitz's corpse until Jackson caught him by the arm and pulled him forward. In the midst of the chaos Chaplain Schreiber stood untouched like some divinely protected madman, blasting at the tanks with his SCMITR. He kept firing long after it clicked empty.

Katz, recognising Schreiber's frenzy, grabbed hold of the shotgun.

'You want to keep killing these bastards, you best bug

out and reload.'

Brought back to his senses, the chaplain slung the SCMITR over his shoulder and drew his handgun. He brought up the rear with Katz, covering the retreat.

As Cooper slid back down into the trench, the returning Defiant attack helicopters passed overhead, firing a barrage of rockets. The lead tank exploded, but the copters came under fire as they banked around for another run, Caliphate infantry emerging from the underground silos in the wake of the tanks. Smoke billowed from the engine of one of the Defiants while another, its tail rotor shredded by rifle fire, spun wildly to the ground. Flames licked up the sides of the downed helicopter, which exploded seconds later when they reached the fuel tank, throwing a nearby Templar to the ground. He let the fireball wash over him before staggering back to his feet, the back of his vest smoking. The burning wreckage of the Defiant silhouetted the fleeing Templar, making him an easy target for the Caliphate forces.

'Shit!' Mackinlay swore, recognising the running figure. 'That's Walker out there.'

Cooper and Mackinlay laid down covering fire as Walker resumed his sprint towards them, bullets kicking up clods of dirt around his heels. Twenty metres out, he went down. Mackinlay handed his rifle to Cooper.

'Don't be crazy, Mac!'

'I ain't leaving Walker to those bastards! They'll torture him and worse.'

Further argument was pointless as Mackinlay hauled himself out of the trench and ran towards his fallen comrade. Cooper opened fire again, with Katz and Schreiber joining in. With the infantry focused once more on keeping the attack copters at bay, Mackinlay reached Walker and lifted him onto his shoulders. He started back at a staggering run, his comrades willing him on step by step as he closed in on the relative safety of the trench. Suddenly, he and his burden were sliding down the trench wall to safety.

Cooper and Jackson lifted their wounded brother and laid him on the floor of the trench. A quick examination revealed two through-and-through wounds in his right thigh, which had missed the bone. Jackson ripped open a coagulant pack and poured the gel onto the wound. Walker moaned as it reacted with the blood to form a thick crust.

'Coop, get a dressing on those wounds while I get him something for the pain.'

Cooper's training kicked in, his hands working from muscle memory as he applied sterile dressings to the entry and exit wounds and bound them in place, provoking fresh cries of agony from Walker.

'Easy.' Jackson reassured him. He punched through the thick material of Walker's combat trousers with a fentanyl pen. The opioid kicked in instantly, relaxing his body.

'He gonna be all right?' Mackinlay asked.

Jackson clapped him on the shoulder. 'Thanks to you, he is. Good work.'

Cooper pressed his right foot hard to the ground to still a treacherous tremble. Why hadn't he gone after Walker himself? They had all taken the same vows and yet Mackinlay was the only one who had honoured them. Was it fear, or worse, a lack of belief that froze him?

An exploding shell ended Cooper's reverie. Now was not the time for self-recrimination. The infantry on the beach was still taking a pounding. Tyler called for the radio operator, Pedersen, and a squat figure with a dark complexion made his way along the trench, unslinging the radio as he came. He hunkered down beside the colonel and powered up the radio.

'Tell the copters to break off the attack and patch me through to command.'

Pedersen relayed the order and passed the set to Tyler.

'Golgotha, this is Apostle One. LZ taking fire from enemy armour – twelve plus units. We need air support with tank busters.'

'Acknowledged, Apostle One. Hellcats are scrambling,

but you need to hold your position. Repeat, hold your position. Golgotha out.'

The trench started to fill up as the survivors of the first landing wave reached cover. Cooper saw he wasn't the only one unnerved by the shelling. Discipline was starting to break down, and if it went unchecked there was a danger the attack would turn into a rout. Tyler, clearly reaching the same conclusion, grabbed the nearest shock trooper by his webbing and turned him around.

'Trooper, who's your CO?'

'Captain Adams, sir. But he's dead.'

'Then who's next in command?' Tyler asked, failing to keep the impatience out of his voice.

'Lieutenant Moore.' The solider looked in both directions before pointing down the trench. 'That's him with the bandage on his arm.'

Moore had the fresh features of the newly graduated and a corresponding look of shock to go with it, having, like many of the Templars, just experienced combat first-hand. He belatedly snapped off a salute in response to Tyler's approach.

'Lieutenant, order your men to start digging in. We need to strengthen the defences.'

Moore opened his mouth and then closed it. Either he was smart enough to work out the importance of keeping his men busy or else he'd thought better of questioning the orders of a superior officer.

'If those tanks close sufficiently to target the second wave of landing craft before they reach the beach, this attack will turn into a massacre. You boys packing any ordnance, Lieutenant?'

Moore nodded and disappeared down the trench. He reappeared a couple of minutes later with an RPG. Tyler grunted his approval and thrust the RPG and ammunition pouch at Cooper.

'Take it you remember how to use this?'

'Yes, sir.'

'Then get going. I'll spot for you.'

Cooper worked his way down the line, doubt and fear evaporating in a surge of adrenaline as Tyler directed him into position opposite the lead T99A. He worked quickly, screwing the propelling charge onto three warheads and loading the first into the launcher. Moving to the lip of the trench, he sighted the tank between the turret and main hull, and fired. The HEAT round exploded on contact, penetrating the tank's armour and transforming it into a fireball. Cooper, acting like an automaton, moved to a new firing position twenty metres away, as directed by Tyler via his earpiece. He sighted the rear of the next tank close to the engine, a known weak spot in the armour. A trail of whitish blue-grey smoke marked the path of the grenade as it shot towards its target. A second, larger explosion followed the initial detonation as the tank's fuel went up.

The remaining tanks responded to this new threat with a concentrated burst of machine gun fire that ripped up the edge of the trench.

'Looks like I've got their attention,' Cooper muttered as he crawled along the trench floor.

Spotting Jackson and Katz, he called for covering fire. He moved past the sergeant and IDF captain as they fired ineffectual salvos at the tanks and took up position a dozen metres away. With the tank crews expecting another attack, Cooper took the first available shot, firing at the flank of the nearest tank and ducking as the grenade hit its target. The rattling clank of broken track which followed the blast indicated he had disabled rather than destroyed the tank. Out of grenades, he had to hope it was enough.

The retaliating fire increased, forcing Cooper to take cover with Jackson and Katz. The engine revs and clatter of the tracks told him the tanks were closing on the trench and, by extension, on the incoming landing craft. Cooper wracked his brains, looking for a solution. To break cover was certain death, but remaining where they were would prove equally fatal. It wasn't supposed to end like this. He looked to Jackson and Katz and saw from their expressions that they had reached the same conclusion. Pa might not want him to take any risks, but there were a whole lot more lives than his own hanging in the balance. He quickly ran through the squad's standard equipment and arrived at the one final, crazy chance.

'You packing any mines?'

Jackson nodded, opened a pouch on his hip and extracted a gunmetal disc five inches in diameter. He twisted the dial on top. 'Two minutes?'

'Reckon that ought to about do it.'

Katz backed away. 'You might be in a hurry to meet your God, but I can wait!'

'Pity.' Cooper laughed. 'Because it looks like He has other ideas. Hope you're tight with Him.'

Katz stopped his retreat and the three men sat and listened as the tanks ground ever closer.

The scream of jets, followed by the roar of incoming missiles, drowned out the approaching tanks. Cooper dived for cover as they struck home, the ensuing explosions rolling over the trench and sucking up the oxygen.

Rivera's voice crackled over his comms: 'Eagle Leader to Apostle One – enemy armour is neutralised. Trust you army boys can handle it from here?'

CHAPTER 15

Schreiber waded back from the listing wreck of the landing craft, leaving the burial detail to recover the corpses from its waterlogged hull. He paused at the edge of the sea, the water lapping around his ankles, and took in the expanse of beach. Truly this was the fire and brimstone of Hell, the corpses of the damned laid out for all to see. And yet there were Christian lambs to minister to. He pressed forward, boots leaving deep indentations in the wet sand that slowly filled with water.

The first of the bombed-out trenches lay a hundred metres from the shore and Schreiber followed its crumbling edge northwards, homing in on the plaintive cries of the wounded. Spotting the sandy tones of desert camouflage, he slid down the edge of the trench to where a member of the Templar ground assault forces lay with his back pressed against a wall of sandbags. A bloody field dressing covered the soldier's right shin, which he had propped up on an ammunition crate. Otherwise, the trooper appeared unhurt.

The soldier looked Schreiber up and down, taking in his clerical collar. 'Say, Padre, you wouldn't happen to have a smoke on you?'

Schreiber, a non-smoker, nodded and took out the

lighter and cigarette pack one of the old hands had advised him to carry for such occasions. He shook a cigarette free and handed it over. The wounded man bent close for a light as Schreiber flicked the wheel of the lighter.

'What's your name, son?'

'Leroy. Leroy Burdell.'

'You in any pain, Leroy?'

Burdell held up a used fentanyl pen and laughed. 'Can't say as I am, Padre. Can't say as I am.'

'Anything else I can get you?'

'Don't reckon so.' Burdell indicated the flashing green LED on his vest. 'I've activated the medi-beacon – lowest priority. Soon as they've dealt with the more urgent cases, I'm sure they'll get around to my sorry ass. Begging your pardon for the language, Padre.'

Schreiber nodded his excusal and moved off along the trench. He stepped over a headless corpse and then crouched beside a second body. No pulse. Cold skin. Schreiber drew the lids down over the staring eyes.

'Another righteous soul gone to God.'

The trench curved to the right, following the lie of the land. Schreiber moved cautiously, checking two further corpses before coming to a stop in front of the entrance to a zig-zagging communications trench. The subsidiary trench led off at a forty-five-degree angle. He unslung the SCMITR and peered around the corner. The first twenty metres of the trench, up to where it turned again, were clear. Schreiber pressed a finger to his ear, trying to cut out the whine of medivac helicopter rotors overhead. Was that a cry? He moved forward, checking the floor and walls of the trench, looking for tripwires or hastily scattered anti-personnel mines. Plenty of spent brass, which meant enemy action, as the Templars used caseless ammunition.

Schreiber turned the next corner. A figure dressed in the olive drab of the Caliphate lay curled in a foetal position midway along the section. Schreiber kept the SCMITR aimed as he approached. Up close, he saw the soldier's bloody hands pressed to his belly in a futile attempt to hold in his intestines. The man's eyes widened in fear as Schreiber pressed the barrel of the shotgun to his forehead and used it to tilt back his head. The sparse beard revealed him to be a youth not long out of puberty. He uttered a few words in Arabic and closed his eyes.

'If it's mercy you're looking for, you're out of luck. Don't rightly know if you can understand me, but I'll say this anyway. Whatever pain you're in right now, it'll be as nothing compared to the torment and agony you'll experience when you're burning in hellfire. And though you burn for a hundred thousand years that won't be enough to atone for what you and your people have done. Truly it is written: woe to the heathen!'

Schreiber shook off the young Caliphate soldier's fingers from his ankle and walked on. He was a merciful man, allowing his enemy an hour or two of respite before his eternal damnation.

The communication trench broke out once more into a defensive trench. Sixty or so metres to the right, Schreiber spotted a medic tending to a wounded trooper. He moved instinctively to the left, navigating broken duckboards and ruptured sandbags. Ahead, the walls of the trench fell away, widening into a crater caused by an air-to-ground missile. Schreiber took in the scattered gobbets of burnt flesh, the still-smoking base, and climbed out of the trench to circumnavigate it. He looked back towards the beach as he skirted the crater's edge and saw the burial detail heaving the corpses of Caliphate soldiers clear of the shattered defences. Dozers were already preparing the first mass grave. Schreiber thought it a good start; nothing more. His anointed duty was to cleanse the evil of Islam with fire.

He descended into the trench once more and continued picking his way along. A pair of boots stuck out where the trench curved again in response to the path of the limestone ridge. Something about the angle disturbed Schreiber and, caution momentarily forgotten, he hurried forward.

Schreiber discovered the feet in the boots, together with the shins and knees, no longer attached to their owner, who rested a few metres distant. The Templar corporal had propped himself against the side of the trench, supported by his right arm, which hung between the staves of a ladder. He had managed to apply coagulant gel packs to his stumps. No easy task, given his left arm dangled useless, blood dripping from a deep wound in the shoulder. Another spreading patch of gore marked a shrapnel wound in the soldier's stomach.

The corporal's eyes flickered open as Schreiber reached out to check for a pulse, causing the chaplain to flinch back. His eyes were near black with agony and his lips cracked as he tried to speak. Pushing aside his revulsion, Schreiber tilted his ear towards the corporal's mouth.

It was as much exhalation as speech, but Schreiber could just make out the words, faint as they were: 'Finish … me.'

Schreiber tried to pull away, but the corporal caught his shoulder with his good hand and gripped him with the preternatural strength of the dying. His mouth reduced to a thin line of pain, he nodded, confirming his desire for the coup de grâce.

It was the one aspect of their training that Schreiber had thought barbaric: to be willing and able to end a brother's suffering, and yet his hand moved of its own volition towards the dagger on his belt. His breath quickened as he pushed down on the spring release and drew the blade. Sunlight glinted from polished steel; a fighting knife should be bright to invoke fear in your opponent. But he saw no fear in the corporal's eyes, only a longing for release. Schreiber pressed the point of the blade just below the corporal's left ear. He pivoted to the side as he made the cut, avoiding the arterial spray of blood. Death followed a few swift, merciful seconds later.

Schreiber detached the corporal's hand from his shoulder and wiped his dagger on the dead man's tunic. He sheathed the blade and sat back on his heels, the words of

Psalm 23 coming automatically to his lips.

A hard day, sure enough, but the cause was just. Why then did he feel he should do so much more to avenge his family? He had personally dispatched a score of Caliphate soldiers to Hell, but sleep came no easier to him of a night. How many would it take; a hundred, a thousand, before he stopped seeing Jessica's face in his dreams, crying out for vengeance? He longed to be with her again, but how to accomplish that in a fitting manner God would approve of? Was he, himself, to be the burnt offering?

Lynch directed the camera drones along the path of the trench, taking in the live feed on his HUD. The bodies of dead Caliphate soldiers lay in various attitudes of agony: burned, shot, crushed and, in one grotesque display, decapitated. His earpiece crackled, instructing him to pause the drones and zoom in for a close-up on the stake-mounted head. Lynch circled the drones and then moved on, taking in the caches of recovered rifles, ammunition and grenades. The support crew had spent three hours dressing the scene, removing the Templar casualties and equipment to create the impression of an easy and near unopposed victory. Total BS, but the viewers back home were not to see anything that might cause alarm.

He panned the drones independently, taking in the shattered bunkers left and right, then zoomed out to display the grid of trenches that connected them across the cratered landscape of the beach. A warning in his ear reminded him not to track too far to the right to avoid showing the destruction of the limestone ridge by Templar missiles. The clean-up had also included the removal of dozens of dead sea turtles, the last vestiges of a once-famous colony, now rendered extinct.

Skirting the edge of the ridge, Lynch directed the drones inland, skimming across the freeway and out into the scrub to examine the shattered remains of Caliphate tanks. The aerial view picked up several black commas in close proximity to the burnt-out armour. He homed in on one which resolved itself into a shrivelled, blackened corpse. The limbs had curled into the body, teeth shining white from a lipless face. Death by fire, the all-too-common fate of a tank crew. He suppressed a shudder.

Lynch circled the bat-like drones back to the beach, where twenty JLTVs were forming up in two fast, mobile columns which would travel inland under cover of darkness to meet up with the heavy armour that had landed at Tel Aviv. Speed was key to the whole offensive, but first the voting public must have their circus.

A countdown popped up on Lynch's HUD, heralding an auto-cue. Lynch focused the drones for a head and shoulders shot and started to read.

'Palmachim Beach – in peacetime this was one of many Israeli resorts famed for its natural beauty. Today, twenty-six years after the Fall of Jerusalem, it is the site of a successful landing by Templar forces led by Colonel Martin Tyler, Commander of the Second Battalion, Two Hundred and Twenty-Seventh Aviation Regiment of the First Templar Division's Combat Aviation Brigade.

'Superior firepower, tactics and training have overwhelmed the Islamic Caliphate troops stationed here and, as you can see around me, the Templars have established a beachhead from which they will begin their deployment inland. The Fourth Crusade has commenced in earnest and the liberation of Israel from the tyranny of the Islamic Caliphate will surely follow. This has been Jefferson Lynch, Fox News, covering the war in detail. Stay tuned for further updates.'

Lynch killed the feed and let out an exasperated sigh as the drones docked at their base station. He ran his hand across his shaved head, feeling the sweat. Above him the sun shone mercilessly from a cloudless sky. Fuck it. The area was clear. He unbuckled his vest as he walked back to his assigned JLTV. No sign of Jackson or that nut-job preacher,

Schreiber. Opening the rear door, he threw the vest onto the back seat, looked up at the sun again and took off his uniform tunic. The milk-pale flesh of his arms shone in the sunlight. He needed some shade. Across the beach, he spotted the awning erected over the ordered ranks of body bags. One hundred and twenty-seven fatalities, the true cost of this insignificant piece of beach. A reality his handlers had warned him not to broadcast. Fair enough, but that didn't prevent him from investigating for his own benefit.

He crossed the sand, stepping around and over the various patches of dried blood. The body bags were airtight and waterproof to prevent escaping odours and fluids. Some were recognisably human in shape, but the worst were no more than a jumbled collection of parts, so much so that Lynch wondered if they even belonged to the same person. Had he spoken to any of them during his acclimatisation at Fort Irwin? More than likely, but he found it near impossible to recall individual faces from the homogeneous mass of young men, predominantly in their late teens and early twenties. Boys united in the common myth of their own invincibility; the youthful delusion that bad things only happened to other people. Trouble was, to everyone else you *were* that other person.

Lynch pulled out his hip flask and gave it a shake. It felt worryingly light. He unscrewed the cap and tipped a couple of fingers of bourbon down his throat. The cheap spirit burned, but out here you had to make do with what you could get. He fought the urge to empty the flask and lit a cigarette instead. The heat of the drink and the nicotine took the edge off, reminding him he was playing the long game. Suck it up. Do what they tell you. And maybe, just maybe, he'd get out of this alive. So long as he didn't let pride fuck with him. And no more thoughts of suicide. He refused to give the bastards the satisfaction. Couldn't leave his daughter solely under the influence of his ex-wife – God only knew what she was saying about him.

He smoked the cigarette down to the filter and flicked it

away. What was the old adage? War is long periods of boredom punctuated by moments of sheer terror? Sounded about right. He certainly knew about the boredom, and once the convoy set off he'd be an active part of the offensive, which meant the terror was sure to follow.

The *whup-whup* of rotors drew Lynch's attention back to the sky, marking the arrival of the first of the transporters. The airlifting of the bodies had begun. He pulled his bandana up over his mouth and nose and made his way through the rising dust clouds. Time to get some food. Maybe gauge the mood of the men.

A mess tent had been set up but there was no galley as yet. Lynch picked up the first MRE pack to hand and scanned the tent for a familiar face. He spotted Cooper, whom Sergeant Jackson had introduced him to as the driver of their JLTV, and crossed to his table. The kid was a tall, gangly youth with a distinct overbite and a thick Southern accent. He looked pale to Lynch, with dark smudges below his eyes. His first taste of combat had gone hard on him.

'Cooper, isn't it? I'm—'

'Jefferson Lynch. The journalist.'

Cooper didn't quite pronounce the word as an insult, but it made Lynch's outsider status clear. Best to let the boy speak on his own terms.

Lynch added water to the ration heater and waited for it to get up to temperature. According to the pack, he was about to have shredded BBQ beef. He spread some cheese on a cracker and ate mechanically, occasionally glancing over at the young Templar. Cooper's own meal of chilli and macaroni sat largely untouched, a plastic spoon standing proud in its centre.

'Do you know how many men I killed today?' Lynch, taking the question to be rhetorical, said nothing. 'No, me neither. You point your rifle and fire or you shove a satchel charge in a bunker and you move on. Rinse and repeat. And if you're lucky, you're still alive at the end of it. We did so much training, so many simulations, but it's not the same. It should be, but it ain't.' Cooper's voice dropped as he looked around to ensure no one overheard him. 'Hell, I know they're the enemy. That we're fighting to liberate a country. But they're still, y'know, human beings.'

'Some mother's son.'

'What?'

'Forget it, kid. Just an old expression. Maybe you ought to have a word with that preacher of yours? That's what he's here for, right? To minster to your spiritual well-being.'

Cooper leaned closer. 'That's his official role, as chaplain, sure enough. But between you and me that crazy fucker is only here to kill as many Muslims as he can. Reckon I don't want to be taking any doubts on the killing front to him.'

'What you gonna do, then?'

'My duty. But last time I checked no one said I had to enjoy it.'

Cooper stood and picked up his tray with his uneaten meal. Lynch turned and watched him walk over to the food waste bin and jettison its contents before stacking the tray. Kid seemed a decent sort, which probably meant they'd be shipping him home in a body bag before long.

Lynch arrived back at the JLTV to find Jackson waiting for him. The sergeant folded his arms across his chest and narrowed his eyes.

'Where's your tunic?'

Lynch pointed at the JLTV. 'In the back there. Too damn hot for it.'

'That's as may be, but you'll put it back on. I don't need you getting your lily-white ass burned to a crisp. Speaking of which, when did you last have a drink?'

'I don't know; maybe an hour ago.' Lynch's voice rose in pitch as he became irritated. 'I'm not thirsty.'

'Wrong answer. Did you listen to a single word of your acclimatisation? By the time you feel thirsty you're already dehydrated. Get yourself dressed. Drink plenty of water. Find some shade. I don't need to be dealing with no heat casualty.'

'That sounds an awful lot like an order. Last time I checked I wasn't part of this army of yours.'

Lynch took an involuntary step back as Jackson stepped in close. He stood a good six inches taller than the sergeant but lacked his bulk and muscle.

'You do not want to be testing me. Do that and I'll see you bounced straight back to the pen. Yeah, I know all about your deal with the Agency, so you better not be giving me no more trouble. You get me?'

Lynch nodded. This deal was getting shittier all the time.

No matter how hard Lynch stared into the dark it refused to resolve itself into anything other than shadows. It dulled the sense of movement as the JLTV sped along the highway, motion instead indicated by the occasional jolt of the shocks. Not that he was missing much: rocks, dirt, olive trees. For the country of God's chosen people, it really was an inhospitable spit of land. Regardless, they had prospered through the diamond trade and, by their own ingenuity, weapons tech and cyberwarfare, the latter of which remained in demand after the Fall. As did their soldiers.

Lynch's gaze flitted to the face of the man sitting opposite him. Even as he approached middle age, Elad Katz retained the dark good looks of his Mediterranean ancestry. Assigned as an advisor by the Israeli government, he had nonetheless demonstrated a willingness and a capability to engage with Caliphate forces. By the time Lynch realised he was staring, it was too late.

'Something I can help you with, Lynch?'

'Guess I was wondering how it felt to finally set foot on your home soil again. It would be good to present the viewers back home with the Israeli point of view.'

Katz appeared to ponder, a man lost in a welter of

emotion. And maybe he was, although Lynch thought it more likely a cover for composing a suitable response, one that toed the party line.

'I was nineteen years old, second year of my national service with the IDF, when those bastards drove us out. I've lived more of my life in exile than in Israel. Yes, it feels good to finally be home, but there's plenty didn't live to see this day. I feel the weight of that. Then there's the guilt.'

'Guilt?'

'The suspicion, the fear, that all of us carry. That we somehow brought this tragedy on ourselves – something we did or didn't do that offended God.'

Lynch shook his head and snorted. 'Seriously? In this day and age, you people are still blaming your misfortunes on breaking some covenant with God?'

'I take it you're not a man of faith?'

'The only spirit I believe in comes from a bottle.'

'Cynicism and nihilism are a poor religion.'

'Maybe they are. But if you ask me, they do a far better job of explaining the world we live in than the existence of some all-knowing big beard in the sky.'

'Then you're to be pitied.'

The vestige of a smile that accompanied the Israeli's words informed Lynch they were meant as a provocation. He bit down on a suitable retort and went back to staring into the darkness. He didn't need Katz's pity. He had more than enough of his own to go around.

The convoy pulled off the road, jolting Lynch from his reverie. He flicked a glance at the IDF captain, blaming him for his sense of unease. Jackson, Cooper and Mackinlay worked quickly to erect a camouflage net over the vehicle, covering the windscreen and other optics to prevent the glint of sunlight from the glass betraying their presence. Even Katz found himself drafted into the work, erecting the lean-to under which they would sleep.

Lynch's mood, which had been sour since his talk with the Israeli, deteriorated further as he found himself standing around like the proverbial spare prick at a whore's wedding. He wandered off into the shadows and took out his hip flask. The last of the bourbon, rough or not, tasted as sweet as any nectar. Stowing the hip flask away, he lit up a cigarette, closed his eyes and inhaled deeply.

'What the fuck is your problem, man?'

Lynch started at the harsh voice as Cooper snatched the cigarette from between his lips and ground it out under his heel. He felt the blood rush to his face under the hostile gaze of the young man.

'That shit is visible for miles. Are you trying to get us all killed?'

'Sorry. Wasn't thinking. Been a long day.'

'Yeah? Well, it'll be a short life if you don't pull yourself together.' The Templar's expression softened slightly in response to Lynch's hangdog look. 'You need a piss or a shit, take them now and then get yourself some sleep. It'll be difficult once the sun's up.'

Lynch stared mournfully at the crushed cigarette. Out of booze, couldn't smoke, and the bastards wouldn't let him have an assault rifle. Didn't trust him. Even though he had five of them back home. Said they were bending the rules letting him have a Glock 9mm for defence, along with one of those wasp-bladed daggers. This war was no goddamn fun at all.

Lynch woke a little before midday, the sun lancing through the canvas of the lean-to. His mouth felt dry and there was a dull pounding behind his eyes. He grabbed his canteen and swallowed a couple of mouthfuls of the now-warm water. It had a faint metallic taste and did little to assuage his thirst. He supposed he'd better dress and see if there was any food on the go. Jackson's earlier admonition came back to him and Lynch reluctantly pulled on his uniform tunic. He reached out for his boots and paused, a lesson from his time at Fort Irwin coming back to him. Grabbing the first boot, he tipped it upside down and shook. Empty. He repeated the procedure.

'Holy mother of fucking God!' Lynch scuttled back on his butt as the scorpion twisted and turned on its back. The commotion attracted the attention of the sergeant, who stuck his head inside the lean-to, took in the situation and laughed.

'Looks like you're learning, Lynch. Breakfast in ten. Get your ass in gear.'

Lynch nodded, unable to speak, his eyes still fixed on the scorpion. Less than two inches long, but still with an excruciatingly painful sting. The scorpion, for its part, was a lot less interested in Lynch. Having righted itself, it scuttled off in the direction of the nearest rock, disappearing into the shade.

Interview Transcript #2: Jefferson Lynch in conversation with Sergeant Tyrone Jackson on the road to Rishon LeZion.

Jefferson Lynch: I did a little digging, call it due diligence, and you have an impressive service record, Sergeant Jackson.

Sergeant Jackson: If you say so.

JL: The facts say so. Sixteen years' military service, including one tour of duty during the Second Crusade, and a further three during the Third. You've been awarded the Purple Heart with two bronze oak leaves.

SJ [sniffing]: All that means is I've been stupid enough to get my ass shot three times.

JL: Wasn't the third decoration for being stabbed?

SJ: Shot, stabbed, what's the difference? I'm out here serving my country and my God. Same as thousands of other men of faith. I don't expect someone like you to understand that, Lynch. The only duty you've ever felt is towards your next drink.

JL: Ouch. I guess I ought to take that one on the chin. Look, I know you don't like me. And for what it's worth, I don't blame you. Must be galling to find yourself stuck with some candy-ass civilian in the middle of a war zone. You say you're no different from thousands of other men out here. That's probably true. But there are thousands more back home who don't get what you're doing. They live what they see as being a good Christian life without getting the urge to pick up a rifle in defence of their faith. I'm trying to help them understand your point of view. Why being out here matters to you and the other Templars.

SJ: All right already. Ask away.

JL: Reckon it's fair to say you're like an older brother, even a father figure to the men under your command. Does that come from training or do you come from a large family?

SJ: It's no secret we Templars swear an oath of brotherhood – a solemn obligation to protect one another. But I'd say that's more in a man's heart than any training. As to my family, I spent most of my childhood in care. Never knew my father and my mother, God rest her soul; she was a … troubled woman. Had a few problems of my own before I came to the army. Don't think it no exaggeration to say it probably saved my life.

JL: It was Pastor Davis who advised you to enlist?

SJ [irritated]: What's this BS, man? If you already know the answer, why are you asking? You trying to catch me out?

JL: Like I said, I did my research. But it never hurts to confirm the biographical details with a subject. It's important the folks back home get to hear this in your own words.

SJ [suspicious]: Yeah, it was ol' Davis who took me aside. Right after we put my momma in the ground. Said he could see I was a good kid at heart, but I needed guidance and structure in my life. Discipline. Course I pushed back at first, like the young fool I was. He wasn't my daddy. What right did he have to tell me what to do?

JL: But a couple of months later – March '73 – you enlisted?

SJ: Took a little time to sink in, but I came to realise Davis was telling me straight – only place gang life was leading me was the grave. Army gave me a home. Gave me self-worth. Didn't have to care about what brand of sneakers or jeans I wore. Didn't have to worry where the next meal was coming from. Still had to be tough, but it was a different kind of tough, mental as well as physical. They taught me shit as well – mechanics, electronics, how to read people.

JL: How to kill.

SJ: See, that's your problem, man. You think we're just out here to shoot Abdul. But we're not the aggressors. We're here to put an end to that shit. Make it so everyone can go home, including Abdul.

JL: That goal always seems a little further away. This is the third crusade you've fought in sixteen years, your fifth tour of duty. Even if you're successful and you liberate Jerusalem, where does it go from there? Jordan? Syria? Do you force the Caliphate all the way back to Iraq? Is regime change on the table? America was fighting wars in the Middle East almost a century ago. Back when we were still the fifty states of the old republic. I get that you've got your duty and part of me can honestly respect that. You're a decent and honourable man who cares for the soldiers under your command. Clearly a man of strong faith. But don't you ever ask yourself where all this ends?

SJ: It ends when there's no more threat to America.

JL: But there's always going to be a threat – real or otherwise. It's how the military-industrial complex operates.

SJ: Don't know about that. Just know I got my duty and my calling.

Transcript Ends.

Lynch hoped to find Tyler in a better mood; the colonel had been prickly since their aborted interview. He lifted the flap of the command tent and guided the camera drones inside. Colonel Tyler stood front and centre, studying a holo-projection of Caliphate positions. Sixty klicks ahead on Route 431 they had amassed a battalion of tanks, with the aim of stopping the Templar convoys. A further ten klicks beyond that, ranks of infantry had dug in along the road, ready to engage any survivors.

Tyler turned to Lynch. 'I hope you're recording this, Mr Lynch?' At Lynch's nod, he took up position at the fire control computer. 'Good, because we have a show for the people back home. One I'm sure they'll appreciate.'

Lynch watched as Tyler co-ordinated radar, IRST and laser rangefinder data to zero in on the Caliphate positions and uplink it to orbital kill-satellites. The top right quadrant of the holo-projector changed to identify the active satellites.

'Targets acquired. Firing in three, two, one.'

Red lines traced the path of the Gehenna missiles through the atmosphere as they arced towards their targets. They became visible on the main satellite image at one hundred klicks, graphic representation matching the real-time footage. Panic broke out on the ground as the tank crews spotted the incoming missiles seconds before impact. Proximity sensors detonated the fuel-air explosive warheads and engulfed the desert in a series of blossoming fireballs. Lynch's HUD automatically polarised against the glare.

The main holo-image switched again to show a squadron of six UAV hunter-killer drones as they flew past the burning remnants of the tank battalion and homed in on the infantry positions.

The comms crackled to life. 'Visual on enemy confirmed. What are your orders, Colonel?'

'Burn them down.'

The Hellfire missile detonations might have lacked the intensity and size of the Gehenna tank busters, but they transfixed Lynch nonetheless. His imagination filled in the sounds of the explosions and the cries of the wounded and dying as he watched the eerily silent display. The drone operators circled back, scouring the ground for surviving pockets of resistance and delivering, where required, fresh death from above. It seemed to Lynch as though the whole world was on fire.

'Reckon that's enough, Lynch. Cut the feed.'

Lynch nodded absently and recalled the drones to the docking station on his belt.

Tyler turned to his aide. 'Give it half an hour and then review the target areas. You see so much as a sand flea moving, bomb it again. We mobilise at eighteen hundred and I expect zero resistance as we progress along Route Four-Thirty-One. Tonight, we liberate Rishon LeZion.' He turned to Lynch. 'What do you think of the show so far? Heard you've got a bit of a thing for blowing shit up?'

'Things. Not people.'

'Didn't see no people. Just enemies of the one true God. Trust you'll make that clear when you write up your report to go with today's footage?'

Lynch gritted his teeth, but managed to spit out a terse 'yes'.

As the JLTV sped along the highway Lynch noticed a difference in atmosphere. The previous banter between Cooper and Mackinlay had ceased as the former concentrated on his driving, using sensors to keep a precise distance behind the vehicle in front. Before, they had been in transit. Now, with a definite combat objective ahead of them, they were preparing themselves mentally. He could feel the tension oozing out of the young Templars. They'd had their first taste of combat on the beach, inevitably found it different from the simulations, and formed fresh doubts. Jackson, by contrast, sat alert on the seat opposite. He'd ran through his weapons and equipment checks and was now studying the mission objectives on his datapad. A career soldier, a true believer; reasons enough for Lynch to dislike him, and yet a grudging respect was forming. Jackson cared for his men, sought to protect them, an attitude that extended even to Lynch himself in the form of his constant scolding. Lynch might have been a self-confessed pain in the ass, but he still counted as one of them. Admittedly, most of it was a soldier obeying orders and doing his duty, but Lynch appreciated it nonetheless.

And then there was the Israeli, Seren Elad Katz. Another career soldier, but one with a completely unreadable visage. His official bio listed him as IDF special forces, which made him at least equal if not superior to the Templars, and a stone killer. But Lynch's journalistic instinct sniffed something darker, more hidden. The advisory role didn't quite ring true, or at least wasn't the whole story. Katz was here at the behest of the Knesset, the Israeli government in exile, and if they had demonstrated only one thing over the years, it was an unflinching willingness to do whatever it took to protect the future of the Jewish people. One to watch closely, for sure.

Lynch heard the incoming rocket seconds before it struck the vehicle in front. He cursed as he turned his head away from the phosphorous white glare of the ensuing explosion. He cursed again; his body catapulted forward against his safety harness in response to the JLTV's auto-braking.

'We're under attack!'

CHAPTER 16

Charles Gerrard, age forty-six, brown hair with hints of grey at the temples, strong jawline, tanned skin, laughter lines around the eyes. Hopkins shook her head and swiped the image to the side. She had no doubt that the senator for South Carolina had a serious shot at the Southern Democrat nomination for president, but the voice in her head kept asking why it couldn't be her. The answer, she knew, lay in the fact that in the thirty-nine-year history of the Religious States of America, a total of seven women had been elected to the Senate, with only two of them currently serving. It had taken talent, hard graft and no little backstabbing for her to rise to spokesperson for the Southern Democratic National Committee, but she wanted more. She wanted VP, but knew Gerrard's backers would never agree to it should he secure the presidency. Instead, they would fob her off with Press Secretary, another pretty face to entertain the media and press corps. But at least she would be at the centre of power and, in its way, that represented influence, given most of these guys still thought with their dicks.

Hopkins swiped to the next image: Senator Michael Hamilton, age thirty-seven, red hair, freckles, youthfully good-looking with his quarterback's physique. If Gerrard, with his hawkish views, represented the continuity candidate to Williams, Hamilton was the liberal alternative: an anti-war voice vowing to bring the troops back home and focus on domestic issues. Public mood, after the initial surge of enthusiasm, was already turning against the latest crusade as the cost and death count spiralled in line with the predicted data-modelling. People struggling to put food on the table while raising second- or even third-generation unemployed kids would reach out to hope in whatever form it took, and right now they were the majority of the electorate. She scrolled up the screen, reading Hamilton's resume. A former defence attorney, he was already a second-term senator for Florida. He had inherited a substantial fortune from his mother three years previously following her death from breast cancer, the bulk of which he had ploughed into a charitable foundation for hospices. He paid his taxes, was faithful to his wife of nine years, Kristen, and had one daughter, Claire, age six. His voting record was consistent, showing no undue influence from lobbyists. In short, the only front they had to attack him on was a perceived soft attitude to the Islamic Caliphate. A strategy that could easily backfire. Probably wisest to imply it by omission, playing up Gerrard's commitment to the restoration of the state of Israel. The Jewish vote, of course, wasn't enough. He'd need to convince the soccer moms, the blue-collar workers and the African Americans and the Latinos, the latter two for which his polling remained consistently poor.

Hopkins scrolled through the list of upcoming primaries and caucuses. The open primaries were too much effort compared to the likelihood of securing delegates, so she immediately rejected them and focused on Virginia, Arizona and Georgia. And that brought her to the caucuses in Nevada and Wyoming on Super Tuesday – March 8 2089 would be make-or-break for Gerrard's run on the presidency. She had four weeks to ensure the party activists were on his side and to secure his name on the first ballot at the Southern Democratic National Convention. At present, with 1,022 delegates required, Hamilton led Gerrard by 47 to 33. But in line with the old adage, the nomination was Hamilton's to lose.

She leaned back in her chair and pinched the bridge of her nose between her thumb and forefinger, feeling the nagging throb of a tension headache behind her eyes. Truth was, they needed good news from the war, something to convince the voters the pain was worthwhile, to get them back behind the hawks. Everything rested with Tyler now, and knowing his naked lust for victory at any cost, she didn't feel encouraged.

Hopkins looked at the results: Georgia had broken 84 to 21 for Gerrard, but after relatively modest victories in Virginia and Arizona, he tallied 186 delegates against Hamilton's 134. The kid was fresh, dynamic, a clean break with the existing administration. Presenting Gerrard as a safe pair of hands at a time when the majority of the electorate wanted change wasn't cutting through, and without any dirt on Hamilton she had nowhere to go. Time for Plan B. Tyler wouldn't be best pleased, but their strategy relied on having the ear of the president, regardless of who actually filled that office. They needed to put their support and resources behind Hamilton in return for him choosing Gerrard as his running mate. A ticket that would reassure the more conservative voters that the new administration would not unduly concede the war. She would have to get Gerrard onboard, of course, and there was no time like the present.

Gerrard answered Hopkins' call almost immediately. 'Take it you're calling to congratulate me about the result in Georgia?'

'No, Charles, I'm calling to ask you to step aside.'

'What the hell, Susanna? You cannot be serious? Look, I'll admit Hamilton's making a better showing than anticipated, but I can still take him.'

'That's not what the numbers are showing – the voters want a fresh face. I know this is difficult, but I'm sure you'll agree we need to put the interests of the party first. Polling has Hamilton as best placed to defeat Patton.'

There was a long pause. 'You really think the GOP will go with that old fossil?'

'You know it, Charles. He's ahead by a country mile now that Haversham has pulled out. Trouble is, you can't out-hawk him. Leastwise not when it comes to the war. Lucky if you can squeeze a cigarette paper between your policies. It's turning our voters off.'

'Then I should just quietly step aside? After all the work we've put into this?'

'Don't be foolish, Charles. You've been in this game long enough to know everything is quid pro quo. You withdraw and give Hamilton your full endorsement, in return for which you get the VP ticket. I know it's a setback, but if we play it this way we're still in government. You go toe-to-toe with Hamilton and lose, we're both out in the cold.'

'And if Hamilton fucks it up?'

'The '93 nomination will definitely be yours. Failing that, you're still a relatively young man, Charles. Eight years as VP will do your standing no harm with the party.'

'Assuming there isn't a new Hamilton by then.'

'That's the game we're in. Always was. But you do this thing now and Hamilton takes the presidency, well, I can promise that won't be forgotten.'

'All right. You can issue a statement in the morning. I'm trusting you on this, Susanna.'

'And I thank you for it, Charles. Good night.'

Hopkins closed down the connection and stared into the darkened depths of her monitor. A setback, yes. But not necessarily a fatal one. In these dangerous and uncertain times, who could say what might happen to Hamilton?

Hopkins clicked the remote and the screen went dark. Her hand hovered over the bowl of chips and then moved to her wine glass; victory always made the grape taste sweeter. Super Tuesday was all but done and dusted, and as predicted Hamilton was romping home with the delegates. He looked good, like a winner, which was just as well, as her other prediction was also coming true: Patton was equally sure of winning the Republican nomination. Seventy-two years of age, a former Lieutenant General in the old republic, he'd served as Secretary of Defense for the Holtzman administration back in the Sixties. A three-time senator and presently governor for Oklahoma. In other times he would have been seen as last year's man, enjoying a winter sinecure in a through-and-through red state. But with the media pushing anti-Caliphate reports 24/7 he'd surged to prominence. If Hamilton won, it would be worth dialling them back. Least for the first few months to avoid any backlash.

Hopkins picked up her datapad and started reviewing campaign tactics and slogans. 'A Clean Break' didn't quite cut it, given they were replacing one SD administration with another. 'Fresh Face'? 'Fresh Start'? 'A New Deal for America'? The last one had resonance, would play to Hamilton's commitment to focus on the domestic issues of employment and manufacturing. She'd even throw him the bone of a reduced military presence in the Middle East during his first term.

Tyler, as predicted, had reacted badly to Gerrard's withdrawal, seeing the appointment of a foe to his ambition, but he'd come around once she had shown him the wider picture. Gerrard would get his moment in the sun, as promised, before vacating the stage to admit a candidate suited to America's darkest hour. A fresh crusade mounted with renewed vigour that would drive the Caliphate back to its origins in Iraq and Syria, leaving them broken and bloodied. And if he failed? No matter. There was no shortage of men desperate to be president. She just needed to back more winners than losers as she edged her way to the Senate.

CHAPTER 17

Cooper slammed the JLTV into reverse and spun it off-road, bouncing across the scrubland until it came to rest by one of the ubiquitous rocky outcrops. As the doors swung open, Lynch felt Jackson's hand on his shoulder.

'Out, out, out!'

Lynch didn't need any further encouragement. He slithered across the ground as another rocket struck nearby, detonating harmlessly on the road. Cooper and Mackinlay passed him at a crouching run, scanning the area ahead with night-vision goggles. Lynch, seeing only differing patches of darkness, kept crawling, reasoning that the further from the JLTV he got, the safer he would be. Katz flitted past him like a shadow, leaving him feeling abandoned. Surely they had some contingency for this?

'Where the fuck is our air support?'

Lynch felt someone grab his MOLLE belt and found himself hauled upright as Jackson hissed in his ear, 'Keep your motherfucking voice down.'

He watched the sergeant scan left and right, doubtless looking for somewhere to offload his charge. Jackson's curt nod to himself confirmed he had identified a suitable location. Lynch peered in the direction of the sergeant's pointing arm to where the outline of an AMPV was just visible. Tyler's Mission Command. A shove left little doubt as to Jackson's expectation.

Lynch stumbled forward, his eyes fixed on the prize, frightened of becoming turned around and finding himself lost. He had little illusion as to the likelihood of the convoy waiting if he wasn't onboard when the order came to pull out. Tyler could always get himself another war correspondent; one more suited to his taste.

He heard the whistle of the incoming rocket a fraction of a second before the shockwave threw him to the ground. His helmet rolled free as he lay groaning from the pain of several fist-like impacts to his back. Despite his agony, he could already hear Jackson's disapproving voice in his head. His fingers closed on the rim of his helmet and he hauled it towards himself. This time he fastened the chinstrap.

By the flickering flames of another destroyed JLTV he spotted the outline of the AMPV and made his way towards it, all too aware those same flames would be painting him as the perfect silhouette. So far, however, he'd heard no small-arms fire and had to assume the attack was long range, similar to their own strikes earlier. He quickened his pace, and as he came alongside the AMPV a hatch opened to admit him. His boots sounded loud on the hull as he clambered up the side, heartbeat thudding in his ears. Then reassuring hands were guiding his feet to the rungs of the ladder inside.

Schreiber dogged the hatch behind him and slid down the ladder. He turned away, Lynch already forgotten, to resume his post behind Tyler.

'Thanks, preacher. Guess Jesus don't want me for a sunbeam quite yet.'

Lynch found himself physically flinching back from the hard blue stare that followed. It was the humourless gaze of the committed zealot. He'd read about Schreiber, how he had lost his wife and unborn son in a suicide bombing. A man, particularly one of faith, could go either way after a thing like that. Schreiber had clearly decided not to turn the other cheek. Lynch stepped away, moving towards Tyler. The colonel's fanaticism was at least of a type he felt comfortable with.

'Looks like your satellites missed a few.'

Tyler regarded him coolly, secure in the knowledge that Lynch's opinion wouldn't travel outside of the Mission Command vehicle.

'Long-range reconnaissance, dug in and camouflaged, biding their time. Nothing we can't handle.' He turned back to his command console. 'Valkyrie One and Two, you are clear to commence your attack run.'

Lynch watched two blips on the screen close on their position, Wagner playing inside his head as the Air Cavalry once again rode to the rescue. Those SB Defiant XV attack helicopters were starting to become the best friends they had out here. Even through the thick armour of the hull he heard the distinctive *whoomph-whoomph* he now associated with Hellfire missiles. One, two, three strikes, followed by the rattle of chain guns on maximum speed. Tyler inclined his head, forefinger pressed against his earpiece, his expression one of grim satisfaction.

'Valkyrie One, you are clear to drop incendiaries.'

'Isn't that a bit of an overkill, Colonel?'

Tyler stiffened and then unexpectedly broke into a wry smile.

'I don't tell you how to write features, Lynch. Don't tell me how to make war.'

Lynch gripped the console instinctively as the explosion cut across the airwaves, even though they were too far away to feel the impact. He imagined the boiling clouds of flame lighting up the night skies. The latest generation of fuel gel explosive was every bit as deadly as its forerunner, napalm, had been.

Tyler's terse commands cut across his thoughts. The Templars were to mount up and resume their journey.

'Colonel, should I—'

'No time, Lynch. Anyway, I want you to do a piece on Mission Command. You can't broadcast details, but let's give the folks back home a sense of what's happening out here.'

Tyler tapped the console and a holo-display flickered to life. He crooked his finger, motioning Lynch forward.

The engine rumbled to life and Lynch stumbled as the driver put the AMPV in drive and steered for the road. Tyler, feet planted wide apart, stood rock-steady and expectant. Lynch felt like a schoolboy flunking his lesson as the Templar commander used a tap of his fingers to zoom in on the projected image.

'This marks our current position and, here, the convoy of the thirty-first infantry division, travelling inland from their beachhead at Tel Aviv. Our rendezvous point is Har HaMenuchot Cemetery, to the northwest of Jerusalem. There, we will form part of a ring of steel about the city, cutting off all supply lines and reinforcements.'

'Maybe my arithmetic is out, but from what I've seen you don't have the troops for a siege.'

Tyler swiped up a second display. Here, blue identified the military forces, opposed to the red of the Templars.

'You're forgetting our allied forces, who have successfully landed in Lebanon and Jordan. Assisted by rebels in both countries, they will open up a second front to the south-east of Jerusalem.'

'You trust the Russians and the Europeans?'

'I trust their hatred of the Caliphate.' Tyler triggered a third display. 'Plus, we'll have air support from the west.'

Lynch stared at the map. After a few seconds he found his voice. 'You're violating Egyptian airspace?'

'Officially, the Elsayed administration will object at the highest levels.'

'And unofficially?'

'There's a rather favourable trade deal hanging in the balance. Coupled with the fact the Sunni population has never been comfortable with having their more radical brethren for neighbours.'

'The enemy of my enemy, huh?'

'I wouldn't go that far. Elsayed is another serpent. We haven't ruled out regime change in the future. I will of course deny that if you attempt to publish it. Now, I suggest you get some rest. I have a special piece I need you to broadcast tomorrow.'

'You join me, Jefferson Lynch, reporting from the liberation of Rishon LeZion. Behind me you see enemy prisoners of war, captured during the Templar assault on the town. I'm joined by our interpreter, Templar-Private Goodman of the First Templar Division's Combat Aviation Brigade, who will assist me in interviewing the prisoners.'

Lynch kept the camera angle tight as he focused on the row of three prisoners sitting against the wall of an abandoned house, hiding the worst of the shell damage to either side. The men wore olive drab uniforms, their one concession to ethnicity the fringed *shemaghs* worn around their necks. One of the men had a bloodstained bandage about his head; another wore his arm in a sling. A Templar was handing out cigarettes to the prisoners. He lit them and then stepped away as Lynch and Goodman approached.

A message on his HUD told Lynch to approach the prisoner on his left, the one with the bandaged head. He stared apprehensively at Lynch through wreaths of cigarette smoke.

'Ask him his name.'

The prisoner responded to Goodman's query, 'Abu Ahmad al-Alwani.'

'Where's he from? How long has he been fighting for the Caliphate?'

A longer exchange followed, which Goodman interpreted as, 'From a small village in Syria. Caliphate soldiers came there when he was thirteen, rounded up all the boys of suitable age to serve in the army. He hasn't seen his family since. He was told they would be punished if he didn't obey orders.'

'How does he feel about the Templars' presence in Israel?'

Al-Alwani was midway through his response when the prisoner with his arm in the sling launched into a long stream of invective. He gesticulated wildly with his good arm, causing al-Alwani to shuffle away from him while the other prisoner looked on furiously.

Goodman raised his rifle. 'Enough!' The prisoner glared balefully at al-Alwani and spat in the dirt at his feet.

Lynch looked expectantly at Goodman.

'He says he's grateful the Americans have come. They fought bravely and with honour. They treat him well. They have given him food, water and cigarettes. He hopes when the war is over that he will be allowed to return to his village.'

'I'm sure the viewers at home feel the same way. That we can constructively work together for peace once this war is over. Jefferson Lynch, Fox News. Reporting from the front.'

'Cut!'

Lynch killed the feed and recalled the camera drones. He took out his hip flask as the prisoners got to their feet. 'Al-Alwani' pulled the bandage from his head and used it to wipe the carefully applied grime from his face. Goodman handed him his canteen and he swallowed greedily before handing it to his colleague, who was busy removing his sling.

'Don't you think that was a little over the top with the wild hand signals?'

'Felt right for the character.'

'If you say so, Stanislavski. Come on, let's get out of the sun. The call sheet says grateful civilians after lunch.'

Lynch watched them walk away, bile burning in his throat. How much did they know? Did they even care? The attack was moving too swiftly to take prisoners – they had neither the men nor the supplies to look after them. Officially, the Caliphate troops were fanatics who fought to the last man and the last bullet. But Lynch had seen a score or so of frightened soldiers, mostly in their late teens or early twenties, surrender in the face of the Templars' overwhelming firepower. Both they and their captors had looked uncertain as to what this unprecedented event meant for them. But the order came through swiftly: they were to move out, leaving no one behind. Lynch's own transport had arrived early, the director keen to make the most of the light for Colonel Tyler's 'special' broadcast, and making them unwilling witnesses to a war crime.

The Templar officer and troops responsible for the massacre were unknown to Lynch, part of the force that had landed at Tel Aviv, but he felt certain the order had originated with Tyler. He had watched from the shelter of the JLTV as the prisoners, hands bound behind their backs, knelt in front of a trench. A captain and a sergeant had started at opposite ends of the line, executing the prisoners with a single pistol shot to the back of the head and pushing them into the ditch. The process had lasted a little over five minutes, Lynch requiring no translation of the men's prayers and pleas for mercy. A waiting D7 dozer had backfilled the earth into the mass grave. Even now, Lynch struggled to accept what he had witnessed. Seethed with rage at being unable to report it. One way or another, he promised himself there would be a reckoning. Even if it meant going to prison.

Lynch panned the drones along the length of the ramshackle convoy, taking in the beaten-up jeeps and ancient flatbed trucks piled high with furniture and food. The adults kept their eyes averted while the children stared with a mix of wonderment and fear. Civilian refugees were becoming increasingly common as the Templar forces pressed on towards Jerusalem. Settlers brought in by the

Caliphate during the last quarter-century to populate and run their newly conquered territory. Their masters had forced them to leave one life behind in order to make another, and now the war was forcing them to leave this one. The Templars, where possible, gave them a wide berth, fearing booby traps and fifth columnists. But today, where Route 431 cut through a deep canyon, METT-TC analysis had deemed the cost of a detour in terms of time and fuel to outweigh any risk. Accordingly, the Templars had ordered the refugees to draw up on the roadside while they thundered past, kicking up choking clouds of dust.

'Waste of time filming,' Jackson said. 'They ain't never gonna let you broadcast this shit.'

Lynch kept quiet. They might have blackmailed him into covering the war from the Templar point of view, but now he was here he intended to document everything. The bastards could muzzle him for now, but once he got back stateside, he would find the means of getting the truth out there. Teach the swine a lesson they wouldn't forget.

'Halt!'

Lynch craned his neck forward to look out of the window. The obstruction was a goddamn school bus. Hard to see through the dirt and dust that caked its windows, but it looked as though they had taken out half the seats and packed it with the grandparents, kids, food, clothes and household goods. Or explosives. Shit! He was beginning to think like these guys.

Jackson pressed him back in his seat when he made to exit, forcing him to continue to peer between Schreiber and Garcia's shoulders. The front tyre of the bus looked flat and he could see what he took for the father and possibly an uncle attempting to get a jack under the chassis. Mackinlay exited the lead vehicle, followed by Cooper. They looked nervous, on edge.

'Maybe we should get Goodman on the horn?'

Jackson shrugged. 'Reckon what we want should be plain enough for Abdul.'

'There's kids on that bus.'

'All the more reason for them not to pull some stupid shit.'

The knot in Lynch's gut hardened as he watched Mackinlay point to the side of the road and shout while Cooper stood with his rifle trained on the two civilians.

'Katz, help me out here.'

The Israeli raised a sardonic eyebrow. 'I should concern myself with the well-being of illegal settlers in my homeland?'

'Yeah, well, I'm pretty sure the Palestinians felt the same way about you, back in the day.'

'In case you've forgotten, the Palestinians lost that war.'

A panicked shout in Arabic drew Lynch's attention back to the bus. The door had opened and a woman, seven or eight months pregnant, stood in the opening, long strands of black hair escaping from her headscarf. The older of the two men spoke rapidly as he waved her back inside, his tone and body language pleading. Cooper gestured with his rifle and she reluctantly turned and made her way up the steps.

Mackinlay, losing patience, snarled, 'Are those rags wrapped about your head blocking your ears? Last time of asking – forget the fucking tyre and get this mobile scrapheap off the road, or we'll move it for you!'

'Cool it, Mac. I don't think they speak English.'

Mackinlay gestured with his rifle. 'If they don't, reckon this is universal. Remember your fuck-up during the MOUT simulation? You can't trust them.'

The two brothers looked from Mackinlay to Cooper, shook their heads and crouched down to check the position of the jack.

'Don't turn your back on me when I'm talking to you!'

The shout caused the husband to whirl round, tyre iron clutched in his hand. Mackinlay opened fire, bullets ripping through both men and the front of the bus. The hiss of hydraulics signalled the opening of the doors and he spun the arc of his fire to the right, with Cooper joining in.

'Your ass stays here!' Jackson warned Lynch as he jumped from the JLTV. He ran towards Mackinlay and Cooper screaming, 'Cease firing! Cease firing!'

Afterwards, they claimed not to have heard him above the gunfire, but Lynch saw both men react to and then ignore the sergeant's order when he reviewed the drone footage, six months of indoctrination kicking in. He'd paused at that point, unwilling to go on, the images already burned into his memory, but he had to be certain that the drones had caught what he saw. Half-speed, the cries distorted, as Mackinlay and Cooper sprayed the bus with bullets that shattered glass, punctured tyres, tore through bodywork into soft flesh. That final damning moment when the emergency exit had opened at the rear of the bus and a child's arm flopped out. Lynch froze the frame, capturing a single drop of blood as it fell from an accusatory finger.

Things had moved swiftly after that. A squad of Templars held the remaining refugees at gunpoint while a second squad pushed the ruined bus from the road. All the while Lynch sat there repeating the word 'fuck' with increasing volume and anger. Then the convoy was moving again, eating up the klicks with a haste driven by what Lynch at first assumed to be guilt but subsequently discovered to be hardnosed practicality when he heard Tyler's voice over the comms giving the coordinates for an airstrike.

'What's the target, Jackson? Come on, tell me what the goddamn target is!'

The sergeant said nothing, his gaze fixed on the floor. Schreiber and Garcia likewise refused to answer, leaving it to Katz. The Israeli's voice was soft but firm.

'You know what the target is.'

Lynch punched the side of the JLTV and buried his head in his hands.

CHAPTER 18

Katz didn't believe in superstition; good and poor fortunes in war were the direct result of planning, tactics, observation and mission discipline. The hairs that rose on the back of his neck were a reaction to the lack of sound and openness of the landscape, which instinctively drew his vision to the ridge with its stunted olive trees. Did he catch the faint gleam of sunlight from the lens of a scope? Unlikely; the sniper was a professional. More likely he recognised the position as one he himself would choose. Either way, he was already diving for the dirt when Garcia's head exploded.

Eight hundred metres from an elevation of one-twenty with no crosswind. An easy kill. Katz knew he would be next if he broke cover. He slithered backwards, seeking to put a small undulation of earth between himself and the sniper's line of sight. The subdued sound of the shot indicated the sniper had fitted the rifle with a suppressor, lowering the chances of anyone coming to his aid. He had left the big sergeant, Cooper and Mackinlay two fields over, investigating the ramshackle buildings of the abandoned kibbutz; his first mistake.

They were in a waiting game now, one which he didn't

doubt the sniper had the patience to win. How many days had he already remained in position, waiting for the opportunity to pick off the unwary? Missing the double kill would have pricked his pride, but he had chosen his kill zone well: a full square klick with no cover at all. Katz's sole window of opportunity would open when another target presented itself. A cold calculation, but his mission took priority over the lives of the Americans. The assassination of al-Qurayshi would be a rallying call to the Israelites, one that went far beyond the reclamation of their homeland. And so he pressed his face into the parched earth of his native soil and waited.

Katz counted a full fifteen minutes between the Templars clearing the buildings and them growing suspicious of his and Garcia's long absence. Jackson's voice sounded over shortrange comms. Katz ignored it; he could blame a transmitter fault. The same slope that shielded him from the sniper would also conceal him and Garcia's body from his comrades, at least until they were on the edge of the kill zone. Katz readied his own rifle. The Israeli-manufactured Tavor X99-L wasn't a sniper rifle per se, but its longer barrel and long-range sight made it ideal for marksman use. He unfolded the bipod and, as the Templars came into view, crawled towards the top of the dip, secure in the knowledge that the sniper's focus would be on the easy kill.

He squinted through the scope, zoning in on the raised area of ridge between two trees. The sniper had dug down, covering his position with timber, which he'd then camouflaged with earth, leaving himself an aperture that provided a 180-degree field of fire. The Israeli respected his skill, but the sniper was still the enemy.

Katz, augmented by hardwired nerves, fired an instant before the sniper let off his own shot. He heard Jackson cry out and ignored it, sighting for a second shot. The sergeant would still be alive or dead regardless of whether he looked now or in thirty seconds. He took the shot, saw the sniper's body jerk back, by which time Cooper and Mackinlay had thrown themselves to the ground and were crawling towards his position. He looked beyond them and saw Jackson lying on his back with a hand pressed to his right shoulder. Today God was merciful.

'Cover me.'

Confident the Templars would obey his command, Katz moved off. Looking out for one another was part of their training, and out here, in the field of combat, he was one of them. He ran in an arc, giving Cooper and Mackinlay a free field of fire until he finally closed on the dugout from the right. He heard the wounded sniper's stentorian breathing as he approached and saw the sniper's left shoulder jammed against the roof in response to twisting away from the pain of the gunshot wound. He met the wounded soldier's gaze and saw not anger or fear, but resignation.

Katz squatted, took hold of the barrel of the ancient Lobaev SVLK-14S rifle and pulled it free. Next, he turned the sniper on his back and hauled his head and shoulders clear of the dugout. Katz had hit him high in the left shoulder – twice. The sniper closed his eyes, a muttered prayer on his lips. Katz unsheathed the Ari B'Lilah knife he wore strapped diagonally across his chest, placing his index finger through the circular guard on its grip. He grabbed a handful of the sniper's beard, jerked his head back and cut his throat. He waited until he heard the last gurgling breath before giving the Templars the all-clear signal.

Tyler looked up from studying the holo-map, his irritation at the interruption clear. 'What is it, Sergeant?'

'It's about our advisor. Reckon he used me and the boys as bait today.'

'If he did – no harm done.'

Jackson felt the throb in his right shoulder together with the stiffness from the extensive bruising. He'd removed the thermoplastic plate from his vest afterwards, saw where the round had penetrated it and entered the soft armour below. Another couple of inches to the left, or even a flatter trajectory, and it would have been a very different story.

'Well, out with it, Sergeant.'

'Who is he really, and what's he doing here? I've seen the way he operates – he's more than special forces.'

'If, and I say this advisedly, he is, that information hasn't been shared with us. More to the point, even if it had, it would be none of your concern.'

'I thought we were brothers? Good Christian sons, looking out for one another? Some Jewish spook puts our boys in the line of fire and you're all right with that?'

'At present all I have is your supposition. Katz says he tried to warn you but his transmitter was on the fritz.'

'Tech support didn't find no fault.'

'Localised interference then, or perhaps the sniper had a signal jammer. And spare me that look, Sergeant. Bottom line is you have no proof and we need to keep the Israelis on side. After all, it's their country we're liberating.'

'In which case you'd think they'd do some of the heavy lifting.'

'You know as well as I that the Israeli forces are small, comprised of veterans like Katz or untried volunteers. It makes more sense for them to join us at the siege than to be part of any prior assault.'

'Better for the viewers back home, anyways. You're saying you won't do anything about Katz?'

'Not without proof. The only fact I'm certain of right now is that one of my most experienced and previously loyal NCOs is verging on insubordination.' Jackson stiffened and Tyler shook his head. 'How long have we known each other, Tyrone? Sixteen, seventeen years? I'm going to have to ask you to trust me on this. But if it makes you feel better, by all means keep a watch on our Israeli advisor. Discreetly.'

Jackson was midway back to the JLTV when his com-unit

sounded. The tone told him it was a high-priority encrypted call. He looked left and right before ducking into the shadow of the cemetery wall and synched his earpiece to prevent anyone overhearing the caller.

'Grand Master, how may I serve?'

'Always straight to the point, Sergeant Jackson. One of your many virtues. I've read your report regarding Apostle One and, much as it pains me, I share your concerns. I fear your commanding officer has lost … perspective. Become complacent in regard to the solemn oath he took to our sacred Order.'

Jackson swallowed, uncomfortable with the direction of travel. But he had taken the same oath just mentioned by the Grand Master and knew his duty.

'Is our brother fallen?'

The sound of fingers tapping on a desk filled the pause that followed. Finally, Vanderbilt said, 'No, not yet. But you must watch him carefully, and, if it becomes necessary, act. It goes without saying, it should look like enemy action. I appreciate this won't be easy for you, given your many years of service together. But remember, the good of the Order must come before any individual.'

'Of course, Grand Master. I will keep you appraised.'

'That's all that I ask. God speed you.'

The line closed with a click, the now inert com-unit a malignant weight in Jackson's hand. He had made his choice when he filed the report on Tyler's increasingly erratic behaviour. From the moment he had hit send there had been no turning back. To believe otherwise was to deny the truth. This unnecessary spilling of Templar blood was a sinful waste and must not continue. He knew where his allegiance lay, but that didn't mean he shouldn't try to steer Tyler back onto the path of righteousness. The Grand Master had said it himself: his commander was yet to fall.

Interview Transcript #3: Jefferson Lynch in conversation with

Templar-Private Dwayne Mackinlay at Har HaMenuchot Cemetery base camp.

Jefferson Lynch: Just relax, Dwayne. Nothing to worry about. I'm just going to ask a few background questions so the folks back home can get a sense of the kind of boys who are out here fighting.

Dwayne Mackinlay: Uh, okay. You go right ahead, Mr Lynch.

JL: You're nineteen years old, Dwayne, and originally from Franklin, Tennessee?

DM: Well, I'm twenty next month, but, yeah, Franklin's my hometown. And, uh, I hope you don't mind, but all the boys out here, they call me Mac.

JL: Whatever you're comfortable with. So what made you join up? Come halfway across the world to fight for someone else's country?

DM: Well, the Caliphate's got to be stopped, right? They're jealous of our freedom, our whole way of life. You can't turn on the vid without hearing how they're torturing their own people – making their women cover their faces, stopping them driving and getting an education. We don't stop them here they'll bring it to us. They want to make us all Muslims. They ain't got no tolerance for folks who is different. Everyone knows that.

JL: But not all followers of Islam are like the Caliphate. You do know that? Only six years ago Templar forces were fighting to help liberate Saudi Arabia from the Caliphate. The Saudis are Muslim, they practise sharia law. Do you think they're a threat to our way of life?

DM: I don't rightly know. I mean, if we were fighting for them then I guess they must be all right. It's the Caliphate we're here for. Ain't it?

JL: Absolutely. But sometimes, particularly when countries are at war, the lines can become blurred. Back in '66, prior to launching the First

Crusade, American Muslim citizens were rounded up and put into internment camps. Similar to what happened to citizens of Japanese origin after the attack on Pearl Harbour during World War Two. The government viewed them as potential enemies within who might give aid to the Caliphate. We're talking third, even fourth-generation citizens, effectively criminalised for their religion. This went on for more than a decade, before they were deported – many of them to countries they had never set foot in before. Were you aware of that, Mac? How does it make you feel?

DM: Uh, I don't know. I mean it's the government's duty to protect its citizens, right? That's why we pay taxes. They probably prevented hundreds, maybe thousands of attacks back home. Got to be a good thing.

JL: Or maybe they radicalised otherwise peaceable citizens?

DM: Hey, anyone who attacks America, threatens our way of life, they deserve all they got coming to them. That's what I say.

JL [long pause]: Okay, I get that. Course you want to protect your country and its freedoms. So maybe we should get back to talking about you, Mac. Wasn't there anything else you wanted to do with your life? Be a teacher, or maybe, given your desire to serve your country, law enforcement?

DM: Well, um, I'm no dummy. I want to make that clear. I got my high school diploma, but I was never that keen on book learning. There are some folks as take to it, and some who don't. Guess I'm that second group. Anyway, as my papa tells it, things have been really hard since the Flood. The amount of cattle we're allowed to raise has been cut right back. Bad for the environment, see? So now we grow most of our meat in vats. Our manufacturing, well, no point beating about the bush, we just can't compete with the Blacks. All that North African tech is way cheaper. They don't have to worry about workers' rights and paying a decent wage. Least that's what I'm told. Even if you find a job outside of the corporate, none of them pays anything worth a damn. I just wanted to do something good with my life. So, yeah, I enlisted.

JL: And has it been everything you hoped for? Do you think what we're doing here is making things better? Making the world safer?

DM: Hard to say, ain't it? We still have a ways to go before we reach Jerusalem. But I got to believe it'll work out. The men in charge, like Colonel Tyler, they have a plan, right? See, I didn't have much back home. Things were tough, and when they are, people look to themselves and their own. Can't say I blame 'em. Being in the Templars has given me, like, this large family, one where we take care of and look out for our brothers. I got pride now, in myself and others. I never had me that before.

JL [low, almost inaudible]: Fuck.

DM: Say what, Mr Lynch?

JL: Nothing, Mac. Just caught some grit in my eye. Damn stuff blows everywhere out here. Thanks for your time.

DM: You're welcome. Hey, you'll let me know when it goes out, right? My folks will be real pleased to hear me on the vid.

JL: Ah, well, it's not up to me. You understand? Editor will make the final decision. But if it goes out, I'll definitely let you know.

Transcript Ends.

Walker grunted as he pushed his legs against the bar, raising the block of weights off the ground. He completed the set of fifteen, rested for fifteen and started on a fresh set. He felt the warm vinyl of the bench through the sweat-soaked fabric of his T-shirt. Told himself one more set. Midway through the seventh repetition his strength failed and the weights clanged to the ground. He wiped a forearm across his brow and concentrated on his breathing, watching his heart rate slow on the monitor beside him. Five more than yesterday. Thirty-three below his personal best.

Walker swung his legs off the bench and grabbed his water bottle. He studied the pale flesh of his right thigh, marvelling that there wasn't a single mark or blemish visible from the two through-and-through bullets he had taken. The nanotech had also, apparently, replaced some worn cartilage in his knee. And yet, in spite of the intensive physio regime and satisfaction of his doctors, he still didn't feel quite himself. He had lost good comrades, sworn brothers, on the beach. Would have been one of them if not for Mackinlay's intervention. The shrink said survivor guilt was perfectly natural, but wasn't his conditioning supposed to prevent such things?

Walker felt phantom pains in his leg and suddenly he was back on the beach, running for his life. The bullets tore through his flesh again and he went down hard. A prayer sprang to his lips as he readied himself to face the worst, then Mac was there, lifting him over his shoulder and carrying him to safety. The details became hazy after that, the warm embrace of the fentanyl dulling his senses. He heard rotors, felt the medics lift him into the evac copter, saw the ground drop away below him. The gunmetal flight deck of the King David replaced the blue-green waters of the Mediterranean as the helicopter touched down. Stretcher bearers hurried him below deck to the hastily converted meeting room that was now serving as a triage centre. A medic checked his injuries, fastened a green tag to his chest and moved on. He drifted in and out of consciousness to the groans and prayers of his wounded comrades and the smell of fear, which he would forever identify as antiseptic mixed with blood and shit. Sometime later the medic returned, supervised his transfer to a gurney and wheeled him through to the ship's surgery. Bland, reassuring voices, a mask over his face, the comforting embrace of darkness. He woke to crisp white sheets and an absence of pain. Since then, both his body and his mind had endured the doctors' endless prodding.

Pushing the memories aside, Walker grabbed a towel and made to hit the shower. The arrival of Doctor Steiner interrupted his progress. He looked up from his datapad on which Walker caught sight of his real-time EEG and ECG stats and fixed him with a wooden smile.

'I know you're keen to resume combat duties, Joseph, but your recovery would actually be hastened if you stopped punishing yourself.'

Walker noticed the stress he placed at the end of that statement and attempted to deflect it with an equally phoney smile of his own.

'Just testing the limits of that recovery. I appreciate you've never experienced it, but you can take my word for it that combat puts plenty of stress on the body.'

'Which is why your progress, physical and mental, is being monitored at all times. I likewise appreciate you're not a physician. But you can take my word for it that you won't be returning to active duty without my signing off on it.'

'I need a shower.'

'Might I also recommend a session in the steam room? You'll find it useful for ... contemplation. Doctor's orders.'

CHAPTER 19

Lynch swore and severed the connection to his implant. It felt like he had spent several hours trying to hack through the layers of ICE, but the time on his com-unit showed he'd been down for less than five minutes. The architecture had Tessler's fingerprints all over it; given time he might crack it, but for now Tyler retained control over what he could broadcast.

Lynch unlaced his boot and rolled down his sock to reveal the memory card taped to his ankle. He peeled it free and inserted it into his com-unit. As well as the bus massacre, it contained a number of unsanctioned interviews with Caliphate civilians. Not fanatics, but ordinary people doing their best to survive. This was a side of the conflict that the American people never saw, and unless he found a way of getting through the ICE they never would. The bastards had everything locked down tight, including outgoing messages on his com-unit. They parsed everything, looking for coded sedition and redacted every name, date and place. His handlers said they were controlling the narrative; propaganda by any other name.

Lynch skimmed through the transcripts, trying to put faces to the names. The heavily lined and sun-darkened features of the logger flashed up in his mind's eye. A man made old before his time by brutal and unceasing physical work. They had discovered him and the sad ruin of his wife in a ramshackle cottage at the edge of the Neve Ilan Forest. A search found no guns, explosives or comms, and the Templars had warned them not to leave the house until the convoy moved on. But no one had specifically barred Lynch from entering.

The man had seemed frightened at first, then suspicious, but Lynch gradually won him round and he had agreed to the interview. The wife, meantime, sat in her chair, smiling and nodding to herself while her husband served them tea in tulip-shaped glasses.

Personal Transcript #7: Jefferson Lynch in conversation with Nabil Tawfiq.

Jefferson Lynch: Mr Tawfiq, I understand you were one of the original settlers brought in by the Islamic Caliphate after the Fall of Israel in '63?

Nabil Tawfiq: My people call this land Palestine. But yes, I come here twenty-two, no, twenty-three years ago to make a new life for my family. Ha! Some joke. Before, we live in Raqqa. I work in construction. This was the time of Caliph Khaled bin Hasan al-Masri al-Qurayshi. He promised land and opportunity to those willing to come here. Building work was not so much at that time, so me and my brother, Tahir, decide to come here.

JL: The Caliphate paid for your resettlement?

NT: We got money to cover transport – not much, it pays for fuel and some food. Once here, they give us houses. We find clothes, personal things – those who live here before have gone in a great hurry. There are bullet holes and broken windows, which we mend as best we can. Power, same as running water, comes and goes. But we are among the first and we think things must get better.

JL: Did they?

NT [lengthy sigh]: Utilities, yes, but a great many things we are promised, these never come. I work with blocks, cement. What you say in English?

JL: Bricklayer?

NT: Yes! Skilled work, but they say they have too much of this kind of worker. So Tahir and me are sent to cut wood. Not so difficult, but we must do very big amount, and always more is needed for war effort. So we work longer and harder, but no more dinar. Food becomes rationed. We see it in the fields, but much of it goes to feed the army, who fight the Americans.

JL: And this happened to all the settlers?

NT: Not all. Those connected to the army or the party get better jobs. Eat good food. The others, we are treated like dogs.

JL: Second-class citizens.

Rima Tawfiq [panicked cry]: Qutiluu tiflay! Qutiluu tiflay!

Transcript interrupted; rapid, urgent Arabic. Unable to translate. Nabil gradually calms his wife.

NT: I'm sorry. She gets confused at times. She has suffered much in life.

JL: What was she saying?

NT [long pause]: They killed my baby.

JL: She lost a child?

NT: We both did. Twenty years ago, my wife is a strong, proud woman. We are angry about our treatment, about the false promises. But what is safe for a man and a woman to talk of in their home is dangerous if spoken in the streets. The Al-Khansaa Brigade come late at night while we sleep. Arrest my wife and take her away.

JL: And this brigade is what? Some kind of secret police?

NT: Not secret. All-women religious police who punish women who do not abide by the law.

JL: Sharia law?

NT [confirmatory nod]: They say she not submit to the will of Allah, that she is not meek as a good Muslim woman must be. They torture and beat her until she loses the baby she is carrying. Then they give her twenty lashes in public. Something in her head breaks and you see her now. I care for her all these years, but…

JL: What about your family? Don't they help?

NT: What you see is all that is left. The great virus took my brother and daughter – ten years ago? I forget exactly. My three sons – the army took those. I'm told they are martyrs, but I never see their bodies, or have graves to visit.

JL: That must be tough.

NT: [looks at his wife]: It is the will of Allah. I have accepted it.

JL: So your life will be better if the Americans succeed and drive the Caliphate out?

NT: It matters little to the slave whose hand holds the whip.

JL: You fear persecution?

NT: I am an Arab and a Muslim. Do you think the Jews will welcome me when they occupy Palestine again? Broken down old men such as I will be driven out. Where do I go? Back to Syria where others live in my home? To Egypt and hope President Elsayed is merciful? No, Mr Lynch, myself and hundreds like me will be taken to refugee camps, where we count the days between Red Crescent parcels. I hope life will be short there.

Transcript Ends.

Cooper picked his way across the rubble that littered the floor of the synagogue. Weeds and small saplings poked their way between the cracked flagstones. He scanned left and right, but IR and motion detection only recorded himself and Mackinlay. He eased his finger off the trigger as he took in the damage. The wood of the Bimah had been burned, as had the Ark and the Torah scrolls it had once housed, the smell of smoke still present years later. Excrement, most likely human, lay scattered about the floor. Only a couple of diagonals remained of the Star of David that had decorated the large circular window behind the Bimah. Cooper had seen the vandalism reflected throughout their journey: the wanton destruction of Jewish culture in the form of synagogues, monuments and museums.

'Guess the Jews won't be worshipping here any time soon.'

'You want to tell Katz that?'

Mackinlay flipped him the bird. 'We better report back to Jackson.'

Cooper caught Mackinlay's arm as he made to walk past, causing him to tense.

'Easy, Mac. Just wanted to take a minute. Talk about, y'know, the bus.'

'Ain't nothing to talk about, Coop. Far as I'm concerned,

we did the right thing.'

'Shooting children is the right thing? Shit, you're starting to sound like that nut-job, Schreiber.'

'Fuck you, man! I don't need to explain myself to you. We gave them clear instructions. They refused to obey. Brought that shit down on their own heads as far as I'm concerned. As for the kids – ten years from now they'd have been fighting for the Caliphate. You saw the videos, listened to the briefings. Just 'cause they're not in uniform it don't mean they're not dangerous.'

'Who are you trying to convince, Mac? Me or yourself?'

'What d'you want me to say? I'm sorry? That I didn't sign up to kill civilians? Damn straight I didn't. But mistakes happen. Sometimes innocents get killed. That's the way war is. And I sure as shit ain't going to beat myself up about it. Better them dead than you, me, or any of our brothers.'

'So we just forget about it and move on?'

'That's my plan, and if you've a lick of sense you'll do the same. You want your ma and pa to know you mistakenly shot up some kids? 'Cause I sure don't want to be laying that shit on my kin.'

'Every time I close my eyes I see their faces staring at me.'

Cooper felt Mackinlay's hands on his shoulders. The other man fixed him with a level and steady gaze.

'You got to let this go. If you don't, it's gonna eat you up. Say Our Fathers and Hail Marys, whatever helps. But you got to get yourself right with this. Meantime, get your shit together. We're almost in sight of Jerusalem. Don't you want to see what we've fought so hard for?'

'Guess so.'

Interview Transcript #4: Jefferson Lynch in conversation with Chaplain Kai Schreiber on the eve of the Battle of Har HaMenuchot Cemetery.

Jefferson Lynch: You volunteered for military service following the terrorist attack in Austin, Texas, on July sixth, 2088.

Kai Schreiber: Correct. I saw the pain and suffering caused by our enemies and knew the Lord had called me to take action.

JL: But, and I'm sorry to bring this up, you also suffered a great personal loss. The death of your wife, Jessica, and your unborn son.

KS: My son's name is David. He sits now at the right hand of God, an innocent martyr.

JL: Interesting choice of words. Wouldn't you agree that martyrdom is a concept we associate more with radical Islam than today's Christian faith?

KS [angrily]: Long before the false religion of Islam, Christian saints were martyred for their faith. Even now, Christian soldiers are laying down their lives to preserve the Gospel of the one true God. For theirs is—

JL [interrupting]: For which our viewers are grateful. Returning, if I may, to the personal. Such a senseless and apparently random loss must have proved a serious test of your faith?

KS: I won't deny I felt rage. What man wouldn't? Not with God but with the heathen instigators of this atrocity. Not only for myself, but on account of all the lambs of God that day.

JL: You blame the Islamic Caliphate for the bombing?

KS: They admitted responsibility.

JL: And yet the bomber, Bradley Foster, had no direct links to any active cell or known radicals. Isn't it possible he acted alone, out of some other sense of grievance and a general misanthropy?

KS: I wouldn't know about that. I leave the conspiracy theories to the left-wing commentators such as yourself. What I can tell you is I heard him take responsibility for that vile and cowardly attack in the name of Islam with my own ears.

JL: And that was the moment you found yourself called to fight the Caliphate? Not with words, with the teachings of the Bible, but in the vanguard of a crusade?

KS: No. I was shocked. Broken. What man who'd suffered the loss of his wife and child wouldn't be? But I took comfort in my faith. Spent many hours in prayer trying to understand what God wanted of me. I realised, at my lowest, that God was surely testing my faith. The doubts, the sense of injustice, the wanting to live that day over and make different choices, they were the whisperings of the Devil.

JL: You heard the voice of Satan in your head?

KS: You sound surprised, Mr Lynch. I doubt there's a Christian man alive who hasn't at one time or another heard the promptings of the Devil. And that's before we get to the sinners; those who give themselves to drink, drugs and loose women. Trading their souls for the pleasures of the flesh in this brief life of ours.

JL: Uh-huh … right. Moving on. Traditionally military chaplains have been non-combatants, their primary concern to minister to the spiritual well-being of the troops. You, however, have elected to fight alongside your flock. Some might question the morality of an ordained priest taking human life. At the very least, it surely compromises your ability to counsel those struggling to reconcile their Christian faith with the actions of war?

KS: That might have been true in the past, but you forget we're fighting a very different war out here. One of survival – total attrition – the very fate of our race hangs in the balance.

JL: Colonel Isaac Vaughan.

KS: Sorry, what was the question?

JL: That last part of your statement – those were the words Vaughan used at his Senate hearing in '75. I covered it as a junior reporter. Seem to recall he also said there was no place for outmoded concepts such as civilians. Do you, Chaplain Schreiber, echo his sentiments?

KS [long pause]: Civilians aren't so much the issue as the definition of non-combatants. A man or woman who takes up arms against America doesn't need to be in uniform for us to identify them as the enemy and therefore a legitimate target. As I said before, we're fighting a different kind of war out here. If mistakes happen … that's regrettable, but necessary in order to achieve victory.

JL: Better a hundred innocents die than a single Caliphate insurgent should escape?

KS [sound of swift, angry movement]: You're twisting my words, Lynch. What's more, I … I don't appreciate your tone! I'm not the one who should be on trial here.

Transcript Ends.

CHAPTER 20

Cooper gazed out over the eastern slope of the cemetery, taking in the sprawl of Givat Shaul, the western entrance to the city of Jerusalem. The flat-roofed architecture, previously so alien to him, had grown steadily familiar with each passing klick. A world of leprous grey and white in a landscape of beige, it looked ordinary in the late afternoon sunlight. Ridiculously so, when you considered the many wars fought for its ownership over the centuries. He had tried to study it online, but the Babylonians, Egyptians, Romans, even their historic brethren, the Crusaders, all blurred in his head. Doubtless it meant something to Katz and his fellow Israelis, but ancient history was just a set of stories to Cooper. The more recent history proved equally opaque to him: the formation of a new state of Israel following something called the Holocaust in the mid-twentieth century and the role of the British, Palestinians and the former United States. Politics – the means by which governments used the so-called will of the people to legitimise their lies. At least, that's what Donny always said. Admittedly, he could see no reasons beyond the political for them being here. Who cared if Jesus Christ had been crucified and buried here? No one Cooper knew in

Jonesboro would think to make a pilgrimage to the Holy Land, even if they succeeded in liberating it. Then there was the moral question: surely the Arabs had as much of a claim to the region as the Jews? Both had spilled plenty of blood over it. From what he remembered of his Bible the ancient Israelites had been particularly bloodthirsty in the founding of their kingdom. History, it seemed, was set to repeat itself.

Cooper jumped down from the grave, another Jewish custom he found puzzling. Even though they buried their dead underground, they insisted on placing these stone-clad concrete blocks on top. He assumed the black-leaded Hebrew inscriptions to be names, dates and other memorial texts. Everyone in Cooper's family and wider circle of friends who died was cremated, the cost of purchasing a plot of land prohibitively expensive. Hard enough to keep a roof over your head and food on the table without spending undue amounts on the dead.

A melancholy crept over him at the thought of home. He pictured his father watching the game, beer in his gnarled hand, while his mother cooked dinner. The twins would be somewhere underfoot, more interested in their own games than the football. And his sister? Shania would probably be on the socials, living through the eyes of vid stars and influencers. When would he see them again? Months, most likely. The Caliphate had dug in deep and all the talk was of a protracted siege. Speaking of which, he'd best get back.

The light faded fast as Cooper made his way down the slope, heading for the base camp on the western edge of the cemetery. Something else he found alien out here: the sudden transition from day to night. A shooting star crossed the sky, followed by another and then another. No, not shooting stars – rockets! The Caliphate forces had launched their counter-attack. He broke into a run, rapidly traversing the slope.

Cooper ducked for cover as a tank exploded, showering the cemetery with white-hot shards of steel. Incoming rockets similarly transformed a second tank and a JLTV into glowing fireballs, sending the Templars into disarray. Through all the chaos he spotted Tyler striding like some vengeful god, screaming into his radio.

'Find out where those rockets are coming from and neutralise them. I don't care – redeploy the satellites! And don't tell me there's no air support – we're sitting ducks out here.'

Cooper felt a hand land on his shoulder and turned to find Jackson standing behind him.

'Don't just stand there, son. Get your ass in that cab and move it. We need to form a perimeter. Long-range scans show we got incoming.'

'More rockets? Armour?'

'Infantry. Looks like Abdul is finally making this one personal.'

The Caliphate must have mobilised the city garrison. But was this a sign of desperation or part of some wider plan? Either way, he would soon find out if the stories about the famed Jerusalem Guard were true; that they were berserkers of unparalleled ferocity.

Cooper kept the lights off as he fired the JLTV to life. He reversed it out of its parking position and onto the main road, where he fell in behind an AMPV. Following its lead, he slewed his own vehicle across the highway, blocking the lanes and creating a narrow pass for the Caliphate soldiers to filter through. Unless, of course, they simply blew them off the road.

Cooper jumped down from the JLTV and listened for the whine of rockets amid the revving of engines and clanking of tracks. Nothing. A lull, or had the colonel's request for kill-sats been authorised? Surely COSCOM classified their force as mission critical? They were at the vanguard of the attack, after all.

A shouted order from Jackson saw him sprinting across the open ground and back to the cemetery boundary wall, behind which the squad was readying its defences. He squatted beside Mackinlay to assist him with assembling the squad's heavy machine gun. Once the tripod was in place, he fed in the first of the .50 calibre ammunition belts. Mackinlay cocked the weapon, sighted it between a broken-down section of wall and powered up the motion sensor. The screen fizzed to life, displaying a wave of dots so dense they almost appeared as a solid mass. Cooper cracked open the cases for the next two belts in preparation while Mackinlay readied the spare barrel. They were going to be busy.

'I don't see why you goddamn bastards won't give me a rifle.'

'Because we've enough to deal with without worrying about friendly fire from a whack-job such as yourself, Lynch,' Jackson spat in response. 'Now do as you're told and take cover up among those graves and leave the fighting to the professionals.'

Lynch pulled out his pistol. 'So if you're overrun I'm supposed to defend myself with this peashooter?'

'Could do. But if I were you, I'd make sure I saved the last bullet for myself. Said it yourself, the Caliphate likes to make an example of journalists.'

The sergeant turned away, Lynch already forgotten as he took in the rest of his command.

'Where's Schreiber? I need him at the wall.'

Mackinlay looked up from the motion sensor.

'Think he's in his tent, Sarge. Said something about needing to pray before the battle.'

'Just what I need, another crazy motherfucker. Cooper – get his ass out here. He can talk to God later.' He added under his breath, 'Maybe in person.'

Cooper checked the machine gun belt again before heading off on his latest errand. Quite when or how he'd become the squad's unofficial runner escaped him, but no point complaining now.

Believing all resistance suppressed and awaiting the arrival of their allied forces, the Templars had pitched their tents behind the protective stone of the cemetery boundary wall. Cooper threaded his way through the impromptu shanty town, making for the chaplain's tent, identified by the red cross flying above it. He paused outside, unsure of the protocol. Schreiber didn't outrank him in military terms but he still found himself wary of the preacher. Intense didn't begin to cut it. On the other hand, the Caliphate weren't about to wait.

Schreiber had his back to him when he entered. He stood up without turning round and fastened the straps of his vest. His voice sounded detached, as if his mind were on other things.

'What is it?'

'Sarge wants you on the wall. We got Caliphate incoming.'

Schreiber nodded, reached out for his SCMITR and pumped a round into the chamber.

'Then we'd best not keep the heathens waiting.'

A lull had fallen outside; the calm before the storm as the Templars waited for the Jerusalem Guard to attack. Ears were strained while eyes focused on motion sensors, watching the moving tide, waiting for it to break on the shore of their defences. It started low but swiftly rose in volume, the crunch of hundreds of feet marching in unison. As the attacking force drew nearer, they heard the creak of harnesses and the rattle of guns and knives. It seemed madness to Cooper for them to approach so openly; these were the fanatics his instructors had warned him about. Ready to take their place in Paradise as martyrs.

Jackson's voice rang out along the line: 'Steady. Steady. Let 'em come a little closer. Now!'

Cooper felt the ammunition belt rattle through his hands as Mackinlay opened fire to devastating effect. The first rank of Caliphate soldiers fell, as did many of the second, but the third pressed on, there being more men than the Templar bullets could account for. As Cooper loaded the second belt he wondered why the enemy had yet to return fire. The answer came in the form of a long whistle that ended in a nearby portion of the wall exploding. Mortars!

Cooper ducked for cover as further mortar rounds exploded along the wall, sending shards of stone and concrete flying. He angled the motion sensor towards himself and stared at the now largely stationary dots.

'Any idea where they're coming from, Mac?'

Mackinlay ignored the sensor and looked up into the sky in response to the incoming whistle of a fresh mortar. He ducked his head as the mortar took out another portion of wall, further eroding their cover.

'Reckon they're using some of our vehicles for cover.'

The rattle of small-arms fire sent both men diving for cover; the Jerusalem Guard were pressing their advantage. Over the persistent chatter they heard Jackson's bellowed order to continue firing. But by then it was too late: the first of the Guards were on their position.

Cooper rolled clear as a heavy boot swung at his face. He felt his back press against an outcrop of rock as he scrambled clear of a second kick and realised he had nowhere else to go. His attacker, realising the same, drew a long and wicked-looking knife from his belt. Cooper reached for his own dagger in the feeble hope of being able to parry the blow.

A SCMITR combat shotgun boomed and the decapitated Caliphate soldier dropped to the ground. A second detonation took out the soldier Mackinlay was grappling with, although Cooper was almost too busy wiping blood and brains from his eyes to see it. Three more blasts followed in quick succession, driving back the enemy and giving Cooper and Mackinlay time to regain their feet and fall back.

'So perishes the heathen!'

Chaplain Schreiber might be the craziest sonofabitch in the squad, but Cooper had never been happier to see him.

Mackinlay looked at the heavy machine gun but Cooper shook his head. 'Forget it, Mac. It'll only slow us down.'

Cooper unslung his assault rifle and fired a couple of bursts to discourage pursuit as they made their way up the hillside. The Templar force was in disarray as it retreated from the savagery of the Caliphate attack. Cooper looked around, desperately seeking a commanding officer to bring order to the chaos. He finally spotted Jackson. The sergeant's helmet was missing and his tunic and vest were bloodstained, a cut on his neck indicating its source. Despite his wound, Jackson was directing covering fire, pinning the Caliphate troops while the stragglers took up position among the graves, the two-foot-high stone-clad concrete blocks offering a reasonable degree of protection.

'Reckon you boys are the last. Better hop to it.'

Cooper stopped while Mackinlay and Schreiber went on ahead. 'What's the plan, Sarge?'

'We hold this hill and hope the colonel manages to call up some air support.'

'He's alive, then?'

'In case you haven't cottoned on by now, the colonel don't die easy. Now find yourself some cover. Abdul's sitting tight for now, but if he works out we ain't got no support…'

Cooper didn't need the sergeant to finish. They were in a tight spot and although no one would say it aloud, it was in large part due to Tyler's insistence on being the first to reach Jerusalem. He had driven the convoy on, outstripping MSRs, CSS and the other units in the hubristic belief that they had already defeated the enemy, and in doing so had played right into the Caliphate's hands.

Cooper picked his way among the graves, counting off the familiar faces and noting the missing ones. Halfway up, he spotted Goodman and Lynch resting against the side of one of the graves. A lighter flared in Goodman's hand and Lynch leaned in to light his cigarette. He nodded his thanks as the translator lit his own cigarette. Lynch's eyes were covered by the HUD shades that seemed to have become a permanent part of him. Cooper looked up instinctively and spotted the hovering drones. He somehow doubted footage of their inglorious rout would be going out on the news. In spite of the imminent danger, or maybe because of it, the journalist's lanky frame twitched with excited energy. Cooper wondered what it was like to be that committed to a job; for Lynch, getting the story meant everything. He envied him that surety of purpose.

He found Tyler hunkered down with Pedersen. The radio operator's expression was dark as he cycled through the frequencies, producing nothing but static.

'Can't you boost the signal?'

'Already at maximum, sir. They're jamming us across the spectrum.'

'Any idea where it's coming from?'

'No, but it'll be pretty short range. If we can bust out of here, I reckon we won't have to travel too far to get a signal through.'

'Then it's fortunate,' Tyler said, 'that one of the best drivers in the squad just showed up. Congratulations, son. You just volunteered.'

Tyler led them back down the hill to the edge of the graves where Jackson, Mackinlay and Schreiber were guarding the perimeter. The sergeant nodded curtly at Tyler, and Cooper sensed a subtle shift of power between them. Providing they got out of this alive, it would be interesting to see where this went.

Tyler lowered his night-vision goggles and scanned the Caliphate positions. Cooper, looking through his own, saw they had dug in along the main cemetery wall, apparently content for now to keep the Templars penned in. The nearest JLTV stood tantalisingly close, a little over a hundred metres behind the Caliphate line. But with the enemy at your back it might as well be a thousand or ten thousand. Tyler appeared to reach the same conclusion as he raised his goggles and sank back below the grave.

'We're going to need some kind of distraction if we're to sneak through.'

All heads turned towards Schreiber as he cleared his throat.

'I've prayed for guidance and received it. So if you'll allow me...'

Before anyone could say another word or stop him, Schreiber pumped the SCMITR and set off at a run for the Caliphate lines. From somewhere inside his relatively compact frame he summoned a deafening cry of rage. Schreiber blasted indiscriminately about himself, reeling back from the impact of bullets striking his body armour. He dropped to one knee and rose up again, seemingly impervious to the storm of bullets directed towards him. But the Caliphate troops, having taken their measure of the man, now directed their fire at his unprotected limbs. Schreiber uttered a guttural cry as the first bullets ripped through his legs, dropping him to his knees. He pumped a fresh round into the SCMITR, took out an approaching guard and tried to pump another round. The SCMITR clicked empty and silence fell.

Cooper watched as a solitary Caliphate soldier stepped out from cover and approached Schreiber. The gold braid and scarlet epaulettes identified him as a captain in the Jerusalem Guard. He stopped ten metres from Schreiber and drew a pistol from the holster on his right hip.

'Should I take him out, sir?' Mackinlay asked.

Tyler shook his head. 'No, let's see how this plays out. Pedersen, Cooper – get ready to move. Whatever our chaplain is planning, reckon we'll only get one shot at this.'

'This should be interesting. Bastard is even crazier than I am.'

Cooper turned at the sound of Lynch's voice. He hadn't heard the journalist approach and wondered how long he had been standing there and what he hoped to see. Lynch seemed oddly nervous and excited at the same time.

Cooper's head whipped around in response to the sharp crack of a pistol shot. A second shot sounded and Schreiber screamed as the SCMITR dropped from nerveless fingers, the Caliphate captain having put a bullet in each of his shoulders.

Satisfied he had drawn the fangs of his enemy, the captain drew a sword from his belt and approached the defenceless chaplain. A dozen men formed a loose circle around the fallen Templar as their leader took up position behind Schreiber and raised his sword to strike.

Jackson made to shoot but Tyler pushed the barrel of his assault rifle towards the ground, the warning look in the colonel's eyes sufficient to prevent the sergeant from arguing.

'Any final words, infidel, before I send you to your Christian Hell?'

Schreiber looked up, a beatific smile on his face. 'Boom!'

The explosion wiped out the circle of Caliphate troops, scattering body parts and shrapnel over a fifty-metre radius. Cooper, ears ringing, stared blankly at the crater that marked Schreiber's final resting place. A hand struck him on the shoulder and then Tyler and Pedersen were past him, running for the JLTV. His own legs kicked into action and he sprinted after them as Jackson and Mackinlay laid down covering fire. The image of Schreiber keeping his back to him in the tent, fastening the straps of his vest, played over and over in his head. The crazy fucker had rigged himself with explosives, planned his revenge on those he held responsible for the deaths of his wife and unborn son. Cooper felt sick at the thought of it. If this was what it took to be a true believer, he wanted no part of it. To hate to the point where your own survival became irrelevant seemed monstrous. If you became just like the enemy, where was your moral authority? Gone, and your humanity with it.

Cooper suddenly found himself clambering aboard the JLTV and firing up the engine. Now there was only the mission, all other thoughts driven aside as his training took over. He slammed the JLTV in drive, spun the nose around as he reversed, and then they were back on Route 1. Small-arms fire rattled off the armour as they sped away, the

Caliphate troops in disarray after Schreiber's suicide bombing.

Cooper glanced in the mirror and saw Pedersen already bent over the radio, fiddling with the dial. The static faded in and out and then a clear voice filled the cab.

'Eagles' Nest, do you copy, Apostle One?'

'We hear you loud and clear, Eagles' Nest.'

'What's your situation?'

'Fubar. We need an airstrike, stat. Main force pinned down by Caliphate insurgents, Har HaMenuchot Cemetery.'

'Copy, Apostle One. Scrambling Eagles.'

'Understood. Over.'

Pedersen ended the transmission and Cooper pulled the JLTV onto the side of the road. No sign of pursuit, but that didn't mean it wasn't following. Should they hold, or keep going until they met up with the Third Battalion? He looked to the colonel, but for now his expression was unreadable. Help was on the way, but if the Caliphate pressed their attack it would come too late. But there was nothing three soldiers in a beat-up JLTV could do to change that.

'Colonel Tyler, what are your orders, sir?'

'Keep moving. We rendezvous with the Third. And may God preserve our brothers.'

CHAPTER 21

Cooper tracked the flight of the F-27 Hellcat through his night-vision goggles as it screamed overhead. He followed each of its five companions as they flew in close formation, speeding to the relief of his comrades. But would they be in time? The distant rumble of explosions carried on the night air informed him that the Caliphate forces had already commenced their attack on Har HaMenuchot Cemetery. Were Jackson, Mackinlay, Goodman, Katz and Lynch already dead? Sacrificed on the altar of Colonel Tyler's ambition? Had Tyler cut and run, or struck out for the Third Battalion in good faith, seeking to bring reinforcements? His anger had certainly been genuine when Brigadier General Stuart had ordered him to hold position, unwilling to lead his own men into a potential trap. Currently he was pacing up and down in front of the JLTV, ignoring the explosions that lit up the horizon.

Cooper sat side-on with the door of the JLTV open, while Pedersen slumped beside him with his knees drawn up and his feet on the dash. His face was underlit as he studied his com-unit, flicking through the various vid-casts. His finger paused mid-swipe and he swore under his breath.

'Colonel, I think you ought to see this.'

The voiceover cut in: 'Broadcast live this evening from the outskirts of Jerusalem, this footage contains graphic scenes which some viewers might find disturbing.'

Cooper leaned in to look at the screen as Tyler pulled open the passenger door. Seen from above, it took a moment for Cooper to place it, then the drones dropped in and he recognised the cemetery and the kneeling figure of Schreiber as the Jerusalem Guard captain approached. The Caliphate officer raised his pistol and shot him in the shoulders.

'Sonofabitch must have hacked through the ICE,' Tyler snarled. 'If that pinko booze hound isn't dead already, he's going to wish he was.'

Cooper held his breath as the captain asked Schreiber if he had any last words. When the explosion came the fireball blossomed outward slowly, the video playing at one-tenth speed. The drones automatically pulled back, capturing the human detritus left in the wake of the blast. The feed cut back to the studio and Pedersen skipped to the reactions.

'Jesus, this is trending off the scale.'

'How bad is it?'

'There's the usual leftist whinging, Colonel, but in the main people are hailing that nut-job as a hero. There's already a petition calling for him to receive the Congressional!'

The sound was hoarse and rough, so much so that Cooper thought Tyler was choking at first, then he realised the colonel was laughing.

'Hoist by your own petard, Lynch. Guess the public isn't with you on this one.'

Three days later the smell of burning still hung in the air: kerosene, white phosphorous and ash overloading the JLTV filters, clinging to skin and clothing. The Hellcats had bombarded the area with MK-97 incendiaries, reducing the land and its occupiers to a uniform black char. The

Caliphate casualties had been left where they had fallen, blackened skulls, ribs and thighbones poking through the blanket of ash. Psychological warfare; let the enemy see the destructive power of their weaponry and the grisly fate of their comrades. Softening them up as a prelude to the second act.

Cooper parked up at base camp and made his way to the siege line. Templar reinforcements had continued to travel inland from the beach heads at Palmachim and Tel Aviv, replacing casualties and increasing divisional strength. They were joined by the volunteer forces of the Greater Russian Collective, advancing through Lebanon, Syria and Jordan, completing the so-called ring of steel about the city. The noose would be tightened in the fullness of time, but first the city's defenders must be subdued, their spirit broken.

The hairs on the back of Cooper's neck stood on end as he heard the charging crackle of the railgun powering up. Soon, an electromagnetic field would hurl a projectile at Mach 6 towards its target, landing with devastating force. As he looked along the line he saw a further nine of its identical brothers being energised.

'Ain't no end to the madness, kid.'

'Not filming this for posterity?'

The journalist gestured dismissively with his cigarette. 'Tyler took away my broadcast privileges. But even if he hadn't, what'd be the point? None of the swine back home seem to give a damn about the right or wrong of what we're doing out here. An American, a preacher no less, blows himself up live on air and people think he's some kind of goddamn war hero. Guess there's no cure for stupid. The system's fucked, kid.'

'Would you stop calling me that? I'm nineteen years old.' A slight hesitation, then, 'I've killed men.'

'I don't doubt it. But there's a subtle distinction between fighting to stay alive and being a killer. Maybe one day you'll cross that line, get lost in the madness. Or maybe you'll come out the other side, a reminder of what America used to stand for.'

'Sounds like you got a touch of the romantic in you, Lynch. No wonder the colonel hates you. Surprised he hasn't sent you packing already.'

Lynch stared moodily at the glowing tip of his cigarette. 'Turns out I'm what the spooks call a useful idiot. They'll upgrade the cams' security with Black ICE to discourage any further hacking and then I'll be back to producing stage-managed puff pieces.'

'I don't get it.' Cooper waved an all-encompassing arm. 'You don't believe in any of this shit; the war, the Christian cause, none of it. What are you still doing here?'

'Same as I've been doing for better part of the last twenty years – attempting to speak truth to power.'

'I'd have thought you could do that just as well back home.'

'That'd be doing what I've always done – hiding behind a screen. Been doing that since I dodged the draft for the Second Crusade. Didn't see why I should get my ass shot up for a cause I didn't believe in. The majority of my college buddies felt different, and most of them returned home in body bags. The few who didn't – let's just say I didn't recognise them as the boys who left. Suppose I should take comfort in the fact history proved me right. Whole thing was a disaster from start to finish, but Acre was the clincher. Sixty-seven per cent casualties – half-trained boys running in panic, live streams of the Caliphate shooting down the evac copters. Forced President Cheney to shitcan the draft he'd introduced at the start of his second term. Cost him both the House and the Senate in the midterms.'

'Sounds to me like you did the smart thing.'

'Trouble is, smart and right aren't always the same thing. Anyway, I railed against the war and for a while public opinion was on my side. But by '79 they'd gotten smarter: airstrikes with minimal boots on the ground liberated Saudi Arabia from the Caliphate and finally gave them a crusade they could call a success. After that, it was only a question of time before we found ourselves here again. Funny thing is, they all but held a gun to my head to get me out here in the first place. But it's given me back my audience and I can't walk away from that without knowing I've given it everything I've got. This time, I'm gonna shake those sons of bitches back home out of their torpor. And maybe, just maybe, there'll be no more lost generations. Beyond that, I guess the journalist in me needs to see how this all ends.'

'Firing in five, four, three …'

Cooper clamped the ear defenders over his ears. Even so, he felt the railgun's discharge as a physical pressure in his breastbone. He looked towards the city where he saw a series of tower blocks come crashing to the ground, sending up plumes of dust and debris.

'For the poor bastards over there it ends in death. Reckon there's a good chance it'll take us too, if we're not careful. Hell, it's a miracle any of you made it out of the cemetery alive.'

'No miracle about it, kid – sorry.' Lynch cracked a wry smile. 'Kinda tough habit to break. Turns out our advisor has some uses after all. Led us down into a bunker concealed beneath the cemetery. Seems they dug it as a command post when the Caliphate first threatened the city. Though if you ask me, parts of it are far older, probably going back to when they were worried the Iranians might lob a nuke at 'em. Whatever it was doing there, it saved our asses.'

The railguns powered up for another salvo and let loose. Cooper watched Lynch watching the destruction. He could almost hear the internal monologue inside the journalist's head as he composed copy for features that he would never broadcast: man's inhumanity to man – the madness of war – the senseless brutality of it all. He heard the phrases in Lynch's drawn-out Southern drawl but knew his own voice was there somewhere in the background.

'Shit. I can't watch this. You want to grab some breakfast in the mess?'

Lynch lit a fresh cigarette from the butt of the previous one and pulled out his hip flask.

'Got all the sustenance I need right here, thanks. Somebody's got to witness this. Reckon it's my watch.'

Cooper searched in vain for some words of absolution, or even comfort, but found none. Shrugging his shoulders, he turned on his heel and walked away. He had a craving for pancakes and bacon with butter and maple syrup. A comforting taste of the ordinary in a land where everything was askew. Halfway to the mess tent he stopped and looked back. Lynch stood transfixed by the destruction of the city they had come to liberate. An object lesson about the dangers of thinking too much. He imagined the bacon fried crisp, the fat shattering between his teeth. God, it was going to taste so good.

Al Jazeera was on the proscribed list, but that didn't prevent the troops from streaming it on their com-units. The channel had picked up the bombardment of Jerusalem on the second day and had proceeded to run it on a twenty-four-hour news cycle. By the fifth day Cooper could no longer tell if he was watching recycled or fresh clips of the horrors the Templars were visiting on the civilian population. Their construction was of a piece: initial establishing shots of bombed-out buildings, focusing on downed power cables and ruptured water pipes, streets clogged with abandoned cars, before a close focus on the signage for a school or a hospital. There would be children staring forlornly into the distance, grieving men and women kneeling beside the bodies of wives, husbands, sons and daughters. Tented enclosures overcrowded with the displaced as Jerusalem Guard soldiers handed out ration packs and ministered to the wounded. Then it would cut to the talking heads from the UN and the Red Crescent, describing the growing humanitarian crisis. Food in short supply, lack of clean drinking water, limited medical supplies. The Templars' apparently deliberate targeting of the civilian population was breaking conventions. The North African Tech Corps had denounced them and, in a rare break, Europa City's Supreme Councillor Birgette Ladegaard had called for a review of the weapons export licenses to the RSA. Even the more liberal news channels back home were starting to question the morality of the bombardment.

As with many things he had grown accustomed to, it took Cooper a few minutes to realise that what he was hearing was in fact the absence of the railguns' continuous sequence of charge and discharge. He put down his com-unit, gathered up his field glasses and exited the tent. A pall of dust and debris still hung over the city, but the rumble of collapsing buildings had ceased. Cooper scanned the horizon, picking out the first tentative survivors emerging from cover, their frightened movements indicative of their suspicions that the lull was some form of trick or trap. The *whup-whup* of rotors drew the eyes of civilian and Templar aloft. He tracked a pair of incoming Red Crescent helicopters as they descended towards the plaza in front of the Western Wall.

Angry shouts by the motor pool drew his attention back to camp. Cooper looked over and saw Tyler and Katz. A change in the wind carried their words to him.

'To be fair, Colonel Tyler, the Knesset has become concerned about the damage to the city's infrastructure.'

'Yeah? Well, it looks like they've got their way. This is what comes of electing a peacenik freak like Hamilton as President. Ordering a ceasefire to relieve the civilian population – what the hell's he thinking?'

'That it's the honourable thing?'

'Not when you're dealing with fanatics. These mutts would wire up their own kids to explode! It won't just be medicine and food on those helicopters, they'll be sneaking in ordnance, possibly even special forces troops. Mark my words, this "humanitarian" gesture will cost American and

Israeli lives.'

'Perhaps, but it seems to me President Hamilton is a pragmatic man. The Religious States of America can't afford to alienate its allies.'

'Seems to me it's more a case of asking ourselves which allies we can trust.'

'It's a fine line between prudence and paranoia.'

'If we're going to quote maxims, being paranoid doesn't mean they're not out to get you.'

Katz nodded in response. Say what you like about the Israeli, he knew when to keep his counsel.

Cooper spotted the cloud coming in with the dawn light, low to the ground, with a faint yellow tinge, and instinctively recognised it as nothing that occurred in nature. He shouted a warning as he sped back to the main body of the camp: 'Gas! Gas!'

The cry spread rapidly as his comrades took it up, but the first wisps of the deadly cloud were already spreading through the tents. Cooper felt it prickle and itch on his skin, catch harshly at the back of his throat. He tried to hold his breath as he threw open the flap of his tent and reached inside for where he'd stowed his NBC gear. The Caliphate's possession of chemical weapons had been well-documented, but no one had thought they were desperate enough to employ them. He pulled on the mask first, knowing it was vital to protect his airways and eyes. The relief was almost instant, but it brought home the burning on the backs of his hands. He saw a faint blistering of the skin as he pulled on the rest of his suit and adjusted the seals. Would the gloves make it worse? Possibly short term, but he knew the protocol – limit his exposure as quickly as possible.

Gloves in place, he checked his rifle and went outside to meet a potential Caliphate counter-attack. He recognised Jackson from the stripes on his NBC suit. The sergeant was holding up a particle scanner.

'What have we got, Sarge?'

'Weaponised chlorine and sulphur mustard. Most of our boys are suited up now – limited casualties. The wind's blowing more to the east.'

'Is that good?'

'Not if you're with the Russkies. As volunteers and irregulars, I doubt they've much by way of protective equipment. Could be Abdul is hoping to punch through their lines and retreat through Jordan. Our air support is already scrambling. One thing's for sure: that's definitely the end of the ceasefire.'

Cooper nodded thoughtfully. Appointed an observer, he'd spent the last four days watching a steady stream of copters airlifting women and children to safety. Safe to assume anyone left in the city, regardless of age, gender or whether they were in uniform, was an enemy combatant.

He felt the cough starting to build and tried to stifle it, but that only made it worse. His shoulders shook and his back arched as he struggled for breath. Panic gripped him as his brain demanded oxygen and his lungs refused to obey. Then, as quickly as it had arrived, the fit passed. He stood bent over, short shallow breaths rasping inside his mask.

'Better report to the MO and get a nano-shot before there's any more damage to your lungs.'

'It's nothing, Sarge. I'll be okay.'

'That wasn't a request, Cooper. An unfit soldier is a liability to himself and his brothers. You're relieved of duty until the doc certifies you as fit. Don't worry, I'll save a bit of this lovely war for you.'

His father's admonition echoed inside his head as he went in search of a medic: Don't you go being no hero. Was this the line Lynch had warned him about crossing: war becoming the only thing he knew, the one thing he lived for? He called up the images of his father, mother, Shania and the twins, reminded himself of the reason he had enlisted in the first place: to make life better for his family.

He didn't care about no Caliphate or people worshipping Allah. Family was everything. He just had to hold on to that. Complete his tour. Go home and live a normal life.

CHAPTER 22

Hopkins scanned the line again. Something was missing, but she couldn't quite put her finger on it. True to his word, Hamilton had named Gerrard as his running mate and now, as his press secretary, it was down to her to craft a suitable acceptance speech in the wake of their victory. How to find the right balance between triumphalism and humility? Too much of either would play poorly with the voters: Gerrard either appearing to grandstand or else appear pathetically grateful to Hamilton for offering him the crumbs from his table, the latter fatal for any future presidential ambitions.

She retrieved her smouldering cigarette from the ashtray and took a draw, pulling the smoke deep into her lungs before breathing it out through her nose. The nicotine hit the spot but failed to provide any inspiration. Her eyes flitted to the empty wine glass on the desk, another creative dead end. She hit the save icon and stood up, stretching her back and arms. Six weeks until Hamilton's inauguration, but the president-elect was already proceeding swiftly with his appointments. Moderate voices. Too moderate for Hopkins' comfort, but at least they had the political experience and clout to avoid appearing weak. Hamilton's sweeping victory in the Electoral College and an increased Southern Democrat majority in the House and the Senate had emboldened him. He would pass the reforms he had promised on the campaign trail into law with little opposition, including the scaling down of military operations in the Middle East. She had at least wrung the concession from him not to lift the siege of Jerusalem. However, it had become clear that the Israelis could expect little support in maintaining their borders following the successful liberation of their country. Still, public opinion was malleable, and if the campaign trail had taught her anything it was that Hamilton liked to be popular. The major planks of his policies were all crowd-pleasers. That was a weakness she could exploit.

She picked up her com-unit and thumbed through her contacts. Hamilton had another weakness he didn't know about, in the person of his choice for the Director of the Office of Administration. She hit call.

'David, Susanna Hopkins. Congratulations on the appointment. Calling to see if there's anything in the president-elect's inaugural speech I should be aware of?'

'And why on God's green earth would I tell you that?'

'Oh, I don't know. Perhaps in the spirit of cooperation. Or to establish openness and transparency. Or maybe because you'd prefer it if your wife didn't find out you've been screwing your intern. You know, the brunette with the strawberry-shaped birthmark on the inside of her right thigh.'

'They warned me you were a piece of work, but I really had no idea.'

'If it makes you feel any better, it's nothing personal. Just politics.'

'I'm sure Brutus said something similar right before he stuck the knife in.'

'Play ball and I'll make sure you're on the right end of the knife. Isn't that what friends are for?'

Hopkins smiled to herself as the connection went dead.

She had Gerschwitz hooked, even if he didn't know it yet. He would have been better taking his chances with the personal and public fallout of marital infidelity. Because once he betrayed Hamilton there would be no going back, and each subsequent betrayal would only dig him deeper. She would send Louise a bonus. The honeytrap – as old as time, and yet it rarely failed to deliver.

Hopkins ran a finger along the inside of her collar. Fifty metres below ground, the windowless briefing room felt airless in spite of the climate control. The weight of the Panopticon's tower seemed to press down on her, adding to her feeling of unease. In the wake of the Jerusalem chemical attack, Hamilton's decision to call a meeting of the National Security Council inside what was effectively an NBC bunker was clearly a statement of intent. But what that intent was remained to be seen.

Hopkins looked around the table, trying to take the temperature of the room. Kordowski, the Chairman of the Joint Chiefs of Staff, wore his habitual hangdog expression. Morrison, by contrast, kept his features neutral: the Secretary of Defense being something of a political weathervane, he would wait to see which way the wind was blowing before taking a position. Gerrard looked, if not smug, then at least pleased with himself. She hoped it was down to schadenfreude and nothing more malevolent. Far too early in Hamilton's presidency for his VP to be briefing against him. As to the man himself, from the throbbing vein in his temple, she could tell he was about to explode. In three, two, one …

'Would any of you care to tell me what the fuck is going on here? How did they get chemical weapons into Jerusalem and the means to deploy them against our troops?'

Kordowski steepled his fingers, lending him the air of a teacher. Appropriate, as he was about to school the president. 'Given they've held the city for a quarter of a century, Mr President, there's every reason to believe the weapons have been in place for years, if not decades. More importantly,' the CJCS paused for effect, 'there's no evidence they were brought in under the guise of the ceasefire you authorised.'

'It's like that, is it, Gene? Funny, I don't recall you raising any objections at the time.'

'That'll be because public opinion was behind it. But the trouble with the public is they're apt to change their minds when the casualty lists are published.'

'Last I read,' Morrison interrupted, 'American casualties were limited.'

Kordowski turned to Morrison. 'Comparatively speaking, they are, Lee. But, regardless of the previous history between our two nations, the public is proving surprisingly squeamish about all those body bags filled with volunteers from the GRC. Seems a Christian soul is still a Christian soul, even when he's a Russki or a Latvian.'

'Yeah? Well, I'm sure it'll all be forgotten come the midterms.'

'Perhaps.' Kordowski smiled coldly. 'Provided we've actually taken Jerusalem by then.'

Hamilton's face darkened again. 'That better be your idea of a joke, Gene, misplaced as it is. In case you've forgotten, this administration was elected on a ticket to retake Jerusalem, secure Israel's borders and bring our troops home – in that specific order. So if you boys are finished with the wisecracks, how about telling me what's standing in the way of achieving that? The chemical attack was a big enough PR disaster – are we certain the IC doesn't possess any nukes?'

Silence.

'Well, Lee, I'm waiting.'

'Intelligence reports state their bases and missile launchers have been successfully eliminated,' Morrison finally responded. 'We've reduced them to conventional weapons only. Infrastructure attacks and blockades have further eroded the morale of the military. By all accounts they're close to collapse, Mr President. One good push is all it'll take.'

'Then what are we waiting for?'

'Data modelling still predicts thirty per cent casualties from a direct assault at this time. I don't need to tell you the public won't accept that sort of loss lightly. The Caliphate's Jerusalem Guard are fanatics – they'll fight to the last man and to the last bullet. We need to break their spirit.' He paused to look at Kordowski, who gave the briefest of nods. 'Fortunately, we have the perfect card to play. Intel confirms Abu Ahmad al-Nasr al-Qurayshi himself is trapped in the city.'

A hushed silence fell across the room. Hopkins instinctively looked towards Gerrard, noting his lack of surprise. A cold weight settled in her stomach.

The president was first to recover. 'You're absolutely certain? The caliph is in Jerusalem?'

'Positive satellite ID. His elimination would be a critical blow to the Caliphate. Our operatives are already working with Mossad.'

'Some good news at last. And we're ready for this?'

'One hundred per cent.'

Hamilton checked his watch and, pushing back his chair, stood. 'In which case, I'll leave it in your capable hands to make it so. Don't disappoint me, Lee. Now, if you'll excuse me, I've other business to attend to.'

Gerrard waited until Hamilton had left the room to remark, 'Heavy is the head that wears the crown.'

'In case you've somehow forgotten, Chuck, we're a republic.'

'It's all relative, Gene. Now, more to the point, I'm sure we're all agreed that this mission is too important to fail. If Mossad drops the ball, I want a contingency in place – maximum plausible deniability.'

'Woah!' Morrison held up his hands. 'You're speaking about undermining the president's authority.'

'I prefer to think of it as delegating. By his own admission, the president is a busy man. But if it makes you sleep any easier, I'll take any flak. Terminating al-Qurayshi will save American lives, and that has to be our primary objective.'

Hopkins waited until they were back in Gerrard's office before confronting him. 'What the fuck was that about? You've barely been in office long enough to take a dump and you're already making power plays? We agreed to wait until at least the end of Hamilton's first term.'

Gerrard took a step forward, deliberately invading her personal space. He leaned in close, ensuring she could feel his breath on her face when he spoke.

'I think you'll find that's what *you* said, Susanna. I never agreed to jack shit. Now, there's no disputing you are one fine piece of ass, and that you know how to play that to your advantage. But unlike some of those other suckers it's going to take more than waving your snatch in my direction to control me.'

Hopkins took a step back and felt the edge of Gerrard's desk press into the back of her thighs. She cursed inwardly. While she didn't feel threatened, she would have preferred some room to manoeuvre. She settled for a cheap shot instead.

'Didn't reckon you for a fag, Charles. Then again, I also didn't take you for a fool.'

'Is that what's worrying you? You really haven't got my measure at all. Let me enlighten you – however this plays out, I'm more than happy for Hamilton to get the credit for eliminating al-Qurayshi. At this point, all I'm doing is making sure of my allies. Because if this all goes to rat shit and Hamilton doesn't get a second term, I aim to make damn sure it's my name on the ticket for the Southern Democrats presidential nomination.'

Hopkins pouted. 'I already told you it would be.'

'Yeah, well, you also told me it would be this time, and look where we are. I'm looking out for myself, and if you don't like it, you know where the door is.'

'Don't forget: I made you!'

'Seriously? I don't deny you whispered in the right ears and greased a few palms here and there, but I'm in this office as much by my own talent and effort as by anything else. You'd be foolish to forget that. Particularly if you want to be elected to the Senate.'

'The Senate—'

'For Christ's sake, don't act stupid. It doesn't become you. You're a lot less skilled at hiding your ambitions than you like to think. There are plenty out there still uneasy about women in the Senate, but I'm not one of them. What say we stop pretending to be friends, admit our differences and concentrate on our mutual ambitions? We don't have to like one another, but there does have to be some measure of trust between us. If you're not capable of that, now's the time to part ways. Deal or no deal?'

Hopkins chewed her bottom lip ruminatively. How far did she trust Gerrard? She had little doubt he'd stab her in the back as soon as it became politically advantageous, but then so would everyone else on the Hill. Better to keep him onside while she dug for dirt in order to be able to threaten him with mutually assured destruction. 'Deal.'

She shook Gerrard's proffered hand. *I just hope to hell I know what I'm doing here.*

CHAPTER 23

Al-Hashimi looked out over Jerusalem. He felt a pain in his heart as his weary eyes took in the destruction wrought upon his city. For, having served here for more than a quarter of a century, he had come to regard Jerusalem as his home. The minarets of the mosques were gone, targeted by the Templar bombardment, as were many of the houses and shops, along with hospitals, schools and substations. He knew the strategy well: denial of services, designed to erode the spirit and break the will of its defenders. Had he not used them himself during the Caliphate's rise to power? An old playbook, but that didn't make it any less powerful. He sighed and turned to face his companion.

'Beware of melancholy, my friend. It will weaken your arm when you need it to be strong.'

'As ever, your counsel is wise, my caliph. But if I might be so bold as to offer some of my own?'

'I have always valued your advice.'

The smile that accompanied Abu Ahmad al-Nasr al-Qurayshi's words was wistful and al-Hashimi saw that the caliph already knew what he had to say and had decided against it. But he had to try, if only to say he had.

'The Jews and their American and Russian lapdogs ready themselves for an assault on the city. We cannot hold against such numbers. You should leave the city while you still can, my caliph. Much as my heart aches for the mortar and stone that surrounds us, it would break irreparably if your light should be extinguished. Remember the words of the prophecy – there will be but five caliphs. You should save your strength for the final battle to come.'

'Even the holiest of prophecies is subject to the interpretation of man, and men are often wrong. Who is to say that it is here, Jerusalem, and not Dabiq, that the army of Rome will finally be defeated? If I am to be the last caliph I must ensure my legacy is one of victory, or at the very least, glorious defeat. As we both know, it is not for man to know the will of Allah.'

'As you say, my caliph.'

This time al-Qurayshi's smile was full of warmth. He reached out and placed his hands upon al-Hashimi's shoulders and looked his military advisor and friend directly in the eyes.

'Have we not lived good lives, Mohamed, my friend? We have raised strong sons to carry our family names and to continue our work once we are gone. Have we not earned our right to enter Paradise? You and I, we are warriors. We will teach the infidels the meaning of jihad and show them how to die!'

'That we will!' al-Hashimi said with a conviction he did not feel.

As the caliph strode away, al-Hashimi turned back to look at the broken bones of the city. He was glad his old friend had relented and allowed the evacuation of the women and children. On a tactical level it was no concession at all; the Americans had bombarded the city with scant regard for its human shield. But for the sake of their long years of friendship he had to believe humanitarian concern had motivated the caliph. It was a poor thing to put civilians in harm's way for the sake of military advantage, no matter the strength of their beliefs. As to himself, was he not of the faithful, a true believer, his place in Paradise assured? And yet, he felt a sliver of doubt worry at his conviction. It would be a fine thing to gaze upon the face of his wife one last time. Not on a screen, but in person. To reach out and touch her, to hold her. But he might as well wish for the moon on a silver platter. No point in trying to deny his fate. He would die defending Jerusalem from the infidels.

'General Volotsky to see you, sir.'

The Russian commander pushed past the orderly and entered the command centre without waiting to be invited. Tyler studied the intruder: a tall man, barrel-chested, with close-cropped hair and a neatly trimmed beard, both of which were silver-grey. His face and the lines of his body radiated disapproval as he came to a halt in the centre of the room and assumed a stiff-legged pose. Behind him, Tyler's orderly, Martinez, pulled the door closed, leaving the two men alone.

'What can I do for you, Mikhail?'

'Do?' The general chewed the word over before spitting out a reply. 'You can commence your assault on the city, as agreed. My men grow restless. They fear another chemical attack. I share their concerns. Our lines of supply are stretched – we are a sitting target for any counter-attack. As are your own troops.'

'I hear what you're saying, but let me show you this.'

Tyler called up a holo-display of the city and its surroundings. He zoomed in using his fingers and rotated the various areas of interest to show the Russian commander.

'All the roads are mined. There's a well-constructed trench system, including bunkers, pillboxes and heavy machine gun posts. Now that that fool of a president has allowed the evacuation of women and children, those left defending the city have no weak spots to protect.' He summoned up a list. 'Projected casualties for your forces in a direct assault are close to forty per cent. Are you really willing to take that kind of damage?'

'The key word here is projected. Our casualties may be far lighter.'

'Or heavier. "Cannon to the right of them, Cannon to the left of them, Cannon in front of them."'

Volotsky sniffed. 'As I recall, those were Russian cannons.'

'And this time they'll be Caliphate ones. I've no desire to play the role of Lord Cardigan, and I'd strongly advise you not to either.'

'So we … what's the English expression? Sit on our hands and do nothing?'

'We wait, but we will be far from idle. A plan is in motion – need-to-know only, I'm afraid, but it will break Abdul's spirit and aid our taking of the city.'

'You're refusing to share this information? After all the blood we've spilled for you? Your lack of trust is insulting.'

'Mikhail, believe me when I say trust is not the issue here. The plan is known only to a select few – the majority of my men know nothing about it. What I will tell you is there's to be an aerial bombardment prior to our final assault on the city. You and your staff will be briefed in the run-up to the attack. Despite what you may think, your sacrifice has been noted and will be rewarded.'

'Just so long as that reward isn't in Heaven.'

Walker fidgeted on the couch. He had long since lost track of his sessions with Doctor Steiner, which seemed to have fallen into a repeating pattern. When he told Steiner what he wanted to hear he dismissed it as fabrication, and when he told Steiner what he actually thought the doctor tried to convert him to what he had said originally. Whatever subtle difference existed between the two escaped Walker and he had begun to suspect that Steiner's intention was to keep him out of action for as long as possible.

'From your silence, I take it you don't wish to discuss the deaths of your comrades?'

'More a case of failing to see how this time will be any different from the other half-dozen or so times I've discussed it.'

'Surely that's for me to decide?'

'All right. What do you expect me to say? I'm relieved to still be alive? Damn straight I am. You can believe in a cause without pointlessly throwing your life away in pursuit of it. It's possible to uphold your vows without dying like a sucker.'

'You think the war is causing needless deaths?'

'No more than any other. Sometimes war is about luck as much as skill. Least it seems that way to me. Who can predict where a helicopter will drop out of the sky?'

'Your wounding was bad luck?'

'Or good, depending on your point of view.' Walker slapped his thigh. 'Here I am, good as new, thanks to the wonders of nano-meds. Then there're the guys in the body bags.'

'And you don't feel you failed to protect them?'

'If the chance had been there, I would have done what I could. Same as any Templar.'

'Same as Dwayne Mackinlay? A sworn brother who ran through enemy fire to rescue you.'

'What? You want me to make sure he gets a medal or something? Don't recall saying I wasn't grateful. But had the tables been turned, I would have done the same.'

'You're absolutely certain of that?'

'As certain as any man could be – you don't know until you're in a situation how you'll react. But, as you rarely tire of reminding me, the RS government spent a small fortune on my training and conditioning, so I reckon I'd be good for it. You ever sign off on me returning to active service, maybe I'll get the chance to prove it.'

'And how do you feel about the Caliphate?'

'Feel?' Walker snarled. 'They're the enemy! The reason we're out here in the first place.'

'Do you ever wonder what they think of you? Are you the enemy?'

'What the hell kind of question is that? Have you spent your life hiding under a rock or something? They hate our faith, they hate our freedom, they hate the values we stand for. Even thousands of miles away we're not safe. Look what they did in Texas. Jerusalem's only the start – we need to drive them back to Syria and Iraq and wipe them from the face of the earth. If we don't, they'll only come back stronger.'

'And the civilians, the women and children. Should they be exterminated too?'

'If they won't accept re-education and renounce their faith, they won't leave us any choice. It's us or them. Has been for decades.'

'Hmm.' Steiner recorded something on his datapad and swiped it closed. 'Okay, I think that's enough for today. Same time tomorrow.'

Walker swung his legs from the couch and stood up, resisting the urge to punch Steiner. Gratifying as it would be, he doubted it would see him cleared for combat duty any faster.

Tyler stood studying the holo-display of Jerusalem, looking for weaknesses in the city's defences, but his mind wasn't on the task. Volotsky's visit had unsettled him. The GRC volunteer force was a sizeable unknown variable. While he was pragmatic enough to acknowledge they couldn't have made it this far without their support, he worried about Volotsky's ability to control them. They might be fierce fighters, but they lacked military discipline. If the Jerusalem Guard put them into a rout all would be lost. Instead of glory, he would return to Richmond a failure, his dreams of power shattered. He thought he'd detected an air of coldness in Susanna's manner during their last call. She had made it clear that she didn't back losers. Perhaps he was reading too much into it. Feelings were apt to cool with thousands of miles between them. Even so, he found himself wondering if she was seeing someone else. He hadn't asked for exclusivity from her, fearing the possible answer. He felt a pang of jealousy at the thought of her lying with another man, but in a way that made things easier. Once she had served her use, he would need to see to her disposal. As the secret mistress of a man sworn to celibacy, she knew too much. That, however, remained a problem for the future. For now, he had more immediate concerns.

He shut down the holo-display and rubbed his eyes. Perhaps some fresh air would help clear his mind. He picked up his helmet, fastened the chinstrap and checked his sidearm. It never hurt to be prepared. He had removed his rank insignia from his helmet and body armour to make him less identifiable to snipers. So far, the Caliphate forces had shown little inclination to engage with the forces surrounding them. But a high-value target might tempt them to make an exception. Two of their sentries had gone missing last week, doubtless picked up by a Caliphate snatch squad. Disciplined and loyal as they were, they might eventually break under torture.

The heat hit him like a physical blow as he stepped outside the command carrier. He scanned left and right, then proceeded to make his way over to where Jackson was supervising the digging of a new latrine ditch. Not strictly necessary, but keeping the men occupied was vital for maintaining discipline. They had built fortifications around the camp, stripped and maintained their weapons and conducted drills.

Jackson snapped to attention at his approach and Tyler told him and the workers to stand at ease. The men gratefully put their shovels aside and took shelter in the shade of an awning. A figure stirred in the hammock erected between its poles, and a skinny arm shot upward, brandishing a hip flask.

'If it ain't our glorious leader,' Lynch slurred. 'Slow day is it, that you're doubling as Superintendent of Shits?'

Tyler pursed his lips. The only thing more irritating than Lynch was a drunk Lynch. The man seemed to have an uncanny knack for sniffing out booze where there should be none. He suspected the men of having set up a still. Maybe God would answer his prayers and Lynch would go blind and be shipped home.

Lynch swung his legs clear of the hammock and lurched towards him, limbs flailing in all directions. 'Cat got your tongue?'

'You're drunk, Lynch.'

'And that means you can ignore me?'

Tyler folded his arms across his chest. 'Strikes me as the wisest course of action.'

'Don't know why you're so pissed. Schreiber's suicide bombing is off the charts. The heroic Templar chaplain laying down his life to save his brothers and smiting the enemy with the righteous anger of the Lord! The dullards back home are loving it.'

'Believe me, that's the only reason you're still here, Lynch. Had my way, I would've packed you back home in a body bag. But you're trending way too high for that. For now, at least. So you're to film what I say when I say, and maybe, just maybe, you'll go home at the end of this, walking upright.'

'That sounds like a threat.'

'Take it any way you like, screwball. But if you know what's good for you, keep out of my way unless I call for you.'

Tyler saw Lynch's hand grope for the pistol holstered on his hip, his fingers scrabbling at the flap as he swayed on his feet. He drew his own pistol swiftly and levelled it. The action saw Jackson reach for his own gun.

'Draw that gun on me, Lynch, and I will put you down.'

Lynch let his hand fall by his side. 'You're a goddamn

swine.'

'And you're a has-been drunk. What's new? Jackson, relieve Mr Lynch of his sidearm and dagger. Seems he can't be trusted to play nicely with his toys. Then escort him to the stockade. Our war correspondent needs a few days to dry out.'

Lynch raised his arms and let Jackson take his weapons. A firm hand gripped his bicep as the sergeant took hold of him.

'I can walk by myself.'

'That's as may be,' Jackson said, 'but we wouldn't want you falling down.'

'You know he's going to get you all killed, don't you?'

'Who? Colonel Tyler?'

'He's on a power trip, risking your lives for his glory. The cemetery wasn't the first time he led you into danger, just because he wanted to be first, and it won't be the last. I've seen his type on the Hill – the naked ambition for power at any cost. He'll use the bodies of you and your men as stepping stones to achieve it.'

Jackson dragged Lynch forward, holding him up when he stumbled.

'Just shut your mouth with that crazy talk, and walk.'

Tyler looked up at the knock and called out, 'Enter.'

The door swung inward and Jackson marched briskly across the command centre and stood to attention in front of where Tyler sat at his console. The colonel could tell from his expression that Jackson had something on his mind.

'Permission to speak freely, sir?'

'At ease, Sergeant.' Tyler flipped over the stylus between his fingers, using the pause to gather his thoughts. 'We've known one another a long time, Tyrone. If there's something on your mind, just come out and say it.'

Jackson swallowed, clearly uncomfortable. He drew a deep breath, held it, then finally exhaled.

'Look, Lynch is a crazy bastard, no doubt about it, and I don't buy his conspiracy theories. But he's right about one thing – you've been pushing too hard ever since we got here. Wanting to be the first boots on Israeli soil, always putting us in the vanguard. I know you're thinking of the mission and your sworn duty as a Christian soldier to achieve it, but we also hold the lives of our brothers in trust. We all swore the same oath to look out for one another.'

'You think I've been remiss in my duty towards the men under my command?'

'I think the … prize might have clouded your judgement. Like I said, we took solemn vows and there isn't a man out here who wouldn't willingly sacrifice his life in pursuit of those vows. But surely it would be an affront to God to surrender the lives of good Christian soldiers wantonly?'

'I see.' Tyler deliberately let the pause stretch, forcing Jackson to fill it.

'You know you have my respect, right? I'm saying this to you as a brother. You need to step back and draw a breath. Maybe spend some time in private meditation and prayer. God wants this victory, so I'm certain he'll show you the way if you petition him.'

'How long have we been encamped on the outskirts of this city? How long have we besieged the enemy?'

Jackson frowned, put off by the sudden change in tack. He did some mental calculation and said, 'Ninety-seven days.'

'A little over three months. And during that time I've spent most of it in this command centre, monitoring the satellite feeds, reviewing intel with the Israelis, the Russians, Jordanian rebels, even the Saudis, while taking the pulse of the public back home. Believe me, Tyrone, I've taken more than a breath here. And I've done my share of praying. But no matter how you try to slice it, taking the city from the Caliphate is going to cost lives. As well you know, the burden of command is sending men to their deaths. I can assure you, it never gets easier, regardless of the size of the prize. But in the name of our friendship and the vows that bind us together, I ask that you trust the plan I've put in place. Jerusalem will fall and we will be the victors. And, God willing, most of us will live to see it.'

The tension drained out of Jackson's stance and Tyler knew he had won him over, at least for now. The aerial bombardment would certainly deplete the Caliphate defences, but he intended the Templars to be at the front of the attack on the city, regardless of the cost.

'I'm sorry, sir. Got to stop listening to crazy people.'

'No need to apologise. You're only looking out for your brothers, including myself. It's been a long campaign – only natural some doubts would start to creep in. As you said, sometimes you need to take a breath and look around to see what's important. And, as always, look to God for support and guidance.'

CHAPTER 24

Steiner had transferred Walker to Akrotiri Air Base to complete his convalescence. He had spent the intervening six days following the same routine: 10K run, breakfast, gym session, lunch, shooting range, R&R. Although, with a comms lockdown in place, there were limited options for recreation. For the most part it involved watching vid-casts in a pastel-painted day room. The furniture seemed deliberately designed to be just the wrong side of comfortable. Not that any of the ground crew or drone pilots seemed inclined to linger once they spotted the red cross pattée on Walker's uniform, or maybe it was the brooding expression he now permanently wore. Either way, it suited him, which was why he turned irritably at the sound of the door opening to look at the intruder. The neat haircut, stony expression and designer black suit/ear-piece combination were unmistakeable. What was less clear was why the spook had come calling.

'Do I know you?'

'Operations Officer Matthew Hannah.'

Hannah thrust out his hand and, after a moment's hesitation, Walker shook it.

'What can I do for you, Agent Hannah?'

'More a case of what I can do for you.'

'Which is?'

'Get you re-assigned to combat. That's what you want, right? Get back out there and show Abdul how it's done?'

'This a service you offer to all the convalescents?'

'Just the ones I deem useful. Quid pro quo is the way of the world.'

'So you're a manipulative prick who uses people's weaknesses to bend them to his will?'

'I prefer to think of myself as a facilitator. I match certain skill sets to opportunities, enabling those individuals to serve the greater good.'

'And what exactly has Doctor Steiner told you that makes you think my skill set is any different from the fifty-three other men who graduated from my intake?'

'You're a believer. Not just in God, but in the mission itself: protect America from her enemies, whatever the cost. A man such as yourself understands that in order to do that, sometimes you have to ignore conventions, rules of law and due process. In short, you're someone who can be relied on to get the job done. No questions asked.'

'Even supposing I agree with your assessment, in case you hadn't noticed, the war is wrapping up. Hamilton wants the troops back home by Christmas.'

Hannah snorted. 'Our new president might not be aware of it yet, but he'll be supporting ongoing operations in Jordan and Syria. That's how the system works. How it always has. Believe me when I say this war is far from over.'

'So what happens next if I agree to sign up?'

'Doctor Steiner will sign off your discharge papers, allowing you to return to active service in Israel. Once Jerusalem is secured, you'll be transferred to Langley for your induction and further training.' Hannah held out his hand. 'Do we have a deal?'

Walker regarded the proffered hand: clean with neatly trimmed nails; no scales, talons or other signs of the Devil. But appearances could be deceptive. He shook it anyway.

Katz had been shadowing the snatch squad for over an hour. Watching them as they crept along the Templar lines, seeking an unwary sentry to capture. Tonight offered slim pickings. The Templars' previous losses had made them wary and the sentries now conducted picket duty in pairs. Three men on two were odds the Caliphate soldiers weren't comfortable with, particularly when the success of their mission relied on silence. Katz, by contrast, found the odds more than favourable.

He waited for the squad to abandon their mission and take shelter in the lee of a rocky outcrop before making his move. The silenced Tavor X99-L coughed twice, dropping two of the men. The third wheeled about wildly, seeking his enemy. Katz stepped in behind him, immobilising his arms while tightening his own forearm across the soldier's windpipe, cutting off any cries of alarm. The Israeli increased the pressure, choking off the supply of air and rendering his opponent limp. As he lowered the unconscious figure to the ground he twisted its head sharply, snapping the neck.

Katz worked methodically, stripping clothes and equipment from the bodies until he had a complete uniform of reasonable fit. He hid the corpses in a shallow depression and covered them with branches from the scrubby acacia trees that lined the ridgeline. By the time the squad's commander reported them missing he would be at his objective. The Russian-manufactured Groza was an ugly-looking and inferior weapon, but if things went wrong even his trusty Tavor wouldn't save him.

Katz picked his way across the plateau, avoiding the ridgelines and taking cover whenever the moonlight filtered its way through the scudding clouds. He climbed the hill, rising up the flank of the cemetery until he reached a certain mausoleum. It took him a few moments to locate the concealed entry plate, which he opened using the tip of his knife. He pressed his palm against the plate and a section of wall slid back to reveal a narrow staircase. Overhead lights fluoresced to life as Katz entered. The stairway descended for ten metres before opening into a small chamber furnished with a desk, on top of which Katz had earlier stored his datapad. He flipped open the pad and logged into an Israeli spy satellite in orbit over Jerusalem. Having zoomed in on the former Tower of David Museum, which al-Qurayshi had converted into his headquarters, he set the satellite to quartering the city and initiated facial recognition software.

Ten minutes passed before a positive ID picked up al-Qurayshi exiting the tower. He stood in conversation with two of his bodyguards for a few seconds before starting to walk north on the Armenian Patriarchate. The men fell in three paces behind the caliph who, judging from the time and direction, was heading for *Isha*, evening prayer at the Al-Aqsa Mosque.

Katz closed the connection and flipped the datapad shut. He pulled the desk away from the wall and accessed another panel, giving him entry to one of the secret escape tunnels that ran between the cemetery and Jerusalem. He regretted revealing the existence of these bunkers to the Americans, but with no means of slipping away from them he'd had no choice but to lead them to safety. The mission came first. Always the mission.

Katz checked the Groza's action and descended into the tunnel. Once again, firefly globes in the ceiling led the way as he descended deep below the city. The tunnel opened onto a short platform with a waiting bullet capsule. Katz lifted the canopy, climbed inside and strapped himself in. The dash readouts were green: primed and ready to launch. He sealed the canopy and pressed the start button. The acceleration pressed him back into the couch as the maglev capsule accelerated towards 500 kph before slowing down almost immediately, relying on residual speed to complete its journey in under two minutes.

Katz exited the capsule next to a shaft fitted with a series of vertical steel rungs leading up to the surface. He climbed methodically, maintaining three points of contact at all times, concentrating on his breathing. The slow, even breaths triggered pre-conditioning, heightening his senses and stilling his mind, a technique taught to him during his Kidon service: the killing trance.

Wedging himself in the shaft, he extracted a fibre-optic camera from one of his vest pouches, attached it to his com-unit, and fed it through one of the manhole cover's lifting holes. He rotated the camera 360 degrees, taking in the full sweep of the Western Wall Plaza and confirming it was empty before lifting the cover.

Katz adjusted his night-vision goggles and orientated himself towards the Mughrabi Gate. He climbed the steps and crossed the wooden bridge leading to the Temple Mount, where he took shelter in a stand of trees adjacent to the mosque. Scanning the grounds through his rifle scope, his eye came to rest on the Ablution Gate. Set mid-way long the western edge of the Mount, it offered the most direct access to al-Kas, the main ablution fountain, situated between the mosque and the Dome of the Rock. Here, al-Qurayshi would perform the ritual washing of his hands, arms, legs, feet and face before entering the mosque.

Katz's patience was rewarded less than five minutes later when his target entered through the gate. He motioned for his guards to remain outside and crossed to the fountain. Al-Qurayshi took his time washing in spite of the cold night air, completing the *wudu* ritual according to long-practised motions. Ablutions performed, he walked towards the central archway of the mosque's ornately carved façade.

Katz had the shot but it felt too impersonal. Abu Ahmad al-Nasr al-Qurayshi, fifth caliph of the Islamic Caliphate, was an enemy who deserved to look upon his killer as he met his fate. He unsheathed his Ari B'Lilah, the aptly named lion of night. For the lion was the symbol of Judah and Jerusalem, and tonight the lion would roar as Israel took her long-sought revenge.

The Israeli gave al-Qurayshi a couple of minutes to settle himself at prayer before entering the mosque. As a holy building, Katz could not deny the beauty of the mosque, with its series of heavy pillars supporting arches inlaid with geometric designs, the stained glass decorating the ceiling, and the great, hanging chandeliers, in the warm glow of which he now walked towards his target.

Katz found Al-Qurayshi kneeling in the central aisle of the nave in front of the semi-circular niche of the *mihrab*, facing Mecca while praying. He slipped around the side of one of the white marble columns, intending to strike down his enemy as he passed by, on completion of his prayers. The Ari B'Lilah was a comforting weight in his hand, an extension of his body. He wondered if al-Qurayshi's prayers would be different if he knew he had but minutes to live.

Katz froze as he felt the cold steel of a gun barrel press against the base of his neck.

'Easy, my friend,' a voice warned him. 'I do not wish to disturb the caliph at his prayers.' The pressure of the pistol on Katz's neck remained steady as his captor took the Ari B'Lilah and Groza from the Israeli. 'Come, let us finish our conversation outside, where we will not violate the sanctity of this most holy of places.'

His unseen abductor marched Katz ahead of him at arm's-length, allowing him no opportunity to manoeuvre. Katz wondered how long he had been following. Had he missed his opportunity by not taking the shot when he had the chance, or merely postponed the inevitable bullet in the back of the head? The hand on his shoulder spun him around and Katz recognised Mohamed al-Hashimi, Commander of the Jerusalem Guard.

Al-Hashimi stepped back, increasing the distance between himself and his prisoner.

'Seren Elad Katz, formerly of the IDF Special Forces Unit 212. Now known to be an operative of Mossad's assassination department, Kidon. Don't look so surprised,

Captain; we have been aware of your presence with the American forces for quite some time. Our satellites may not be as advanced as your own, but they do their job well enough.'

'Have you been tracking me all this time?'

'More from curiosity than necessity. We've had a quarter of a century to explore this city, during which we found all of the Knesset tunnels. A few simple seismic sensors were all we needed to detect their use. We thought you might utilise them to lead a strike force into the city, but we forgot how little you trust even your allies. It matters not. The tip of the spear has been truly blunted.'

'And now I'm to be executed as a spy?'

Al-Hashimi motioned up and down Katz's body with his free hand. 'You are wearing a Caliphate uniform behind enemy lines. For what it's worth, one soldier to another, I bear you no ill will, even though I judge your actions cowardly and dishonourable. But we each discharge our duties in accordance with our faith. I must kill you, even though I know it will make no difference in the end. This city will fall into the hands of the Americans and be returned to the Jewish people.'

'Can you return something that is rightfully ours?'

'Ownership is a matter of perspective. This land, even this city, has changed hands many times over thousands of years. The Babylonians drove your people out, as did the Romans, bringing another long exile for your people. And yet our two faiths have not always been at odds. It was Caliph Umar ibn al-Khattab, after its conquest, who allowed the Jews to return to and live and worship in the city for the first time in four hundred years. You would also be wise to remember that when the first Crusaders captured the city, they put most of the Muslim and Jewish inhabitants to the sword.'

'I know the history of my city. We have been driven out many times, but we always return.'

'My point is, for how long? The city has been captured

and recaptured forty-five times throughout its history. It must be obvious to you that the Americans will only help maintain your borders for as long as it remains politically to their advantage. If history has taught us anything, it is that this land is destined to be continually fought over. And yet somehow the city endures. But for you, my friend, the end is here.'

Al-Hashimi had reached first pressure on the trigger when the whine of an incoming drone made him look up. 'It would appear the Americans have taken matters into their own hands.' His eyes widened as a pair of missiles streaked toward the mosque. 'No, they would not dare!'

The explosion threw both men to the ground amid a rain of rubble. Neither witnessed the slow collapse of the lead dome into the smoking ruins.

CHAPTER 25

Rivera lowered the IHADSS and commenced the pre-flight checks on her console. Behind and to her right, her two wingmen were also readying their aircraft, the UAS pod at full capacity. A member of the support crew motioned towards the door and Rivera gave him the thumbs-up, signalling that he could close the hatch. The door shut with a clang and Rivera felt the air-con rise a notch as the lights dimmed, triggering the console backlighting. All systems good to go.

Checks complete, she focused on her screens, where a member of the ground crew was directing her out onto the flight deck. She taxied the Hellcat forward and took up position. Her wingmen fell in line behind, ready to fly the first sortie of the day. With the Caliphate on the ropes, they were pressing them hard in preparation for storming the city. Rivera pulled back on the joystick and the power readings jumped as the engines throttled up. The ground controller waved her Hellcat forward with his paddle and she let the jet lift off. The plane climbed high above the Mediterranean with the two wingmen hot on its tail. She banked through a playful roll before heading inland.

Most of the anti-aircraft guns had been destroyed during

the previous raid and flak was minimal as Rivera zeroed in on her target: a squat concrete pillbox guarding one of the main approaches to the city. At a klick out she released the first of her missiles, a fire-and-forget variant using radar-seeking to home in on its target. Banking hard left, she came in on the next of her targets, a line of concrete tank traps, the pillbox exploding behind her as she released the next of her missiles.

Rivera pulled up and circled round, noting the series of explosions on the ground as her wingmen also hit their assigned targets. It almost felt too easy. Her console beeped as it received data from the spy-sats: the pillbox required a second strike. She panned round her cams as she turned in for a second run. Tracer fire arced above the Hellcat's canopy from one of the few surviving heavy machine gun emplacements, and then she was past and clear to fire. Still, she didn't like loose ends.

'Eagle Two, this is Eagle Leader. Scratch that gunner.'

'Confirmed, Eagle Leader.'

She closed to half a klick before launching, hauling back hard on the joystick and looping the Hellcat away from the explosion. As Rivera evened out, cannon fire cut across the rear of the plane and she threw it into another roll, causing the enemy fighter to overshoot. Now that it no longer had the sun behind it, she recognised the plane as a Chinese-manufactured Shenyang interceptor. The Caliphate had finally got some birds in the air. Not that those museum pieces, with actual pilots onboard, would do them much good.

The pilot, realising his error, attempted to bank to safety but turned instead into a hail of fire, Rivera having anticipated the move. Smoke and flames billowed from the port engine as the Shenyang plummeted towards the earth, the ejector seat launching the pilot free. Rivera let him go, judging the threat neutralised. She already had a fresh target in her sights as a second Shenyang dived out of the sun. Give them their due, these Caliphate flyboys had balls. But that wouldn't make them any less dead at the end of the day.

Rivera flipped the left aileron down and the right one up, making the Hellcat roll to the left and causing a volley of 30mm cannon shells to pass below the left wing. Undeterred, the Shenyang continued straight on, forcing Rivera to climb out of the way. As she evened out, the Caliphate pilot was already turning to follow her. Rivera looked out of her canopy and spotted Eagle Two at three o'clock.

'Eagle Two, I could use a little help here.'

'On it, Eagle Leader. Fox two.'

Rivera forced the Hellcat into a dive in response to the code word; Eagle Two had just launched an infrared-guided missile. She accelerated towards the ground, putting as much clear sky between herself and the Shenyang and the incoming Sidewinder as she could. The explosion above her was a secondary concern as warning lights flashed and the ground sped up to meet the Hellcat. She hauled back on the joystick, almost standing the aircraft on its tail before it started to climb again.

Rivera congratulated her wingman. 'Looks like you've got yourself another confirmed kill, Dugan.'

'Like shooting fish in a barrel. Only not as sporting.'

'I'll have a word with Colonel Tyler, see if he can find you a war more to your liking. Okay, boys. Close up. We still haven't got our quota for the day.'

Three attack runs later, she was out of missiles and turning for the aircraft carrier. The wingmen fell in behind, leaving a landscape pockmarked with burning craters. Turnaround for refuelling and rearming would be forty minutes; then the fighters would be back in the air, methodically working their way around the city, bombing the Caliphate back to the stone age.

Rivera dropped the plane on deck and hit the brakes as it slewed into the kinetic webbing. With the Hellcat at a standstill, the webbing drew back into the deck as a turntable rotated the plane. Inside the UAS pod Rivera removed her IHADSS and stretched. She had time to visit the head and grab a coffee before the next sortie. It was going to be a long day.

Tyler watched the symbol for Al-Aqsa Mosque blink out on the holo-display. The drone strike against al-Qurayshi was the herald of the wider aerial bombardment of the city. He tracked the progress of the incoming F-27 Hellcats on one screen, marrying up their missiles with the targets on a pair of secondary displays. One by one he watched the tank traps, pillboxes and machine gun posts blink out, while listening to the whoops of excited drone operators on the radio. He pulled up a fourth display, a live satellite feed, and checked off each of the targets in turn. Where the destruction wasn't complete, he ordered a second attack run. Scorched earth. Nothing that might oppose the Templar forces was to be left standing.

Multiple sorties over a three-day period reduced the outskirts and surrounding lands of Jerusalem to a lunar landscape, the likes of which had not been seen since the First World War. The lulls were deliberate; an enticement to identify where the Caliphate forces would attempt to re-entrench, to further deplete the forces that emerged from hidden underground bunkers, along with the ragtag dribble of weary volunteers sent from the city to reinforce the siege line. Tyler felt neither remorse nor pity as the piles of corpses mounted, bodies bloating in the midday sun. Grand Master Vanderbilt had tasked him to recapture the city, and if that meant exterminating every last Muslim within its boundaries, he would not flinch from his duty. Besides, it was good press.

The Templars and their allies assembled in the pre-dawn light of the fourth morning. Tyler, having transferred his command centre to his personal AMPV, led the initial strike force, comprising the First Templar Division's Combat Aviation Brigade and fifteen hundred members of the Israel Defense Forces, led by his Israeli counterpart, Aluf mishne Shimon Baruch.

General Volotsky's face appeared on Tyler's com-screen in a crackle of static and in defiance of the comms blackout. The Russian commander raised his assault rifle in the air and fired a volley. At this signal the Russian armour ground forward through the eastern fringes of the city.

'Damn that Russian madman!'

Tyler had no choice but to issue his own command to attack. M3A2 Abrams tanks led the assault, rolling forward in front of the JLTVs carrying the Templar and IDF troops. The tanks' CROWS III systems automatically acquired targets on-the-move and launched first-burst engagements. Tyler watched on his displays as they drove the enemy before them. He noted that the majority of the Caliphate troops were not in uniform and identified a number of women among them. Volunteers, fanatics, who had refused the civilian evacuation. Soft targets designed to lull them into a false sense of security. Al-Hashimi was no fool; he would have stationed the seasoned troops, together with the Jerusalem Guard, in the centre of the city. That was where the fiercest fighting would take place.

Lynch cursed behind Tyler. Sobriety had not improved the journalist's demeanour, but at least he wasn't trying to kill him.

'Quit grousing, Lynch. You'll get your fifteen minutes soon enough.'

'Don't you mean *your* fifteen minutes?'

Tyler ignored him, concentrating on the readouts in front of him. Once the tanks were in position, cutting off all avenues of retreat, it would be time to deploy the troops. Military Operations in Urban Terrain; this was where the casualties would rack up. Every doorway and window a potential field of fire, and each building a source of booby traps. With no means of retreat, the Caliphate forces would sell their lives as dearly as possible, each believing their martyr's death would assure them a place in Paradise. Easy to dismiss them as fanatics, but wasn't it merely a variation on a theme? Hadn't the Pope informed his own troops that God would forgive all their sins in return for their service in this holy war? The soldiers of both sides relied on promises of pie in the sky, but Tyler was determined to get his reward in the here and now. He gave the order for the troops to disembark.

'Okay, Lynch, you're up.'

'Fuck you! I'm done filming this horror show.'

Tyler drew his pistol. 'I'm going to make this real simple. Either you get out there, get those drones in the sky and start filming, or I put a bullet in your head. Martinez, keep an eye on our friend here. He steps out of line, you put him down.'

Martinez opened the hatch and thrust Lynch out in front of him. The journalist landed on his hands and knees and it took a boot up his ass to spur him to his feet. Tyler watched him out of the corner of his eye as he synched the camera drones to his HUD display and launched them into the air. They hovered malignantly overhead for a few seconds before buzzing off in pursuit of the Templar fireteam assigned to Tyler's command.

Tyler patched his own HUD into the fire control system and took a virtual tour of the city. He took in a series of skirmishes as the Templars cleared the street house by house, resistance remaining light as they travelled almost due east. A couple of klicks to the northeast the IDF forces were blazing a rapid trail, their tactics and movements marking them as augments; the beneficiaries of cyber implants and nanotech. As cutting edge as the tech coming out of the North African manufactories was, the Israelis were at least one, if not two, generations ahead. They had clearly learned the lessons of Europa City's aborted Delta troop programme and improved autonomy while increasing speed, endurance, accuracy and reaction times. He had lobbied through Hopkins for augments of their own but the Senate had refused to pass the budget. He hit record, gathering evidence for such a time as he was able to bring the proposal back before the House.

Time to see what his own boys were up to.

CHAPTER 26

Cooper, along with Jackson, Walker and Mackinlay, formed a line on the street corner. The movement flowed smoothly: Jackson stepped out, covering the street at the same time as Mackinlay pivoted to guard the rear, allowing Walker and himself to cross to the opposite side of the street. No danger being present, Jackson turned the corner while Mackinlay backed his way round to join him. Cooper watched Walker's six as he ran on ahead, the game of leapfrog ensuring the squad maintained a 360-degree field of fire.

A volley of shots rang out, scattering the fireteam. Cooper hunkered down and patched into Lynch's feed, getting an aerial view of the action. Mackinlay was down, Jackson crouching over him, while Tyler and Martinez directed fire at an adjacent shop front. Smoke billowed from the shattered glass, making it impossible to confirm how many enemy targets they were engaged with. Cooper felt Walker's hand on his arm as he made to rise.

'The sarge has got this. You stick your head up, Abdul will blow it off.'

Cooper shook Walker's hand off. He was right, but that didn't make it sit any better with him, not after Mackinlay had risked his own life to rescue Walker. But something had been off with Walker since he reported back for duty, his manner colder and more aloof than before.

Tyler's voice sounded over the comms, ordering a kill-sat strike on the shop. The Templars took cover as a missile streaked from the heavens and detonated on impact.

Lynch caught Tyler's arm as he attempted to move forward. 'Guess we're not worrying about civilians any more?'

'There are no civilians. We let the Caliphate evacuate them all. Remember?'

Tyler shook Lynch off and pressed on, leaving the journalist and Martinez to catch up as he pulled ahead of the fireteam.

Cooper looked down at Jackson, still kneeling with his hands pressed to Mackinlay's neck. The blood had reduced from a spray to a trickle, the colour and quantity indicative of an arterial wound. Jackson shook his head in response to Cooper's questioning look and lifted his bloody hands clear of the body. The sergeant removed Mackinlay's dog tags and tucked them into one of his belt pouches. Unlucky, the bullet catching him above the vest like that.

Cooper tried not to think about Mackinlay as he moved off, aware of their exposure on the long, open street. Time enough to mourn him later, if he survived. He patched into another feed and yanked his earpiece out in response to the sudden burst of explosions and machine gun fire. He muted the sound on the channel and screwed the earpiece back in. The Russians were closing rapidly on the Temple Mount from the north, their tanks rolling across any and all opposition, infantry following in their wake. Cooper watched as the soldiers quartered the ruins, dragging out visibly shellshocked and unarmed survivors and executing them with bayonets and pistols. They clearly wanted revenge for the chemical attack and, as such, there would be no reasoning with them. He looked to Tyler and the sarge, but both appeared indifferent to the slaughter.

The sound of the Russian tanks grew louder as the Templars closed in on the Western Wall, the rattle of weapon exchanges increasingly one-sided. Cooper felt the oppressive atmosphere of the Old City as they navigated its narrow stone streets. Evidence of the IDF's passage before the Templars stared back at him from every arch and vault, the hastily erected barricades littered with the bodies of Caliphate soldiers. They checked each corpse, fearful of leaving an enemy at their back, and found only the pinpoint accuracy of the small-arms fire that had dispatched them and the occasional slit throat. Throughout it all, the bat-like drones flitted high and low, streaming a succession of corpses. Cooper looked at Lynch: the journalist's expression was numb, his actions automatic. He wondered if the war had finally broken him. Cooper felt near his own limits.

Ahead, the gunfire tailed off and an ominous silence fell. Cooper led the fireteam forward to where a squad of Russian troops stood guard over the shattered remains of a shop front. Screams sounded from inside – high-pitched, female – followed by coarse laughter. A couple of seconds later, two Russian soldiers emerged carrying a struggling woman between them. Her trousers were about her ankles and her tunic torn open to expose her breasts, her nose and mouth bloody from repeated blows. One of the men called out something in Russian and the men formed a queue, with the exception of the sergeant. He held his weapon casually, but Cooper noted it pointed in their direction. The Russian sergeant's eyes remained fixed on the Templars as the first of the men took his turn.

Cooper looked around the squad in search of support. The men, with the exception of Colonel Tyler, refused to meet his gaze. 'Tell me we're not just going to stand by and watch these animals?'

'No,' Tyler replied, 'we're moving out. The mission objective is still ahead of us.'

'They're raping her!'

'Then they'll kill her, and there will be one less Caliphate fanatic in the world. I said move out. That's an order.'

Cooper held his ground for a few seconds and then the discipline instilled in him by his training took over. Walker, Jackson and Martinez followed him. Tyler turned to find Lynch still staring at the rape, the drones hovering above as they broadcast it to the world. He caught hold of one of his MOLLE straps and dragged him away.

'Save your pity for the living.'

'She sounds goddamn alive to me!'

'You're mistaken. That woman was dead long before we arrived. She just hadn't stopped moving.'

Cooper moved on in sullen silence, the woman's cries fading into the distance. They were supposed to be fighting for freedom and democracy, for Christian values, and yet it seemed the war had stripped them of the better part of their humanity. The Templars might not personally be executing the wounded and raping survivors, but the act of walking by surely made them complicit. Was he the only one who saw that?

Jackson nudged him with his elbow, ending his reverie as they finally caught up with the Israelis at the entrance to the Western Wall Plaza. A circle of Jerusalem Guards stood waiting behind the barricade of burnt-out vehicles and mattresses they had erected, closing off the plaza. History, it seemed, was about to repeat itself, with the roles reversed. Only this time there would be no final airlift for the wounded.

Shimon Baruch, the IDF commander, was supervising the laying of charges along the barricade. Cooper had expected to find Katz here as well, but saw no sign of their advisor. Was he dead, or engaged in whatever his true mission was?

'Colonel Tyler, you and your men have arrived at a most propitious moment – the end of the Islamic Caliphate's occupation of Jerusalem.'

'Do you want my men to join you for the final assault, or are we going to deploy the Wrath of God?'

'We are indeed, Colonel. Enough Jewish and Christian blood has been spilled this day.' Baruch flipped open his com-unit. 'Zion One, you are clear to commence firing. Repeat, you are clear to fire.'

Cooper looked up and saw the flash in the sky as the first of the missiles streaked towards the plaza.

Baruch, noting Cooper's apprehension, smiled at him.

'Don't worry, we are quite safe.'

Cooper counted three separate strikes, less than a second apart. At first, he thought they were duds, as the impacts did little more than throw up chunks of stone and earth. The Jerusalem Guard appeared to think the same, the men gesturing defiantly with their rifles. Then Cooper spotted what looked like smoke or mist rising from the craters. It swirled upward, growing in density and moving towards the circle of defenders with the intelligence of a swarm. Then the screaming started. Cooper stood frozen as he watched it strip the flesh from the Caliphate soldiers, the swirling tendrils changing from grey to dark crimson. The men clawed at their own flesh and beat at their clothes, but this only seemed to speed up the process. Cooper's stomach gave a lurch and bile splattered onto the ground next to his feet. He saw Lynch being similarly sick, but the drones remained trained on the Jerusalem Guards' agonising deaths. The cloud had stripped them to the bone, which meant the screaming had stopped, although the silence added to the horror of the spectacle, with even the skeletons slowly dissolving into grey slime.

Baruch's attention remained fixed on the screen of his com-unit throughout the grim spectacle, analysing reams of data.

'What the hell have we just seen?' Cooper demanded.

'A targeted nano-virus. Genetically encoded, limited to a ten-metre radius, and designed to consume itself.' He glanced at his screen. 'One hundred per cent mortality achieved in fifty-three seconds. A most effective demonstration. Wouldn't you agree, Colonel Tyler?'

'Indeed. With such a weapon at your disposal Israel's borders will remain secure.'

The Israelis and the Templars fell back to the street while Baruch supervised the demolition of the barricade, shaped charges blowing it into the plaza. Cooper's stomach threatened to turn again as he walked past the burning wreckage and saw what remained of the Caliphate soldiers. He stopped to pick up a scarlet epaulette that had become detached from a slime-soaked uniform. His fingers brushed the gold braid and captain's pips; so much for the feared fanatics of the Caliphate's Jerusalem Guard.

'A trophy?'

'No.' Cooper dropped the epaulette and wiped his fingers on his trousers. 'Just curious.' His gaze drifted up towards the Temple Mount, where the end of the mission awaited him. He left the Israelis to their victory.

Lynch circled the drones over the ruins of Al-Aqsa Mosque. The south wall stood strangely unaffected, but the dome and the façade and porchway had collapsed into the building, the stumps of its marble pillars reaching imploringly to the sky amid fragments of stone and stained glass.

'What have we done? Even the Crusaders of old left the mosque intact.'

'Yeah?' Tyler sneered. 'Guess those old-time Europeans were weak.'

'Colonel!'

Jackson's shout drew their attention to the fringes of the devastation, where he and Walker were sifting through the rubble. They pulled the corpse clear and turned it over. Katz's sightless eyes stared up them.

Cooper shook his head. 'Why's he in a Caliphate uniform?'

'Because he's a damn Israeli spook, that's why.'

Lynch squatted down beside the corpse. He closed Katz's eyes and folded his arms across his chest. He began to speak, quietly at first, his voice rising as he gained confidence.

'Exalted and hallowed be His great Name.

'In the world which He will create anew, where He will revive the dead, construct His temple, deliver life, and rebuild the city of Jerusalem, and uproot foreign idol worship from His land, and restore the holy service of Heaven to its place, along with His radiance, splendour and Shechinah, and may He bring forth His redemption and hasten the coming of His Moshiach.

'In your lifetime and in your days and in the lifetime of the entire House of Israel, sword, famine and death shall cease from us and from the entire Jewish nation, speedily and soon, and say, Amen.'

'Didn't take you for one of *them*, Lynch,' Tyler sneered.

'On my father's side of the family, which apparently doesn't count. But it seemed the right thing to do. Didn't we come here to get this poor bastard's country back? At least, I think that's the mission. Maybe we should ask Baruch?'

'Got another one here, Colonel. And he's breathing!'

Tyler took off his bandana and soaked it in water from his canteen. While Martinez held the unconscious man upright, he wiped away the blood and dust from his face to reveal a familiar set of features.

'Lookee here. We're in luck, boys. We got ourselves our number two priority target, Mohamed al-Hashimi, Commander of the Jerusalem Guard. Martinez, Walker, get this piece of shit on his feet.'

As the Templars held him upright, Tyler slapped al-Hashimi on either cheek, provoking a groan and a flutter of eyelids. Tyler slapped him again and again, rocking his head back and forth.

'Sir.' Cooper pointed at the hovering drones. 'The world's watching. Al-Hashimi is an enemy prisoner of war.'

'What he is, Cooper, is a terrorist and a war criminal.' Tyler turned. 'Lynch, make sure you capture this for the folks back home.'

Lynch shook his head and called the drones back to their docking station. 'Do what you want to me, but I'm done. I've fed the world enough of this shitshow to last a lifetime.'

Tyler drew his pistol and pointed it at Lynch.

'When are you going to get it through that thick redneck skull of yours that you're done when I say you're done? Start broadcasting or, as God is my witness, I will put a bullet between your eyes.'

Lynch folded his arms across his chest. 'No.'

Tyler's jaw clenched as his finger tightened on the trigger. At the last moment he pointed the Sig Sauer at the ground and the bullet kicked up a cloud of dirt at Lynch's feet. He levelled the pistol.

'Last time of asking.'

Cooper darted forward and stepped in front of Lynch.

'Whoa, let's all calm down.'

'I am calm, son. Now step aside. I've had all the insubordination I'm going to take for one day.'

As Cooper hesitated, Jackson reached forward and took the drone remote from Lynch's belt. Lynch stiffened for a second and then the fight went out of him. He shook his head in disgust, removed his HUD display and handed it to the sergeant.

Jackson settled the wrap-around glasses on his head and activated the remote. The drones rose uncertainly from the docking station as Jackson familiarised himself with the controls, initially overcompensating on the joystick.

'Damn, this isn't as easy as it looks. Can see why you use that neuro-link.'

'I'm sure the viewers back home won't mind some shaky handheld cams,' Lynch replied, his voice laden with sarcasm.

The sergeant brought the drones in tight as Tyler emptied the contents of his canteen over al-Hashimi's head. The Caliphate commander snorted and coughed and threw back his head, his eyes suddenly wide open.

'Welcome back to the waking world, Commander.'

Al-Hashimi looked around, taking in the soldiers that held him captive, the ruins of the mosque, and the dead-eyed stare of the Templar officer in front of him.

'I had hoped our roles might be reversed when we finally met, Colonel Tyler. *C'est la guerre.*'

'Your caliph is dead,' Tyler said, looking in the direction of the ruined mosque, 'and whatever remains of your men are surrounded, with no means of escape. In such a situation there's no dishonour in surrendering. Give the order and I give you my word your men will be spared.'

'Spared the death of martyrs in exchange for lingering death in a concentration camp? I do not think so.'

'Had a feeling you'd see it that way.' Tyler patched into his comms and issued a channel-wide order: 'All units, I want the city secured by nightfall. Liquidate all surviving Caliphate soldiers. No quarter. No mercy.' He smiled coldly. 'Back to the business at hand.'

Tyler nodded and Martinez and Walker hauled al-Hashimi forward and secured his wrists behind his back with plastic ties.

'Commander Mohamed al-Hashimi, I'm arresting you for war crimes committed against the state of Israel and the people of the Religious States of America.'

'And will I be tried by a jury of my peers?'

'Consider yourself fortunate you're getting any kind of trial. If the roles were reversed, you'd be hacking my head off during a live vid-cast. Take him away.'

Cooper fell in step with Jackson as Walker and Martinez marched al-Hashimi back towards the plaza. Lynch sat slumped in the ruins of the mosque, looking into the middle distance. Cooper let his hand drop onto his shoulder as he walked by. The journalist looked up and nodded, eyes bleak and empty.

They wound their way back through the rubble-strewn streets of the Old Town, making for the Chain Gate Hotel, where MPs would detain al-Hashimi prior to his rendition. Cooper felt the hostile glances of both Russian and Israeli troops as the prisoner passed through their ranks. Ahead, there was some kind of disturbance. Cooper tightened his grip on his rifle as they approached a line of Russian troops who had formed a cordon across the street. He thought they meant to block the prisoner escort, but realised they were facing the opposite direction, holding back a line of civilians. The men and women were pitiably thin: arms and legs like sticks, eyes huge and sunken in sockets. They wore ragged grey jumpsuits, covered head to toe in dirt and filth. A susurration rose from the crowd as they recognised al-Hashimi, which swiftly grew to a hate-filled roar as they stabbed accusatory fingers towards the Caliphate commander.

Cooper stared, dumbfounded. 'I thought all the civilians were evacuated?'

One of the Russians, his head cocked as he translated the Arabic, said, 'These men and women are political prisoners. We found them in the cellars below. They have been beaten, starved, kept as slaves. They demand justice.'

Tyler spoke to the Russian: 'Tell them this man is my prisoner. We're taking him to America to stand trial for his crimes. They will have justice.'

Before the Russian could translate, another angry roar went up from the crowd, indicating that some, at least, understood English.

One of the living cadavers raised his fist in defiance. Clumps of long hair dotted his scalp and face, and when he opened his mouth to speak his gums were black.

'We don't want justice on a screen. Images can be faked.' He raised his right hand, showing the ragged stumps where his pinkie and ring fingers had been. 'We want justice we can touch.'

'Move aside. We won't ask twice.'

An ominous silence fell as the crowd shuffled back. Cooper did the maths: five Templars and eight Russians; an unlucky number. Their movements made them hard to count accurately, but he estimated at least forty civilians.

These people had been through hell. Surely they wouldn't open fire on them? Images of the dead children on the bus flashed before his eyes and his stomach retched in dry heaves, its contents long since emptied.

Cooper looked at Colonel Tyler, noting how his hand rested on top of his holstered pistol. What that hand did or didn't do would decide their fate. Cooper willed the hand to move. Tyler was no fool. He recognised a zero-sum game when he saw it, particularly one with no political advantage.

Tyler turned from the crowd to face al-Hashimi.

'Guess you're getting a trial by your peers after all.'

Al-Hashimi's eyes went wide.

'What? No! I had nothing to do with what happened to these people. That was the Hisbah police. The military weren't involved.'

'But you knew about it and did nothing?'

Receiving no reply, Tyler gave the signal to fall back and the Templars and Russians retreated along the street, leaving al-Hashimi standing alone. Realising his fate was sealed, he straightened his back and faced the crowd. Long moments passed and then the first stone struck al-Hashimi on the shoulder. He turned with the blow, uttered a low grunt and straightened himself, the challenge unmistakeable. The fierceness of his gaze held them at bay for a few seconds longer and then a volley of stones flew at him. One struck his right temple, dropping him to his left knee. He swayed uncertainly before collapsing to the ground as the other stones hit.

Cooper made to start forward, but Jackson held him in check as a fresh salvo of stones rained down on the prone figure. Finally, the man who had addressed Tyler staggered forward, cradling a block of masonry in his mutilated hands. Cooper turned away as he dropped it on al-Hashimi's head, but he still heard the sickening crack of bone. He turned back in time to witness several of the men urinating on the corpse, the steaming pools mingling with the blood on the street.

Walker was the first to break the silence, reciting in a flat monotone, 'And if it is true and certain that such an abomination has been done in Israel, then you shall bring out to your gates that man or woman who has done this evil thing, and you shall stone that man or woman to death with stones.'

Tyler nodded. 'Reckon justice has been done according to the Good Book. Move out, boys.'

CHAPTER 27

Blood and brain matter froze midway across the holo-screen as Hamilton paused the video at the moment of the block's impact. Hopkins looked away, her face pale, while Gerrard stared impassively. The feed had been broadcast live less than ten minutes before and he had summoned the vice president and his press secretary straight to the Central Office. His body shook with barely restrained fury as he regarded them across the wooden expanse of his desk.

'I want that stupid bastard recalled to Richmond immediately! You hear me? On the next flight out of Jerusalem.'

'Is that wise?'

'What the fuck has wise got to do with it, Charles? The troops under Tyler's command have been exposed as killers of women and children, not to mention destroyers of historical and religious sites. Even the Israeli government in exile has voiced its disapproval.'

'To be fair,' Hopkins said, 'the majority of the atrocities were committed by our allies.'

'Don't you try to defend him as well, Susanna. He's on film ignoring the atrocities, and that's before we even get to al-Hashimi. A high-value target like that – we should have had a show trial, not a summary execution at the hands of a rabble. Then there's the drone strike on al-Qurayshi.' Hamilton glanced meaningfully in Gerrard's direction. 'It's still unclear who authorised it, but whoever it was has turned al-Qurayshi into a martyr and made suppressing the Caliphate much more difficult. Tyler is to be relieved of his command, pending a Senate inquiry. And while we're about it, have that treacherous lunatic Lynch arrested and thrown in the deepest hole you can find.'

Hopkins shifted in her seat. 'About Lynch …'

'What is the point of being president if everyone around me is going to argue with what I say?' Hamilton released an exasperated breath. 'Come on then, out with whatever it is you have to say.'

'While Lynch's broadcasts have done us no favours with the international community, they've played out well back home. Very well. His approval rating is so high he's essentially untouchable. In light of which, the wisest course of action is to spin that we're grateful for him shining a light in the darkest places. I'd go as far as to publicly thank him for his service.'

'Seriously? You expect me to reward that nut-job?'

'For now, why not? Lynch is a serial fuck-up. He'll fall out of favour with the public, and when he does, we'll be waiting. As to the other … issues. Just remember it's the victors who write history. The static we're catching from Europa City and the African Tech Corps will die down, particularly once the Israelis start to reoccupy their country. Once that happens the only thing the voters will remember is that you're the president who liberated Jerusalem.'

'That's as may be. But I can't have the face of the crusade handing over prisoners to the mob. Christ, those savages stoned him to death.'

'Yes.' Hopkins glanced meaningfully at the screen. 'You've made that rather hard to ignore.'

Hamilton swiped the screen closed with an irritated

wave of his hand. 'Point is, we're in the middle of a PR disaster here. One we've little hope of spinning thanks to Tyler broadcasting it to the world.'

'Is it a disaster?' Gerrard interrupted. 'You'd have preferred Tyler to give the order to open fire on a bunch of unarmed torture victims? Besides, al-Hashimi was dead whatever happened. Probably for the best his blood isn't on our hands. What we have is Tyler acting to preserve the lives of his men and our allies. You said it yourself, Mike: Tyler has been the face of this crusade. In the eyes of the public, he's a war hero. Do we really want to be seen punishing him for serving his country?'

Hamilton narrowed his eyes. 'No doubt you have a better suggestion?'

'By all means call a Senate inquiry, but put Grand Master Thaddeus Vanderbilt in front of it.'

Hamilton shook his head. 'I don't know. Vanderbilt has powerful friends in the Senate. He'll take being hauled up before them as an insult – to himself and to the Order.'

'Not if you compensate him for the loss of face.' Hopkins placed her hand over Hamilton's. 'Trust us on this. It's the right way to go.'

'Goes against my better judgement, but we'll do it your way.'

Hamilton locked his datapad and looked directly at Gerrard. 'Now, Susanna, if you'd like to give me and Charles the room.'

Hopkins arched an eyebrow in Gerrard's direction as she stood, to which he shrugged in response. If Hamilton caught the interaction, he gave no sign. The door of the briefing room closed with a soft click. Gerrard sat, letting the silence stretch, enjoying the younger man's growing exasperation.

'Nothing at all you want to say to me, Charles?'

'Depends what we're talking about here, Mike.'

Hamilton, finding an outlet for his frustration, jabbed a finger at Gerrard.

'Your damned insubordination is what we're talking about. A united front before the staff is one thing, but don't you dare sit there, piss in my ear and then tell me it's raining. You ordered the drone strike on al-Qurayshi.'

'I did what I had to do. Keeping your hands clean and giving you plausible deniability. You're welcome.'

'You arrogant sonofabitch!' Hamilton spat. 'Don't think I can't have you removed from office. No one is untouchable.'

'No, they're not. But I reckon it would look pretty bad for you to lose your vice president so early in your term. You need to pause and take a breath, here. I've strengthened your position, not undermined it. You're the president who took out a dangerous terrorist and liberated Jerusalem. The president who finally drove the Caliphate out of Israel and forced them into a retreat. Less than twelve months into your administration and you've already got your second term in the bag.'

'And what about the Israelis and the rest of the public condemnation? We blew up the third holiest site in Islam, for Christ's sake.'

'Ben-David will make noises in public, as is expected of him, but do you really think he gives a damn about one less mosque in Jerusalem? As to UNESCO, the average American voter has never heard of it, doesn't know what it stands for, and cares even less for its opinions. History is written by the winners.'

Hamilton leaned back in his chair and took a deep breath. Like it or not, Gerrard had presented him with a fait accompli. To do anything other than accept the victory as his own would make him appear weak and fatally compromised in the eyes of the electorate.

'This is your one and only warning, Charles. You ever go behind my back again and you're out. Regardless of the fallout. Are we clear?'

Gerrard permitted himself the ghost of a smile. 'Crystal.'

Vanderbilt deliberately angled the desk lamp to shine directly on the chair opposite his desk. A cheap power play, but intuition told him he needed every advantage he could muster. His old friend, Chester Williams, had not come calling simply to shoot the shit, whatever the now former president might claim to the contrary.

Satisfied, Vanderbilt pressed the intercom.

'Lachlan, please be so good as to show President—sorry—*Mister* Williams in.'

Vanderbilt stood as the door of his office swung inward to admit Williams. The former president squinted as Lachlan directed him to the chair in front of the desk before beating a hasty retreat.

'Sorry for keeping you waiting, Chester. Please, take a seat.'

'Payback for all the times I made you wait when I was in the hotseat?' Williams' tone was jocular but the lines of his body were stiff.

'Just some business to tidy up. The Order doesn't run itself.'

'Indeed. About that – your running of the Order. As you'll have seen, quite the mess in Jerusalem with your boy Tyler allowing a mob to execute al-Hashimi live on air. We're also experiencing pushback from Europa City and the African Tech Corps over our failure to intervene in what they view as atrocities committed against the civilian population of Jerusalem. Then there's the deployment of the nano-virus, contravening the North–West Frontier Accord. Admittedly, it was the Israelis who pushed the button, but the question is naturally being asked as to who supplied them with it. Plausible deniability will only go so far.'

'You think I should censure Colonel Tyler? Relieve him of his command?'

'Had I still been president that would certainly have been my choice. The new incumbent, I'm afraid, is otherwise minded. He feels it would play badly with the voters, given the majority see Tyler as a war hero.'

'Then al-Hashimi's execution isn't such a mess?'

'Domestically, no. But it's hurting international relations. Enough that we must be seen to take action.'

'In other words, someone must shoulder the blame. And as I am the supreme commander …'

'Thad, it's nothing personal. Look, you know how this works. The findings have already been written – lack of oversight, failure of intel, conflicting mission objectives, acting in concert to put Tyler in an invidious position. He gets exonerated, you acknowledge there are lessons to be learned, and then it's back to business as usual.'

'With my authority shredded.'

'Hardly. Dulled perhaps, but based on the remarkable way that you've transformed the Order in the time it's been under your leadership, I'm certain you'll soon put a keen edge back on it.'

'Apparently that transformation isn't remarkable enough.'

'I'm afraid that's just politics.'

'Yes. A far dirtier business than war.'

Williams ignored the barb. 'I get this isn't ideal – no one likes taking the blame for another man's mistakes. If you'd rather step down after the inquiry, I'll see you're taken care of. After all, we go way back.'

'We do, which is why I know you've already got someone in mind for my successor before mentioning my stepping down.'

'I'm that transparent, eh? Well, given his popularity with the public, and in spite of the current issues, Tyler would still seem to be the logical choice.'

'You can't be serious? He's a good enough soldier, but he's not one of us. It … no, it won't do. Won't do at all. I forbid it.'

'It's an option, is all. And it's a moot point unless you decide to step down.' Williams held up placatory hands to forestall further protest. 'Just think about it, Thad. No obligation. I can find you a quiet sinecure somewhere in the diplomatic service. Minimal effort, while you sit and count the money. We'll throw in generous stock and share options and a bonus – make it quite the golden parachute. Doesn't that seem like a just reward for your service?'

Vanderbilt thought it anything but just, but perhaps he had some future as a diplomat, for he said, 'I'll think about it and give you an answer by the end of the week.'

Some of the tension left Williams' body.

'I told them you'd understand. That you weren't one to shirk duty, no matter how onerous. Whatever you decide, I'll see to it personally that you're looked after.'

'I'm sure you will, Chester. Isn't that what friends are for? Now, if you don't mind, perhaps you can see yourself out? I'm still Grand Master and I have matters to attend to.'

Williams stood. Still not entirely at ease, he smiled and nodded before making his exit. Vanderbilt's adjutant, Lachlan, apparently responding to an invisible summons, met him at the door. He handed Williams his coat and umbrella and bade him good evening.

Vanderbilt had already dismissed Williams from his thoughts. His old college roommate would keep for another day. One where he could pay him back with interest. He picked up his com-unit and keyed the line, Apostle One Has Fallen. He hesitated briefly before hitting send. No room for sentiment at the top. He had the success and health of the entire Order to consider. Besides which, he had worked too long and too damn hard to be a patsy for someone else's errors in judgement. Was that pride again? Perhaps. But Vanderbilt tempered it with godly wrath. He would show them where the true power lay.

CHAPTER 28

Lynch had wanted to duck out of the ceremony but Tyler had insisted he film it as his final piece of coverage of the war before they shipped him home. With the end finally in sight, it didn't seem worth the argument. He synched the drones to his HUD, ignoring the foul taste in his mouth, and sent them to hover in line with the top of the two newly erected flagpoles in the centre of the Western Wall Plaza. A panning shot took in Shimon Baruch and Tyler standing next to their respective poles. As agreed, the Israeli commander took the guidelines and raised the flag of Israel to fly above the city of Jerusalem for the first time in twenty-six years. Stepping back, Baruch saluted the flag, accompanied by the assembled honour guard, and together they sang 'Hatikvah'.

Tyler took up position as the final notes of the Israeli national anthem died away. He saluted Baruch and then proceeded to raise the American flag. Bile burned in Lynch's throat as he watched the flag unfurl: a red Christian cross on a blue background with twenty-nine stars distributed between the four quarters, representing the twenty-nine states of the RSA.

Lynch kept his mouth stubbornly closed as the Templars

launched into 'God Save The Republic'. Arguably, though reduced, the flag was still a star-spangled banner, but he was glad they hadn't sullied the anthem that had accompanied the stars and stripes of the old republic by pressing it into service for the new. Not that you could lay the death of the American dream solely at the door of the RSA. In truth, it had been dead for almost a century, with the populists and xenophobes inciting hatred against the very principles on which the country had originally prospered. Who now remembered the words of 'The New Colossus'?

"Give me your tired, your poor,
Your huddled masses yearning to breathe free,
The wretched refuse of your teeming shore.
Send these, the homeless, tempest-tost to me,
I lift my lamp beside the golden door!"

Words from another age, and yet the idea, if not the reality, remained indestructible. The opportunity to start afresh and prosper in a welcoming country through hard work and diligence. Trade wars, embargoes, climate change and deindustrialisation had destroyed that hope. The few jobs that remained were poorly paid, robbing workers of the dignity of labour that paid sufficiently for them to support themselves and their families. In such straitened times it was easy to stir up fear of the other, demand the closing of borders. They had killed everything that had made America special, made it great. Yes, the dream was dead, but in mourning its passing Lynch ensured it was not forgotten.

'Ceremony's over. You can stop recording.'

Lynch directed the drones to make a final circuit around the flagpoles before recalling them to their docking station. Time to go home.

Lynch reached out and ran a hand along the side of the JLTV. Against all the odds, he had actually made it out alive and was going home. All he had to do was drive out to the airstrip and board the plane. Why, then, did he have to spoil it? He turned around and looked back toward Jerusalem, saw the ruined buildings, the dozers pushing bodies into the mass graves, and knew why. There were some things you couldn't allow to stand.

He checked the broadcast status of his implant: green for go. It had taken him weeks to hack the Black ICE without triggering the intrusion detection protocols or frying his synapses. His first instinct had been to broadcast the bus massacre footage immediately, but with the assault on Jerusalem raging, he'd decided to wait for the dust to settle, reasoning that it would have more impact in the calm that followed.

'Hell, Lynch, you've got a face that's tripping you. Thought you'd be only too glad to see the back of this shithole?'

'Walker.' Lynch greeted the Templar. 'Believe you're also heading stateside?'

'Special assignment. Say, heard you'd been nominated for a Pulitzer?'

'Yeah,' Lynch replied sourly. 'By the same media that wouldn't have pissed on me if I was on fire twelve months ago.'

'You're turning it down, then?'

'Hell no! At the end of the day, it's all part of the game.'

'And that,' Walker chuckled, 'is why I prefer being in uniform. People give me orders and I carry them out. No gameplaying or politics. Well, I better get back and finish packing. Don't want to make you late for the homecoming parade.'

Lynch watched Walker walk towards the camp, apparently without a care in the world. Just another brainwashed Templar fanatic, blind to the carnage he left in his wake while playing the game of war. But Lynch had seen the bodies: Christian, Muslim, Jew, man, woman and child. Would continue to see them whenever he shut his eyes. And what for? A city in ruins that would take decades to rebuild. A city that might well change hands again in six months' time, initiating a fresh cycle of horror.

Lynch pulled out his hip flask and unscrewed the cap. He looked up at the sky and then upended the flask, allowing its contents to trickle out.

'Here's to us. Who's like us? Damn few, and they're all dead.' The whiskey soaked into the dust and disappeared. He lit a cigarette and squinted through the smoke as Tyler approached, flanked by Jackson and Cooper.

Overhead, he heard the *whup-whup* of an inbound helicopter. What had started as a trickle two weeks previously had turned into a steady stream of flights as members of the IDF returned from across the globe to protect their city. The Knesset, led by Prime Minister Ben-David, would arrive next week, and then the Jewish diaspora would start to return home. For the Templars this was only a brief respite prior to redeployment: to their mission to fight alongside the GRC and Saudis to liberate Jordan and help secure Israel's borders. The horror would rumble on without him.

Lynch nodded a curt greeting.

'Tell me, Colonel, was it worth it?' He pointed to the mass graves and the stretcher loads of casualties awaiting transport back home. 'How long do you think the Israelis can hold the city, even with the nano-virus? What will be the cost of holding it? Seems to me this goddamned war has turned both sides into monsters.'

'If you're hoping for some sort of moral superiority to end your coverage on, I'm afraid you won't find it here. But seeing as you're shortly going to stop being a pain in my ass, I'll let you into a little secret. This conflict is the same for both sides – it's about giving the people a common foe to hate, about keeping the economy on a war footing. Nobody is trying to win the war, just enough battles to make the leaders look good. You've been around long enough to know the score, Lynch. Just be thankful you're getting out alive. I'd trade you in a heartbeat for one of the boys we're sending home in a casket. But I guess the Devil takes care of his own.'

Lynch spat, 'You really are a swine of the first order. I should have shot you when I had the chance.'

'Too bad you bottled it. For all that you run that mouth of yours, you're no killer. Just a self-aggrandising redneck loser. Go home, drink your whiskey, snort your cocaine and play with your guns. See how long it takes your adoring public to forget you when you got nothing to say.'

'Maybe they will. Maybe they won't. But,' Lynch pointed to the blinking green LED on his implant, 'I'm making one final report from the front, and I reckon it'll bury your political career before it's even begun.'

Tyler drew his pistol. 'Stop broadcasting.'

'Too late for that, it's already gone out.' Lynch smiled. 'You maybe want to check the newsfeed on your com-unit.'

'Like I'm going to take my eyes off you. Cooper, see what our whack-job friend here is gibbering about.'

The colour drained from Cooper's face and his hand started to shake as he heard Mackinlay's voice crackle from the speaker: 'Don't turn your back on me when I'm talking to you!' Gunfire and screams followed the warning and continued for long seconds before giving way to a deathly silence. The camera panned along the bus, taking in the shattered glass and bullet-riddled bodywork, finally coming to rest on the child's arm dangling from the emergency exit.

Lynch's voiceover cut in: 'The footage you've just watched was filmed on Route 1, some ninety klicks east of Jerusalem. In war, where men who have been trained to kill and indoctrinated to hate the enemy operate for long periods under extreme stress, such tragedies, while shocking to civilian eyes, are inevitable. We should neither condone nor condemn the young soldiers involved. But the next voice you will hear is that of Colonel Martin Tyler,

Commander of the First Templar Division's Combat Aviation Brigade, calling in the coordinates for an airstrike. This is not a spur-of-the-moment life or death decision; it is the cold and calculated destruction of a vulnerable refugee column in order to suppress evidence. Some two hundred men, women and children ruthlessly eradicated to preserve the public image of a so-called war hero. This war, this crusade, is being fought without mercy, without honour. We, the American people, cannot allow this to continue.'

'I think we've heard enough of that crap, Cooper.' Tyler pointed his pistol directly at Lynch. 'Seems to me it'll be my word against yours, Lynch. So if you're not around to contradict me...'

Cooper stepped forward and raised his rifle. 'Can't let you do that, sir. Lower your weapon.'

'Always took you for a weak-ass liberal at heart, Cooper, but pointing a weapon at your commanding officer? I'm giving you one chance – lower your rifle, or I'll see you before a court martial.'

'No more than I deserve, after what happened at the bus. Truth is, it's a relief to have it out there at last. Now I can face up to it instead of lying to myself.'

Jackson, taking advantage of Tyler's distraction, stepped in close and took hold of his gun arm. He spun the colonel around and twisted his arm upward in one smooth movement. Tyler snarled and tried to resist, but Jackson was physically stronger and the pistol crept inexorably upward until it was level with his temple. A single shot echoed across the desert as blood and brain matter splattered onto the sand. Jackson let Tyler's corpse crumple to the ground.

Jackson stepped back from the body. 'I did what I had to do.'

Lynch raised his hands. 'Don't get me wrong, I'm cool with that. But what happens now?'

'If you ask me, looks like Colonel Tyler shot himself to avoid facing a court martial. As for you, better hurry. Don't want to miss your plane.'

Lynch shook his head. 'Gonna be too hot stateside for me after this. Reckon I'll take my chances on the road. I hear they still have what amounts to a free press in Morocco.' He looked over to where Cooper stood staring at Lynch's corpse. 'Probably made it hot for you. Sorry about that. Maybe you should come with? You know this war isn't for you.'

'That it ain't. But I was never out here for myself or my beliefs. Don't reckon my folks would understand me being listed as a deserter. Assuming they let me, gonna complete my tour and cash out. There's honour of a sort in that.' He fished a fob from his pocket and thew it to Lynch. 'Better assign me punishment duty, Sarge. Looks like I've been careless enough to leave my keys in the JLTV and someone has stolen it.'

'That sure is mighty careless of you, Cooper. Course, I reckon it might be some time before we notice it's missing in the confusion that'll follow the discovery of Colonel Tyler's suicide.'

Lynch gripped the fob tight in his hand. 'Last words of advice from an old hack, kid. Don't ever let them make you a part of this war.'

CHAPTER 29

The temperature inside the hangar was a cool fifty-six degrees Fahrenheit; it read a hundred and ten the other side of the double-metal skin. But it wasn't the cold air blowing down on him that chilled Cooper as he surveyed the rows of cryo-caskets waiting to be loaded onto the waiting Ultra Galaxy. He walked down the line, checking the temperature readouts and remembering his fallen comrades. When he thought of Mackinlay, Garcia or Schreiber it struck him how easily fate could have reversed their positions. Templars might lay claim to being the most expensive and rigorously trained soldiers in the world, but sometimes war came down to dumb chance. Cooper's luck had held and he'd lived to see Jerusalem restored to the Israelis.

He swiped across his pad and a robotic loader moved into position, picked up the first casket and loaded it side-on to the conveyer belt. Cooper watched Arturo Garcia's earthly remains disappear into the Galaxy's cargo hold. Mackinlay was next, followed by Schreiber, although what exactly they had found of him to bury was a mystery Cooper had no desire to know the answer to. Tyler's casket was the last in line. It remained to be seen what honour he would be awarded as a war criminal and suicide, although many would doubtless still hail him as a hero. Was it really less than a year since he first met him at Fort Irwin? It seemed a lifetime ago, which it literally was for those in the Galaxy's hold. Like the other recruits, he'd looked up to Tyler, had been desperate for the approval of this shining warrior. But war had shown him the colonel's true face: brutal and cold ambition, dedicated only to his own self-aggrandisement. At least Jackson and Walker actually believed in the God in whose name they were fighting. He would be glad when he was done with the hypocrisy, but meantime he had duties to perform.

Cooper made his way into the Galaxy's hold and proceeded to the casket at the beginning of the line. He picked up the carefully folded flag stored at the head of the casket and removed it from its covering. Placing it on the centre of the casket, he unfolded it towards himself three times, away from himself three times, and then twice to the left and twice to the right, exposing the red cross and draping the casket in the process. Satisfied, he secured the cargo netting across it, fixing it into place for the long journey home.

He repeated the process for Mackinlay and Schreiber before arriving at Tyler's casket. The gunmetal box, with the exception of his name and service number, was identical to the others; in death, rank held no privileges. Not for the first time, Cooper wondered what would have happened if the sarge hadn't intervened. Would he have shot Tyler to protect Lynch? Would the colonel have shot him? Thankfully, he'd never know.

Cooper found it equally perverse that he was in more trouble for the theft of the JLTV than the bus shootings. By accident or design, his back was to the camera throughout Lynch's recording. The official word was that they were still attempting to identify those involved, but Cooper knew the reputation of the Order came before truth or justice. He suspected there would be few objections when he chose to cash out at the end of his tour.

The sound of boots on the deck plating made him look up. Rivera smiled awkwardly as she drew to a halt. He thought she looked tired, the seven or eight years she had on him suddenly weighing heavy.

'Sergeant Jackson told me I'd find you here.'

'Something I can do for you, Rivera?'

'Finally got some shore leave. Been flying sorties around the clock, harrying the Caliphate retreat and patrolling the borders. Anyway, thought I might take you up on that offer of a cup of coffee. If it still stands?'

'Said it yourself – not a good idea.' Cooper's voice sounded cold even to his own ears, but it was too late to take it back.

'I thought … Well, I guess it doesn't matter. For what it's worth, I'm glad you're not dead.'

'Me too.'

Cooper swallowed as Rivera shook her head and turned away; thought he must be crazy to turn her down. But whatever vulnerability she displayed now, he knew that being with him would ultimately just be the scratching of an itch for her, and he was tired of people using him.

Cooper pulled down his goggles and adjusted his bandana as the latest transporter dusted down on the outskirts of Jerusalem. He had long since lost count of the hoppers ferrying a stream of civilian workers anxious to reoccupy the city. An estimated ten thousand already, with perhaps double that still to come. Engineers, architects, doctors, nurses, teachers and construction workers, ready to play their part in the reconstruction of the war-torn city. Incredibly, they brought teenagers, toddlers, even babies with them to a country whose borders were still not secure. Cooper couldn't quite decide if that made them dedicated patriots or fools. Perhaps it was possible to be both? Whichever it was, the newly restored state of Israel had once again invoked the Law of Return and the *olim* were answering the call in the hope of securing land, jobs and a fresh start.

He watched the latest batch exit the transporter. For the most part they were in their late twenties to early fifties, the younger exiles already conscripted into the IDF and serving alongside Templar forces. News-vids had broadcast the destruction of the city worldwide and, as part of the wider Jewish diaspora, the settlers were sure to have seen it. Yet each of them stopped to stare, shaken by the scale of the damage, any illusion of coming here in the hope of an easy life now shattered.

Cooper counted them off against his datapad: twenty-seven adults and twelve children. He nodded to Pedersen, also on punishment duty, although Cooper thought there was a world of difference between his 'losing' a JLTV and the looting of Caliphate dead. He wondered if Lynch had made it across the border into North Africa. Certainly, he'd heard no word of his capture or death. Bastard was crazy, but right now the world needed crazy. He hoped Tyler was right and the Devil did indeed look after his own.

'Gentlemen, ladies.' Cooper addressed the settlers. 'I am Templar-Private Cooper, and my colleague here is Templar-Private Pedersen. We are your security detail and are here for your well-being, but primarily for your safety. If you would form up into a double line, we will escort you to the registration centre, where your documentation and IDs will be checked prior to the assignment of your accommodation. This zone has been swept and cleared, but you are advised to remain within the demarcated zone and not, I repeat, not, to touch anything.'

A grey-haired man with a pot belly raised his hand tentatively.

'Are you saying the area is unsafe? We were told the city was secure.'

Cooper's mouth twitched in an approximation of the type of smile his media training had described as positive and reassuring.

'The city is secure, sir, and all demarcated zones are safe. Outside those zones there remains a possibility of live ordnance. Acclimation following registration will advise on all risks and their mitigation. Now, if you would like to follow me and TP Pedersen.'

Pedersen rolled his eyes at Cooper as the man's wife patted his arm. 'We talked about this, Saul. Knew there'd be some adjustments to be made.'

Cooper shook his head, a warning not to make a scene, and then set off at a brisk walk, the settlers falling in step behind. He led them along the path, demarcated with cones and plastic chains, heading towards the two-storey block of the registration centre. An area two kilometres square had already been cleared adjacent to the centre, the skyline dominated by plascrete tower blocks that grew by the day. Cooper watched as another section was craned into place, the prefabricated sections arriving fully fitted out. Wind and solar farms were already in situ together with water boreholes to provide services. Hard to believe the bombs had been falling four short weeks ago; since then, construction had been progressing 24/7. If the buildings were functional and unlovely to look at, they offered a degree of comfort far beyond the initial tent city that had greeted the first wave of settlers.

An IDF army officer was waiting outside the centre to greet the settlers, the oak leaf on his epaulettes denoting him as a Rav seren.

Cooper saluted. 'Major Levitt, settler flight Alpha Echo One Nine Zero Zero, sir.'

Levitt returned the salute, glanced at his datapad and nodded. 'Very good. I will see to our new citizens from here.' He checked the time on the pad. 'Next transport is due in at fourteen hundred. Suggest the pair of you get some lunch beforehand.'

'Sir, thank you, sir!'

They were ten metres from the settlers, making for the

mess tent, when Pedersen said in too loud a voice, 'Might be on jankers, but I don't see why we have to kowtow to one of them.'

'Other than we're in their country and he's a superior officer? Guess you must like PD.'

'Wouldn't have their piece of shit country if we hadn't kicked Abdul's ass for them. And this PD is pure bullshit, man. Unbecoming conduct. Bringing the uniform into disrepute. Those mooks were dead. What did they need watches and rings for? That shit was just going in the hole with them.'

'And the gold teeth?'

Pedersen stopped and grimaced. 'Like you're one to talk. Least I didn't let no faggot journalist steal my ride.'

'There's no proof Lynch took the JLTV.'

'No? They just happen to both go missing on the same day. The day Tyler decides to eat his gun. You're dumber than you look if you're willing to buy that as a coincidence.'

'All right. He probably did steal the JLTV. But do you really think he could get the better of the colonel?'

'Thing is, if someone's out to get you, you have to be lucky all the time. They just need to be lucky once.'

'You're forgetting the sarge was there when Tyler bought it.'

Pedersen fell into a sullen silence and Cooper cursed himself inwardly. This was precisely the reason Jackson had warned him off talking about it. If a mutt like Pedersen smelled a rat, there were plenty more in the squad who did as well. Get labelled as an oath breaker out here and pretty soon no one would have your back.

'Shit, maybe you're right, and Lynch bushwhacked him. Maybe the sarge is just trying to protect his reputation.'

'Yeah, he and the colonel went a long ways back. I can see how he might do that.'

They walked on towards the mess tent in silence, Cooper's heart rate returning slowly to its normal level. Much as he hated to throw shade on Lynch, he reckoned he would understand. After all, he'd as good as told him to use any means possible to survive his tour.

Pedersen peeled away after they picked up their MRE packs, and Cooper was thankful for the privacy as he sat at an empty table. Time was, Lynch would have been here busting his balls about the war and Cooper's role in it. Needling him, not out of spite, but in the hope of making him think. Trouble was, Cooper had already spent time enough worrying about the war. But he missed Lynch challenging him. Hell, he even missed Walker, with his simple black and white view of the world. Felt a little envious of his ability to believe they were the good guys. Not that Cooper necessarily thought they were bad. If war taught you nothing else it was that there were a multitude of shades of grey.

Cooper mixed fruit flavouring into his water and unlocked his com-unit. He swiped to messaging and opened a long-neglected conversation thread.

Hi Ma & Pa,

Sorry I've not written you in a long time. Been kind of hectic over here, as you might imagine. Not that I can say much – all comms are filtered. But I guess it's no secret we're in control of Jerusalem. I'm based here just now, providing security for the resettlement. It's a boring job, but someone has to do it. Hope to join my unit in Jordan in a couple of weeks. Just wanted to let you know I'm well and thinking about you. Word is we'll be kept on active duty right up to the end of our tour, so it'll be some time before I'm home to visit. Give my love to Shania and the twins. Hope they're all behaving themselves.

Your loving son,
Billy Ray

Cooper's finger hovered over the send icon. Wasn't like he was actually lying; more that he was being economic with the facts. War had its own specific truth. Something the folks back home would never understand. Lynch had warned him about becoming part of the war, letting it become his life. But the truth was he would carry a piece of war inside him for the rest of his days. Hide away the things he could only speak about with those who had shared the experience. He wasn't a killer, but he had killed.

Cooper added a heart emoji after his name and hit send.

The lights were deliberately low, casting pools of shadow throughout the office. A touch melodramatic, Hopkins thought, but there was no denying those assembled were here on dark business. She watched the spook as he completed his sweep of the room, attention focused on the screen of his handheld scanner. The crackles of static continued uninterrupted.

'Clear,' he announced, placing the scanner on the table. Gerrard opened his mouth to speak and the agent waved him to silence. He took an egg-like device from his suit pocket, flicked a stand from its base and placed it in the centre of the table. A half-turn of its top brought forth a blue glow from its centre. He checked the scanner again and nodded. 'Signal jammer is active.' A finger went up to his earpiece and he said something inaudible before taking his seat at the table.

Hopkins looked around the table: in addition to Gerrard and Hannah, Kordowski and Morrison, the Chairman of the Joint Chiefs of Staff and Secretary of Defense, were also present. A small number of conspirators to effect regime change, but that was probably for the best, all things considered.

Gerrard cleared his throat. 'Gentlemen, lady. Final chance to leave the room.'

Hopkins' eyes flicked to the door. Ignorance might be bliss, but it also meant being out in the cold. She'd pretty much bet everything on Tyler, and now he was coming home in a flag-draped casket. Warning Hamilton was an option, but one, judging from those present in the room, with a very limited return. Loathsome as she might find him, Gerrard was the only game in town. Adapt or die: the golden rule of politics.

'Then we're all agreed on the course of action?'

Signal jammer or not, the conspirators limited their responses to a series of nods. Golden rule number two: never commit your sins to tape.

'Then,' Gerrard said, 'as we are in agreement, it's over to you, Mr Hannah. How long do you think it'll take to action?'

'The action part is easy, sir. The Agency has a permanent contingency plan in place.' Hannah looked meaningfully in Gerrard's direction. 'As we never know when such measures might become necessary. Just a matter of finding a suitable window of opportunity.'

Gerrard's smile was brittle and his voice lacked the lightness of tone he was going for. 'Guess we'll have to trust your judgement on this, and future, matters.'

'Rest assured, Mr Vice President, the Agency will take whatever steps are necessary to protect this great country of ours.'

CHAPTER 30

Lynch pulled onto the side of the road and checked the mirrors for what felt like the thousandth time. He had probably spent more time looking behind than at the road in front, ever fearful of pursuit. A hard knot of fear would form in his gut whenever he spotted a dust cloud stirred up by an approaching vehicle or the glint of sunlight off glass. The silhouette drawing nearer and nearer until it resolved itself into the benign shape of a civilian truck or a bus. Three hundred klicks along Route 90 with only refugees for company. He didn't doubt there were Caliphate troops and sympathisers in their number, but the Templars and the IDF appeared happy to let them flee. Good news for him. And so here he was, on the outskirts of Eilat, waiting for his contact.

The sun was dipping towards the horizon when a white jeep with a chromed bull bar and exhausts rumbled out of the desert and spun to a halt next to the JLTV. The passenger door opened and a man of average height dressed in army fatigues stepped out. Dark glasses hid his eyes and a red-checked *keffiyeh* covered his head. Ignoring Lynch, he walked around the JLTV, tapping it here and there with a knuckle and nodding to himself.

'Good,' he said finally. 'Follow me.'

The jeep was already rolling by the time the Arab clambered back aboard, and Lynch hurriedly threw the JLTV in drive and followed it off-road. They drove ten klicks into the desert, approaching what Lynch first took to be a giant dune until it resolved itself into an old aircraft hangar covered in camouflage netting. One of the doors slid aside as the jeep drew near, exposing an interior lit by powerful arc lamps. The jeep disappeared inside and Lynch reluctantly followed.

A gangly youth, the lower half of his face concealed by a *shemagh*, directed Lynch to park over an inspection pit. He noted the QBZ-95 slung across the boy's chest and belatedly wished he'd armed himself with one of the assault rifles from the JLTV's weapons locker. A shadow moved across the windshield as the hangar door slid closed again. Looked like he was committed now.

Lynch exited the JLTV to find the jeep's passenger waiting for him. The man smiled, revealing a gold eye tooth.

'Welcome, friend, to my little Aladdin's cave of desert transport. I'm sure I have something to suit your needs.' He motioned with a crooked finger. 'Come, come. Don't be shy. Farouk will complete your vehicle inspection, but there is most certainly a deal to be done.'

Lynch followed his guide past the inspection pits, noting a further two armed men as they passed into the rear of the hangar where the outlines of four tarpaulin-shrouded trucks were visible. The Arab stopped in front of the first and flipped up the edge of the tarp to expose a rust-spotted wing. He shook his head and moved on, fingers gesturing left and right as he tried to zone in. He took a step to the left, stopped and then pivoted right. Decision made, he walked briskly to the rearmost vehicle and threw back the tarpaulin with a theatrical flourish. Lynch took in the boxy but solid silver bodywork, his eyes coming to rest on the Mercedes badge fixed to the grill.

'G-Wagon. Precision German engineering. Solid. Like a

tank. With full solar deployment for battery charging. Fair trade. No robbery. Yes?'

It was certainly a lot less conspicuous than the JLTV and looked up to the job of driving across North Africa to Morocco. But there would be palms to grease along the way, and transferring money from his account stateside was sure to raise a flag.

'Throw in five thousand dollars and you've got yourself a deal.'

'Five thousand? I like you, my friend, but not enough to let you rob me. We will have to strip and repaint your vehicle, purge the electronics. All time and money. But never let any man say that Jalaal is not generous in business. Two thousand. A credit more would take the food from my children's mouths.'

'Three thousand and I'll throw in a couple of assault rifles. Modern EC tech. Not those Chinese antiques your boys are carrying.'

'Very well, my friend. Let us inspect these "modern" weapons of yours.'

Lynch led Jalaal back to the JLTV, opened the rear door and pressed his palm to the weapons locker. He heard the mag-bolts release and cracked open the lid to expose three assault rifles and a stack of pre-loaded magazines.

Lynch handed Jalaal one of the rifles. 'M42 IAR – Infantry Automatic Rifle. It's 5.56mm select-fire – single shot or fully automatic, fed from a standard 30-round STANAG magazine. Fitted with a 3.5 x 35 Squad Day Optic.'

Jalaal hefted the rifle experimentally. 'Lighter than you would expect. This is a Templar assault rifle?' Lynch nodded. 'And you are offering me all three?'

'The deal is for two. I've a long road to travel – might need a little firepower myself before the journey's over. These are top-of-the-line firearms, easily worth two thousand dollars apiece on the black market. I'll give you ten magazines per rifle as well – six hundred rounds in total.'

'You drive a hard but fair bargain, my friend,' Jalaal said, holding out his hand.

Lynch shook the proffered hand. 'Said it yourself – fair exchange, no robbery.'

The Arab smiled, treating Lynch to another flash of gold. He stretched up in order to wrap an arm around Lynch's shoulders. 'Come, we have coffee while you wait for my men to prepare and load your new truck. I take it cash is all right?'

'Cash?' Lynch couldn't keep the incredulity out of his voice.

'Cash, my friend.' Jalaal pressed his forefingers and thumbs together and made a rubbing motion. 'In this part of the world the tangible is preferable to numbers on a screen. As it says on the money, In God We Trust. In ecommerce, not so much.'

Lynch shrugged. What choice did he have?

Lynch stood staring up at the red, white and black stripes of the flag outside the Consulate of Egypt on Ephroni Street. As Muslims, the Egyptians had been allowed to maintain a presence in the Caliphate-occupied territories of Israel, but it had come at the cost of living as second-class citizens. Hence the ugly and somewhat dilapidated block of concrete that rose above him. Fortunately, Lynch had no intention of staying in Eilat any longer than he had to. He pushed through a fly-flecked revolving door and presented himself at the reception desk.

'Jefferson Lynch. I have an appointment with the consul.'

The receptionist tapped the screen in front of her and then pointed down the corridor. 'Mr Salah's office is the second door on the right.'

Lynch found the door ajar and knocked briskly before entering. The Egyptian looked up from his terminal and motioned for his visitor to take a seat. Ink-black hair, swept back to form a pair of wings, rose above heavy-lidded eyes and a high forehead.

'You are a journalist, Mr Lynch?'

'That's right.' Lynch handed over his press credentials. 'I'm travelling through Egypt en route to Morocco to take up a post with the *Casablanca Herald*. It's an English language paper.'

Salah gave the press pass a cursory glance. 'I can certainly issue you a visa for Egypt, but the additional papers of transit are more … difficult. I have many cases to consider and even working dawn till dusk I must choose what to prioritise. At the end of the day, I am but a lowly paid cog in the machine with little influence. You understand?'

Lynch understood well enough and extracted a bundle of plasticised notes from his pocket. He peeled off a hundred-dollar bill and placed it on the table. Salah said nothing, and so he continued to place bills on the table. On the count of eight, Salah reached out and swept the money over to his side of the desk.

'Come back tomorrow after lunch, and ask for Baahir. He will sort out the necessary documentation for you.'

Lynch slept in the G-wagon, trusting his safety to its locks. He woke with the dawn and wandered down to one of the beach cafes, where he ate a simple breakfast of cheese, olives and flat bread while overlooking the Gulf of Aqaba. The clear, clean water made the war seem a long way away. But reality, in the form of beggar children, was never far away. Bitter experience had taught him to ignore the proffered hands and pleas for help. If you put your hand in your pocket for one, you might as well do it for a hundred, and to little overall effect. He stared pointedly above their heads as he ran the gauntlet back to the G-Wagon. Cries of '*baksheesh!*' followed him all the way.

Having time to kill, he soaked a spare uniform tunic in oil and cut it into strips, which he wrapped around the disassembled parts of the last M42. Best not to take any chances with potential border searches. His initial thought had been to strap the rifle parts beneath the Merc, but it offered poor concealment and too great a chance of being lost. In the end, he sacrificed the spare tyre that hung on the rear of the truck, slashing an opening on one side and stuffing it with the rifle parts, ammunition and rags. Satisfied it looked the part, he zipped up the cover and checked his watch. A little after twelve. Time to make his way back to the consulate.

The receptionist smiled knowingly when Lynch asked for Baahir and pointed him to a door that led down to the basement via a plascrete staircase. The firefly globes cast just enough light to pick out the cracks and the damp. Lynch's hand strayed to the small of his back, where he had concealed a Templar fighting knife. The nickel-plated brass hilt offered him little comfort. If he were walking into a trap the chances were that they would have guns. A door swung open, casting a wedge of light into the corridor, and Lynch reluctantly stepped forward.

Baahir turned out to be a sullen youth in his late teens. Lynch saw a family resemblance between the boy and the consul, which put him a little more at ease. Salah was unlikely to have sent a son or a nephew if he were expecting trouble. Honest corruption Lynch could cope with.

'You have your com-unit with you, Mr Lynch?' he asked.

Lynch nodded.

'Place it on the desk and I'll synch your papers of transit to it.'

Lynch did as Baahir asked, unlocked the screen and watched the document download. He clicked on it and scrolled through, checking it looked in order.

'Don't worry, Mr Lynch, the documentation is all present and correct for your journey to Morocco. But if I might offer a little friendly advice – American passport not so good in Africa. Your journey would be much smoother with a Moroccan one.'

'And how much would such a passport cost me?'

'For you, a thousand dollars and two days' wait. But rest assured, it will pass all border checks.'

Lynch saw the sense of it, felt tempted, but knew he needed what money he had left for food, water and the likelihood of having to pay more bribes between here and his destination.

'Going to have to pass on that.'

'As you wish. I hope you won't have cause to regret it.'

Lynch transmitted his documents to the border guard, who checked it on his terminal. He offered up a yawn as he sent back an approval code and raised the boom across the road. Lynch thanked him and put the truck into drive. The authorities, it seemed, had little interest in who was choosing to leave Israel. That could change soon enough if they put out a watch list. Lynch found the Egyptian authorities similarly disinterested on their side of the border. He left the Taba crossing behind as he manoeuvred the truck onto the Nuweibaa Taba Road, heading for the turn-off onto Route 50.

Whatever misgivings Lynch had had about Jalaal, he proved a man of his word with regard to the Mercedes' performance. The G-wagon ate up the freeway on auto-drive, the towns and desert passing by on either side. All the same, it came as something of a relief seven hours later to hit the coast road just before El Alamein and gaze out at the tranquil waters of the Mediterranean. From here, it was four thousand klicks along the International Coastal Road.

He drove through the first night, enabling him to rest through the heat of the day, conserving water and charging the truck's batteries. Names such as Alexandria, known to him only from the pages of history, swept past as he allowed the auto-drive to take most of the strain. The tension drained from him slowly with each passing klick until he hit the Libyan side of the border.

The guard examined his passport and papers of transit, simultaneously taking in Lynch's desert camouflage fatigues and vest emblazoned with 'PRESS'. He spoke into the radio clipped to his breast pocket in Arabic and one of his colleagues detached himself from the gatehouse and walked across to the truck. While his rifle wasn't pointed directly at Lynch, he held it in such a way that said this could easily change.

The first guard switched to English and said, 'Switch off your engine and step out of the vehicle.'

Baahir's warning came back to Lynch as the guard returned his attention to his passport. Had he come this far only to end up rotting in a Libyan prison, held ransom to a government that had more than enough cause to leave him there?

'What reason does an American citizen visit our country?'

Lynch repeated his cover story about taking up a post in Casablanca. The guard looked Lynch up and down again.

'You don't look like a journalist. More like a mercenary.' He turned to his colleague. 'Search his vehicle.'

Lynch stepped aside as they systematically emptied the G-wagon, removing food, water, clothing, spare parts and his lean-to. The guard finally reached the spare tyre. Lynch felt the sweat run down his spine as he unzipped the cover and looked inside. He shook his head in the negative and zipped the cover back up.

'Am I free to go?'

The guard handed back his com-unit. 'We have your route logged. Do not deviate from it. My comrades will be expecting you at the Tunisian border, so I would advise against any sightseeing or detours along the way.'

Lynch repacked the truck and drove off. He was twenty klicks from the border when he spotted the drone hovering above. It tracked him for another two hundred or so before its controllers called it to duty elsewhere. Lynch kept up a steady pace regardless, aware a kill-sat could just as easily have locked on. It was with relief that he left Tripoli behind, heading for what he hoped would be the friendlier territory of Tunisia.

A ruddy glow on the horizon indicated the coming dawn, and Lynch drew the truck off the road and parked up. He worked fast, keen to avoid the coming heat, unpacking and deploying the solar panels to charge the truck's batteries. With the batteries on charge, he turned his attention to erecting the lean-to, pacing out six steps from the side of the truck before hammering in the steel posts. He tied off the heat-reflective sheeting between the roof rack and the poles, then hung additional sheets on the front and sides, leaving a gap at the front through which he could watch the dawn.

The day was already heating up as he opened a self-heating ration pack and forked up its contents. According to his com-unit, he was ten kilometres from the border between Libya and Tunisia. Still no sign of pursuit. But why would there be? The spooks back home would be content to let him die alone in the desert. Well, they were going to be disappointed if Lynch had any say in the matter.

Lynch scrolled through the news channels on his com-unit and eventually picked up an American one. The signal was weak, pixelated, but there was no mistaking the breaking news that cut across it: President Hamilton assassinated! The studio cut to live coverage of a press conference with Vice President Gerrard.

'I can confirm that the president was shot earlier today by a lone assailant. Despite the heroic intervention of medical staff, his injuries were too severe and he passed away a little after two pm. The Islamic Caliphate has already claimed responsibility for this heinous act of war on American soil. While this is naturally a time of grief and rage, we ask the citizens of America to show restraint. Our response to this unprovoked attack is already in motion, commencing with the deployment of an additional fifty thousand troops to Jordan and Syria. Their mission, to root out our enemies and ensure there is no hiding place for them. Anyone foolish enough to offer them succour will feel the righteous wrath of our great nation. Rest assured, those responsible will be brought to book.'

Lynch disconnected the feed as the assembled press started to ask questions. He threw his com-unit onto the ground. He needed a new one; his only had fake news on it.

APPENDIX A: TIMELINE

2030

Israel annexes the West Bank. International outcry follows and Jordan, Lebanon and the UAE sever diplomatic ties, leaving Israel increasingly isolated. Egypt admits thousands of Palestinians through the Rafah border crossing. US President Harris attempts to broker a withdrawal but fails to follow through on her threat to cut military aid in the wake of an increased threat to Israel from Iran.

American airstrikes target Iranian airbases. Iranian forces target American troops in Iraq, resulting in 53 fatalities. America seeks to legitimise war with Iran via the UN Security Council, but China and Russia use their vetoes. America responds by vetoing a resolution condemning Israel's annexation of the West Bank.

2031

China applies pressure to broker a peace deal after the escalating conflict closes the Straits of Hormuz, affecting trade. America reluctantly ceases military action against Iran in a bid to avoid a growing trade war with China.

2034

Hamas rocket attacks on Beersheba, Jerusalem and Tel Aviv kill 63 civilians and 11 IDF soldiers. Israel responds with airstrikes and a ground invasion of the Gaza Strip. Operation Bronze Spear lasts for three days, with 23 Israeli and 2,732 Palestinian fatalities. The operation destroys critical infrastructure, along with housing and hospitals. The US government again defends Israel's right to self-defence.

Defeated and destitute, much of the surviving civilian populace begins the exodus to Egypt.

2041

A resurgent ISIS in Iraq and Syria gains control of Lebanon and Jordan and cements itself as a new Islamic Caliphate. The USA deploys an additional 100,000 troops in an attempt to relieve Jordan and assist rebels in Syria. High casualties generate negative headlines in the US.

2043

Escalating tensions between India and Pakistan result in a minor nuclear exchange. Although targets are primarily military, civilian casualties are estimated at 250,000. Fallout affects areas of China and Afghanistan. China responds by sending relief aid and 'peacekeeping' troops to Afghanistan and Pakistan, strengthening the ties of the early twenty-first century Shanghai Cooperation Organisation.

The UN General Assembly attempts to broker an agreement on multilateral nuclear disarmament. China, Russia, the USA, Israel and North Korea refuse to sign. The UK, France, Pakistan and India disarm.

2044

The killing of 84 Turkish troops by Russian-backed forces in Syria results in escalating conflict between Russia and Turkey.

2045

Russian forces withdraw from Syria as part of an agreed peace deal with Turkey. The Islamic Caliphate takes advantage of the power vacuum to seize total control of Syria.

2047

American forces, brought to a standstill by the Islamic Caliphate, withdraw unconditionally from the Middle East. The withdrawal proves highly divisive with the American public, many of whom at a time of growing ecological disasters and global pandemics have embraced Creationist forms of Christianity

2049

No one admits responsibility for the aerial detonation of a nuclear device over the Arctic Circle. Opinion remains divided between terrorist attack and the mal-operation of a military defence satellite. Either way, it makes little difference to the victims of the tidal wave that follows the vaporisation of the Arctic sea ice. North America and Western Europe bear the brunt of the disaster, with large tracts of Alaska, California, Hawaii, Maine, Massachusetts, Rhode Island, New York, Connecticut, New Jersey, Delaware and Maryland remaining under water. England, Norway, Denmark, the Netherlands and the west coasts of Belgium, France and Spain are similarly devastated.

US President Santiago Garcia is killed by the tsunami. Vice President Kecia Williams assumes the presidency, but with much of the infrastructure of the northern states destroyed she is powerless to prevent the country descending into anarchy. A short and bloody second American civil war ensues when 26 American states (South Carolina, Mississippi, Florida, Alabama, Georgia, Louisiana, Texas, Virginia, Arkansas, North Carolina, Tennessee, Kentucky, Missouri, Delaware, West Virginia, Maryland, Oklahoma, Nevada, New, Mexico, Arizona, Utah,

Wyoming, Nebraska, Illinois, Indiana, Ohio), secede from the Union and form the Christian fundamentalist territory of the Religious States of America, with Richmond, Virginia as the capital. The secessionists' intention is to continue the decades'-long war with the Islamic Caliphate in the Middle East.

Construction of Europa City begins, to provide emergency accommodation for millions displaced by the Great Flood.

2050

Woody Lyndhurst is sworn in as the First President of the Religious States of America. The remaining US states request financial aid from the International Monetary Fund, while refugees flee across the border into Canada. With no functioning federal or state governments, the former US states became lawless no-go zones ruled only by the gun.

The RSA withdraws from the United Nations. Russia follows suit, together with a number of the former Soviet Republics, which proves to be a precursor to what follows.

2051–2053

Following the financial collapse of many of the eastern European Union countries, Russia steps in with financial and military aid, effectively annexing Estonia, Latvia, Lithuania, Belarus, Ukraine, Georgia and Kazakhstan into the Greater Russian Collective.

2052

Having requested direct military aid to restore law and order, South Dakota, Idaho and Oregon are formally admitted to the RSA.

2054–2055

Following the collapse of oil prices in the wake of green technologies, the majority of Saudi Arabia falls to the Islamic Caliphate. Oman and the UAE help preserve its southernmost regions. Diplomatic channels are opened with the RSA in the hope of securing military assistance.

2055–2070

A series of typhoons and rising sea levels devastate Japan, Taiwan, Singapore, Indonesia and the Philippines. An influx of refugees fleeing the damage allows North Africa to establish itself as a cyber technology capital, and the foremost supplier of the emerging nanotech market.

2056

In response to the expansion of the Islamic Caliphate, RSA President Lyndhurst signs off on the creation of a new military order of Templars. Drawn from existing special forces units across the military, they are an elite force dedicated to defeating the Islamic Caliphate. Like their predecessors, they take a vow of celibacy, believing that the lack of dependents will make them more willing to make the ultimate sacrifice.

2057

Templar forces establish operational bases in Jerusalem, Haifa, Tel Aviv and Eilat at the behest of the Israeli government.

2061

The Islamic Caliphate attacks Israel. Backed by the RSA and supported by an unprecedented airlift of vital supplies, Israeli forces hold out for two years.

2063

Caliphate forces finally overrun Jerusalem. A detachment of Templars covers the final air evacuation of Israeli forces. The Templars, led by Commander Maxwell Lewis, fight to the death. The Caliphate broadcasts images of their mutilated corpses worldwide.

2065
An accidental deployment of a targeted nano-virus kills in excess of two million people in the Khyber Pakhtunkhwa region of Pakistan before it is contained. In the wake of the disaster, governments around the world sign the North–West Frontier Accord, which outlaws all weaponised nanotechnology.

2066
First Crusade. Utilising Cyprus as a spearhead, the RSA launches a series of air strikes targeting military installations in occupied Israel and the surrounding countries of Lebanon and Jordan. A ground assault on Haifa led by Templar forces ends in a bloody defeat with sixty per cent casualties. The campaign is abandoned amid public outcry.

2069
Seeking fuel for its war machine and a staging point for future military action in the Middle East, the RSA annexes Kuwait, initiating a series of conflicts that will be known collectively as the Oil Wars.

2070–2075
RSA special forces engage in a series of covert actions in Iran, Iraq and Jordon, primarily with the aim of intelligence-gathering for a fresh crusade. Operations, including the assassination of high-ranking Caliphate officers, continue in these territories until the middle of the decade.

2071–2073
Second Crusade. Air strikes and a prolonged ground assault allow the RSA to take control of Israel and parts of Lebanon. Jerusalem remains out of reach and Islamic Caliphate counter attacks soon wrest back control of the territory.

2074

Kuwaiti insurgents rebel against the American occupation. The RSA's response is led by Templar Captain Isaac Vaughan. Vaughan takes less than three months to put down the uprising, executing its leaders live on air. Vaughan is promoted to the rank of colonel.

2075–2076

Dubbed 'Vicious Vaughan' and 'Colonel Killcrazy' by the tabloid press for authorising the use of heavy ordnance and fuel-air strikes against the civilian populations of Iran and Iraq, Vaughan is recalled to Richmond in August following an official complaint by the United Nations and asked to account for his actions before a Senate inquiry. Believing himself betrayed by a government that will not commit to a war of total attrition to defeat the Islamic nations, Vaughan resigns his commission and embarks on a public-speaking tour of the RSA to promote his book, The Enemy Within.

2079

Vaughan assumes the position of Chairman of the Board of the Tessler Corporation in Europa City. Over the next three years he triples its profits by using his military contacts in the RSA to secure contracts for the supply of experimental cyber-ware.

2079–2083

Third Crusade (Saudi Campaign). Having twice failed to take Jerusalem, the next Crusade focuses on liberating Saudi Arabia from the Caliphate and depriving it of the oil reserves used to fuel its war machine. Islamic Caliphate forces are successfully driven back to Syria and Jordan.

2089–Present

Fourth Crusade. Bolstered by Christian recruits from Eastern Europe and the Greater Russian Collective, the RSA amasses an army of one million frontline troops.

Saturation bombing lays waste to Lebanon and the western borders of Syria and Jordan. RSA forces then launch a three-pronged attack through Lebanon and Jordan in the east, via Egypt in the west, violating Egyptian airspace to land ground troops on Israel's western border, and by sea with direct beach landings. A protracted and bloody ground war of attrition follows as they fight to retake Israel foot by foot.

APPENDIX B: MILITARY ACRONYMS

AMPV: Armoured Multi-Purpose Vehicle
COSCOM: Corp Support Command
CSS: Combat Service Support
CROWS: Common Remotely-Operated Weapon Station
ECH: Enhanced Combat Helmet
E-SAPI: Enhanced Small-Arms Protective Insert
E-SBI: Enhanced Side Ballistic Insert
FASCAM: Field Artillery Scatterable Mines
GEMSS: Ground-Emplaced Mine Scattering System
GSR: Ground Surveillance Radar
HEAT: High-Explosive Anti-Tank
HUD: Head-Up Display
IFFN: Identify Friend, Foe or Neutral
IHADSS: Integrated Helmet and Display Sight System
IOTV: Improved Outer Tactical Vest
IRST: Infrared Search and Track
JLTV: Joint Light Tactical Vehicle
LZ: Landing Zone
METT-TC: Mission, Enemy, Terrain, Troops available, Time and Civilian Considerations
MILES: Multiple Integrated Laser Engagement System
MOUT: Military Operations in Urban Terrain

MRE: Meal, Ready-to-Eat
MSR: Main Supply Routes
OCT: Observer, Controller, Trainer
OPFOR: Opposing Forces
POL: Petroleum, Oil, Lubricants
UAS: Unmanned Aircraft Systems

ABOUT THE AUTHOR

Leon Steelgrave is the author of the *Europa City* series – hardboiled science fiction that traces its genealogy back to the pulp stories of the 1930s. This dark and satirical world serves as a warning of the dangers of ecological disaster and totalitarian regimes.

Leon's early work includes articles and reviews for music fanzines *Take To The Sky* and *Glasperlenspiel.* But it was his attempt to secure a commission for writing one of a series of *Judge Dredd* novels published by Virgin Books that kickstarted his fiction writing career. Although ultimately unsuccessful, the editorial feedback was sufficiently positive and encouraging for him to complete his debut novel *White Vampyre.* He has published a further three books in the series and is currently working on the first of a new series set in the wider *Europa City* universe.

Leon is a member of the Alliance of Independent Authors and self-publishes his work through Ice Pick Books – fiction to make your ears burn!

Writing being a solitary profession, Leon loves to engage with his readers, so feel free to join his mailing list for releases, updates and exclusive material.

CPSIA information can be obtained
at www.ICGtesting.com
Printed in the USA
LVHW091443140322
713408LV00004B/200